Echoes
of
Eurydice

By

MARCELLO IORI

Instagram

@m.a.iori

Iori & Co Publisher
Copyright © 2022 by Marcello A. Iori. All rights reserved.
Third editions 2024
Original Title: The Mushroom Effect

Editing and Proofreading
by A. and Ravenwingedits

Chapters

Who I Was

010

Sentient

060

The Mushroom Effect

110

Faults

219

Atonement

288

The Secret Eternity

306

The Mushroom Effect is the modern version of the myth of Eurydice and Beatrice.

Orpheus descends into the underworld to bring Eurydice back from the realm of the dead to the living. He loves her. Armed with his Lyre, Orpheus' music enchants all hell, so much so that Hades gives him a chance to save her muse: he may bring her back to the surface provided that during the ascent he does not turn around to look at her face.

Dante Alighieri falls in love with Beatrice at first sight. A silent, eye-only love. Beatrice, however, is later given in marriage to another man and, still in her prime, dies. Dante has visions of her in his dreams and during the day. Beatrice's soul knows the Poet's love and wants to guide him to salvation, out of torment. So, Dante writes his Magna Opera, the Divine Comedy, to save himself and make his love for her immortal, a love so strong that, at the end of his literary work, the great poet dies.

The main character in my story has much in common with Orpheus and Dante. In fact, I could say that The Mushroom Effect is the modern version of the myth of Eurydice and Beatrice.

After a fatal car accident, Francesco almost completely loses his memory. At first, he remembers a few things, he recognizes family members, for example, but there is a ghost that keeps appearing in his dreams; it torments him all the time.

Determined to see once again the face of the woman he loves, who died during the accident, he is persuaded by an old school friend to try a unique *substance* able to take him into a parallel reality to meet his lost love. But in this new reality, Francesco meets another love and new friends.

To A.

She read this above-the-lines-novel first.

And Marco,

he said: "Go on and break the Infinity"

Vai e spacca l'Infinito

Thank you

The entire world is

a collection of memoranda that she did exist,

and that I have lost her.

Emily Brontë - Wuthering Heights

We cannot change anything until we accept it.

Condemnation does not liberate, it oppresses.

Carl G. Jung

1

The cell phone is vibrating on the wooden table in the room, shifting a few millimetres. Francesco looks for it with his eyes, dumb. In his stoney expression seems to have gathered all the silence of the world. He grabs it but lets the call die.

Giulia is in the bathroom with Matteo. She has prepared dinner. Only Sebastiano is missing, and he will arrive within half an hour.

Francesco already wants to leave, often being set down in a room makes him dizzy. He hasn't always been like that.

The mobile's vibrating again. Losco.

Francesco moves his thumb onto the display towards the red circle to close the call, but hesitates, thinking that his friend is not the kind of person to call him a second time. His finger searches for the green circle and presses it. He watches the seconds progress to an unknown future. There is a croaking voice in the background asking to be heard but Francesco wavers: the distance between his ear and hand comforts him.

The headache has tormented him all day long.

Ten seconds.

If he doesn't answer, Losco will hang up.

Giulia's still in the bathroom, Matteo's acting up as he doesn't want to wash his face.

Fifteen seconds.

He puts the phone to his ear, but Losco has hung up. Maybe he should call him back.

At first, Francesco was comforted by his friends. Now, the only thing that relieves him is family. He comes to Giulia's for dinner at least three times a week. He moved back in with their parents just after the hospitalization.

Once at mom and dad's house, he never wanted to see his friends again.

Francesco gets up and walks to the french window to look at the neighbourhood.

Giulia and Sebastian live on the fifth floor. Underneath there is a small street that crosses a residential district. He pulls the curtain aside to watch a car park in a driveway.

Something vibrates, again, for the third time. He doesn't realize he is holding the cell phone in his hand.

It's Losco.

That insistence reminds him of something, a memory buried in the headache that has haunted him for months, a memory that makes his heart beat faster.

"What do you want from me?" he whispers.

He answers the call.

"How are you?"

"Hi, Lo. Not bad. What's going on?"

"I heard, you know?"

"What? What did you hear?"

"About the accident. And that you attempted suicide."

"I can't remember."

"I know you don't remember the accident."

"Yeah, I don't remember that."

"You don't want to talk about it, but..."

"Yeah, I don't want to talk about it. Sorry."

"But I need to tell you, tell you that I know and I'm sorry."

"Do you know how it hurts?"

"No."

"One day you wake up in a room that's not yours and you wonder - what am I doing here? Then someone comes and tells you what you did the night before, but you just don't remember. It's like something ripped your memory out, so you're forced to believe somebody else's version."

"But you want to remember?"

"Yeah, I mean... no, I don't think I want to remember. It's terrible what happened. But I guess I have to. I've been to a psychologist, you know, but it hasn't helped."

"What did he say to you?"

"It's not easy. You know what I did?"

"No."

"I smiled and left."

"What if I told you I know a way? Would you laugh at me by putting the call down?"

"Sorry, Lo, a way to do what?"

"To remember. A safe way that can help you."

"Who told you that story?"

"Is it really important?"

"My sister, right?"

"She just wanted you to talk to someone, a friend. Don't get mad at her."

"I won't."

"I insist. You want to remember?"

"What am I supposed to do? Don't talk about psychologists, they don't work for me anyway."

"This is not medicine for migraine or depression. This is the solution."

"Lo?"

"I'm here."

"You're not fucking with me, are you? I'm not in the mood for jokes."

"I know, man. It's like drowning and not seeing the surface or the bottom."

"Is that supposed to comfort me? I don't need to know that."

"You need to know about this solution."

"What should I do?"

"Come here, to me. Take a few days off, leave behind the world you've lived in for 30 years."

"That's your solution?"

"This is the beginning. It will allow you to see things from another perspective."

"It's no use to me."

"Do you remember Damian? Did I ever tell you about him?"

"He was a friend of yours, but you never told me much about him. What's that got to do with me now?"

"After his death, I spent the next three years in therapy. Two hours a week at a psychologist's, taking pills, and it was all for nothing. That's why I understand you."

"But coming to you won't change anything. I don't remember. I only feel an endless desolation for something I did and I don't remember doing it."

"Do you want to know the rest of my story? I mean, do you want to know how I came out of it?"

"I'd like to say no."

"I met someone, a healer. He showed me the solution."

"What's this about?"

"If I tell you, you'll slam the phone in my face."

"I'm already doing it."

"Come to me. Trust me. I would never make fun of you. You know me. This person saved my life. Things don't happen by accident. Our friendship, for example, was no accident. We bonded from the first moment we met. It's always been easier between us, and even though we haven't seen each other for years, it still is. We are like fluids that bathe the same sea, we don't need so many words. Do you understand?"

"I understand."

"And the same goes for what I want to tell you now.

I've never told anyone about this. Not Damian and not this curator. Many times I thought about telling you, but I didn't have the guts. Now it's different. Now I know you can understand."

"I'm sorry, I never knew anything about your pain. I knew you were close to Damian, but I had no idea that..."

"I attempted suicide."

"When?"

"It doesn't matter. You're the second person who knows this story."

"Did that guy help you?"

"Yes, he did. But it happened later, much later. You want to know how?"

"Yes, alright, but not now. My sister's coming back and I'm having dinner with her tonight. I'll talk to you later."

"I'll call you in two hours. Don't fall asleep."

Francesco ends the call.

"Who were you talking to?" Giulia asks him. Matthew's stuck to her leg and she drags him, limping.

"A friend."

"Good. Anyway, I heard Sebastiano's on his way. He'll be here in a few minutes. Do you want tea or coffee?"

"No, thank you. Just water."

2

Sanremo. Italy. A few months later.

Losco is a weirdo, I've always known.

"Are you ready for this?"
"I am."
"Then this is what you need to know…"

I'm listening to his conditions, his rules. Losco's voice comes out loud and clear from the recorder, mitigated only by the whirring of the spinning tape.

Someone said that writing condemns a part of the writer's soul to stay alive with his books. Writers do not rest in peace; their bodies degrade, but their words remain forever, or at least as long as memory lives.

I turn off the tape recorder because Losco's voice gives me chills, but I keep smiling. I smile but I feel a heartache deep inside.

"Are you ready for this?" This is Losco. It's like a continuous warning, his voice torments me even while I dream.

And yes, my friend, I'm ready for It.

3

Losco worked part-time as a customer service advisor and in the evening, especially at weekends, he was a DJ. Although he was half Italian and half Romanian, he had integrated well in Bournemouth: he knew the places, people and customs of the area. If you were looking for someone or something, he could help you.

"It wasn't easy to get started," he said.

We met in the first year of university. I did biology and he studied foreign languages. Losco dreamed of travelling, discovering the world, he was a wanderer in his mind. I don't remember if he already had a particular fondness for music, nor do I recall him ever having mentioned the possibility of becoming a DJ.

We had certainly been to more than one party during our college year and I never did imagine he would like being behind a deck. And then came last summer, just before August, when he announced that he was going to give up university to leave for London. There he was sitting on a low wall on the campus, with his gaze turned toward the vastness of Milan, using the smoke from his cigarette as if they were the thoughts that he must have hatched long ago.

"I'm not learning anything here." He was sure he didn't need a degree.

He asked me to follow him to London for a week. A holiday.

"Just to see how it is." Losco was fascinated by the idea of travelling. "Everyone has been to some fucking place. Have you seen Instagram? It's full of people who make themselves beautiful here and there, and the only thing I can post is Bimba pooping near Chicca's kennel."

Chicca is a dog and Bimba is a cute grey cat. I could not have animals in my house; my sister was allergic and mom was afraid of becoming attached because, when she was a child, her dog had ended up under a truck.

"Never cried so much in my life," was her comment every time we talked about pets.

At that time, I knew Losco simply as Lorenzo Marsili. He was known as Losco among friends. A kind of reserved and introverted guy. He didn't speak much but was really practical.

His father was a mechanic; Mr. Marsili ran a small workshop in Milan with a business partner. Losco had learned from there.

"I don't give a shit about engines, it's idiotic stuff."

"So, your dad is an idiot?"

"Yes, he is. But, I mean, his interest is in business. If you come to the workshop, you don't see him with dirty hands."

I should have understood many things in those days.

I didn't go with him to London. I should have taken Lisa too but for sure Losco wouldn't have wanted her between us. There was a reason. From the beginning his purpose was to stay. His ultimate destination was Britain.

Years later, he told me that the word *Britannia* meant New Babylon, and New Babylon also became his DJ brand. NB for New Babylon. Soon it would become Now Baby; not for Losco, though, he was concerned about his reputation.

"I'm like my father, *cazzo*!"

It was one of his quirks to start and end a sentence with the slang term for the *male appendix: Cazzo* or dick in English. When he spoke in English, instead, he used the word *shit*, said it sounded like *dick* and gave him the same feeling.

"Why do you do that?"

"My father is a blasphemer. Don't get me wrong, I'm not one of those Catholics who prays about bullshit, but I don't want to curse." Then he seemed to reflect a little, recalling his own private memories. "Even my grandparents blasphemed." He laughed, hiding a grin behind his hand.

Losco had a kind of morality, believed in his principles. I saw him as a straight, determined and driven person. I never knew what he was obsessed with, but sooner or later everyone gets obsessed with something. Society forces us into it, all together we are accomplices. He taught me that. When I think about it, Losco taught me a lot.

He spent hours on social networks studying the lives of others, he looked at them inside his silence of plaster, smoking and tapping his fingers on the tables of the bars we frequented together. Cigarettes and coffee: this was Losco. The drugs would come later.

In high school, during the first and second years, he had smoked a few joints, tried cocaine but then he stopped. I never knew why. The only possible clue that led me to believe that there was a reason was related to the death of a close friend of his, a Romanian named Damian. He never mentioned it openly, but I had seen some pictures of the two of them after a party: the pictures were scattered on his bed. He told me he had forgotten to put them back in the drawer.

"Mum doesn't come in here unless I give her my permission."

"Afraid she might see your Asian porn collection?"

"Don't talk crap, she knows I watch those things."

"Get a girlfriend."

"To be as unhappy as you?"

"What?"

"Did you know I was seeing Dounia?"

"Yes, I did."

"Yeah, but then with this college thing, we broke up."

"Couldn't see each other anyway?"

He shook his head as I watched him put those pictures of Damian back in order. They both looked the epitome of youthfulness, shining like supernovas, pale, dreamy, with elastic smiles and souls already delivered to the devil. It wasn't just them in those pictures, it was all the company they were in.

Echipa, he called them.

I didn't dare ask how he died, how they all walked away from those days like men with one-way tickets to different places. The way Losco put those pictures away and his harsh silence frightened me. I didn't even know much about his family. He told me that one of his grandmothers was a kind of witch, a curator in her parents' hometown, but little else, and that was the only exciting thing. He was tired of talking about his family even though I'd sometimes been to their house. Never at dinner, never with his parents sitting at a table. He didn't like the way his mother talked to his friends.

"She's nosy. She'd even ask you how much money you have in your bank account."

"You exaggerate."

His father had large hands and a huge head. I could see him working with engines, but the vehemence of Losco's shaking head stated precisely the opposite.

"Grandpa grew up on the street. To survive they

repaired everything that could be broken and put back together. Dad had to learn, but he doesn't have much patience. His motto is - You don't work for money, money works for you."

"So, what is he doing at the garage all day?"

"Grandpa taught him to listen. He understands the problem, but then he makes someone else solve it."

"What does he get out of all this?"

He shrugged, turning his back on me. As a result of all the time he spent on social media, he tended to carry his head forward, a bit like an older man.

His mother was thin and tall, and when she spoke, she alternated between Italian and Romanian. Losco made no effort to translate, he nodded and as soon as she left, he raised his eyes to the ceiling. His father was the complete reverse, a slow but witty *marchigiano*. I saw him a couple of times in front of the TV blaspheming for a penalty not given or a score against his beloved team.

After all, I got Losco's reasons, he did believe there wasn't much to say about his parents.

I'm not an only child, but there's not much to say about my family either. My brother works in a real estate agency and my sister is raising her first baby, Mattia. Giulia's engaged to a bank clerk a little older than her: Sebastiano. We used to hang out, in the early days, we'd go together for dinner at the Japanese or we'd go on long trips to some Adriatic or Tyrrhenian beach. Lisa, however, soon got tired of that unbridled life; one evening, she confessed to me that we had been together for eight years and that maybe it was time to put some savings aside. We loosened our grip.

After university, I found a job in a research laboratory. They paid me an internship and in less than a year I was hired. Losco, who was still living in London at the time, said that I had an impeccable fortune, that I had to have some god on my side.

"Fusaro recommended me." My biology professor.

"So it's true?"

"What?"

"That in Italy you need to *kiss ass*."

"I've never done that."

Giulia met Sebastiano during my final internship at the lab. We got carried away by the power of money, by greed, we wanted to live without thinking about the future, without having to ask ourselves if there was something else we had to do. University was often synonymous with restrictions, Dad gave me the minimum and paid my tuition fees. I did my best, I came out with the best grades and a job I thought was secure.

You never know when things may fall apart, but experience makes you soon realize that everything is precarious, nothing can last forever in the same way. At that time, I was far from understanding that, though. The experience with Losco and other friends at university hadn't taught me much. There had been some bereavements in my family during my growth but not close enough to develop an understanding of life. It was as if my mind saved everything in a unique storehouse that kept filling up without me noticing.

Sebastiano had studied political science but thanks to a contact he had found a place at Intesa San Paolo. Intelligent, cultured, articulate and well-to-do, his family had two clothing stores inside Milan, selling important goods, pieces worth thousands of euros or prestigious brands of bags.

"Dad asked me to work for him, but I wanted to go my own way."

Another Losco. Sebastian was very different from my old friend, but in that respect they were very similar. I found it bizarre. Sebastian's problem was that you could never have a confrontation, his ideas were unshakable and he seemed to have an opinion on everything. Lisa felt uncomfortable, sometimes she told me he looked at her in a certain way.

"How?"

"That way..."

"I don't understand. He's my sister's boyfriend."

"Yes, but sometimes he looks at me like he wants something else."

Maybe it was true, maybe women always think that men want them regardless, and I can't say that they don't, I never gave it much thought and the reason was quite sad. An idea popped into my mind one night when I was talking to my sister. She asked me if I still loved Lisa after all those years. I was about to answer but then caught my tongue. I was going to say yes, I still loved her, but the truth, which was brimming up like water in a glass, was that I was bored.

Eight years.

It was the night I confessed to my sister that Lisa and I were thinking about moving in together.

"Maybe next month she will get a permanent contract, and we thought… maybe leave our families."

"It's about time," was Giulia's comment before she shot me with that question.

"So what?" she asked, pushing that bullet even further into my flesh.

I spent the night wondering whether I really wanted to live the rest of my life with her, if I really wanted to make a home, have children. The truth behind my sister's question was something else, which I discovered a week later: Giulia felt too young to have a child, she was still in college, after all.

There were some quarrels at home but it did not take long before we all accepted the news. Giulia was pregnant. Her life would change forever, she had to say goodbye to her carefree, youthful twenty-four years of age, and arm herself with the patience of a mother, the strength of a goddess and the audacity of animal nature because a child is an atomic bomb waiting to explode.

I remember Lisa hugging Giulia and telling her that everything would be alright, that she would support her every day, that she would be like a sister, that my sister could wake her up at night if she needed help.

"Right, love?" Lisa said, looking at me with a big smile.

We were outside a restaurant in Corso Como, on an evening full of light in Milan, cold and crowded with unknown faces.

On second thoughts, I was despondent.

Mattia was born in June. We were all in the hospital. We were there for them. We were there to sanction something we didn't know the name of, but we felt it. Lisa kept her promise as far as she could. She often slept at my place and only went home on weekends. She'd get up every time she heard Mattia scream. Giulia, Lisa and my mother would go to the kitchen in the middle of the night with only the stove light on, looking after Mattia and chatting quietly; sometimes I peeped at them and secretly smiled at their pleasant harmony.

At that time, I no longer asked myself how I felt about Lisa. Mattia was a magnet, able to draw around himself everything about us, like a sponge mopping up our emotions, our fears, boredom, worries and everything else.

There are so many moments I'd like to tell...

Lisa probably wanted a child, but the first step was to move out.

"In a few months we'll do it," she told me one afternoon while she was sitting on the sofa in the living room cuddling Mattia. Giulia was in the bathroom. She was talking to me as I watched my nephew close his eyes for a nap. And we did. Lisa wanted to wait until my sister's son was old enough to be left in Giulia's and my mother's care.

It's kind of weird to say this, but my sister and I left our parents' house at almost the same time. Lisa and I found an apartment to rent while Sebastiano took my sister to one of the houses owned by his family that had recently been vacated by the tenants.

For a while that new change was fun too, it swept some of my thoughts away while I was filling my mental storehouse.

We spent more than a month going back and forth from Ikea although, in the end, we bought the kitchen in another place. Lisa's enthusiasm was so overwhelming that she made up for the weariness I felt about work. One evening, sitting on our new sofa, I told her that I wanted to change jobs and she said *I should think about it*, that *I shouldn't throw my luck overboard*.

"My brother's been home for a couple of years."

"So before you quit your current job, find a new one."

Lisa had no ambitions, no passions, she was committed to the kitchen. She was a good cook but didn't excel in anything. Since our move, she had been taking singing lessons once a week, the rest of the time she practised at home sitting in a corner of the living room as if she didn't want to be disturbed and wanted to go unnoticed. Lisa had dropped out of college to work part-time wherever the agency sent her and often it was to promote some product or assist clients at the call centre. So when I talked about changing jobs, she said that I would end up like her, that it had taken years to get a decent contract. She wanted me to understand my luck, but I kept thinking I needed something more stimulating.

One night we argued. It didn't happen often, but on this occasion, despite my attempts to ignore Lisa's foul mood, I couldn't resist the pull of fatigue, and I fought with her without even understanding if I was really angry or just pretending. Sometimes we quarreled over nothing; it would have been less stressful to simply acknowledge the bad day we had both had and settle any grudges before we went to sleep.

"What's wrong with you? You never say I love you."

It was true. I'd started to put on weight, grow a beard and brush my teeth on alternating days, prompting Lisa to reprehend me for my bad breath. That was it, *bad breath*, the fuse that started *all hell to break loose*. But my breath wasn't the real problem; it was who I was becoming: an apathetic, empty, scruffy man who was gradually getting worse.

After a year of living together, I found no stimulation in anything. Of course, there was still Mattia, who sometimes revived our mood, united us, encouraged us to smile even if we didn't want to; but now we were far away, and the days at Pascucci's house looked more like dreams than reality.

For a while Losco and I stayed in touch, I knew what he was doing, the jobs he found and his thoughts. He tried to push me to follow him, to pair up in London, to break habits, but I resisted. My relationship with Lisa was still in its infancy, the fire was at its peak even after two years and no wind seemed strong enough to put it out.

With the work at the research lab, I lost my connection with Losco. Then he moved to Bournemouth following a famous DJ on tour, a Romanian friend who played in front of important crowds. He learned the business and kept in touch with many of his followers. Bournemouth was the final destination for Losco.

One summer, he wrote to me even though we hadn't talked for ages, telling me that I had to go and see him, that there was life in Bournemouth, there was a beautiful beach and it wasn't as chaotic as London. I promised to visit him, but Lisa was the pivot, holding me back from any good purpose.

I only saw Losco during those summers when he went down to Milan to meet his parents. One year he came back thin, dull, with dark circles under his eyes, but the next year, he was perky and fattened up. At that time, it seemed that he had found balance and harmony. I thought he was finally in his element.

I missed a lot about my friend; and every time I met him and we went to one of our college bars, I noticed how much I missed him. But even those moments ended too.

With the move, I completely lost my only chance to see Losco again. In those two years, he called me and told me that he was in Milan for a couple of weeks, but I never found the time to run to him as I had done in previous years. I was confused. Confused about many things in my life: it was as if I suddenly realized that I could never grasp life and fully experience all the joys it had to offer me.

And then it happened. I hadn't seen the storm coming or heard the distant rumblings of thunder, so when it was overhead, soaking me and enveloping me in its power, I found myself unprepared. The storm overwhelmed me and left me empty for a while.

It was Losco who pulled me out of the river in flood. Even though I had not been a good friend, sometimes I didn't answer his calls and often glanced at his messages with little interest, he held out his hand like a great god descending from the clouds to give his support, and I took it. I did not hesitate. I didn't even hesitate in the face of his words, his revelations. I thought he was a bit mad, yes, but he had told me that I would find an answer to my pain, and that was enough for me to buy a ticket to London and seize the new opportunity he was offering.

4

Dad told me that I had to study if I wanted to find a good job. He had made sacrifices to allow me and my siblings to get an education. I was the only graduate, though.

Giulia tried before she got pregnant.

Fabrizio, instead, with fists on his hips, after the summer of his diploma, while we were all having dinner together, declared that he would find a job because he needed money to buy a car. He spent hours in the bathroom combing his hair. Giulia said he was the woman of the three and Fabrizio would get pissed off, telling her to shut her mouth as she didn't understand anything. They bickered, always did. I watched them grow up with these chicken-eyes, I watched their stories invent and reinvent themselves when they fell apart. They made me understand that between childhood and youth, there is a moment of perdition that I faced, without really realizing I was drowning. Some end up underwater, some are fished out before it's too late, most are lifted to the surface by an unknown force, perhaps the same one that puts pimples and the first hairs under your nose. I hated those moments. You have hair that wasn't there before and wonder how it appeared; then history repeats itself, you've white hair for months and maybe you only find out when someone points it out to you. They start to appear and there's no warning.

That's life.

Besides, I've never been one to pay special attention to these kinds of things.

Fabrizio was the opposite, he immediately noticed pimples and that day he cried, begging mum to find a cure. They spent months asking dermatologists for advice without much success. They said it was all to do with growing, that he was developing faster than others. In fact, at his age, I was less developed. His torment didn't last long, a friend of our father's advised him to do sports and drink a lot of water. Fabrizio didn't waste any time. He played as a striker for a few years before realizing, on his eighteenth birthday, that if he had a car and a wallet full of money, there could be far more to life.

And I still remember that nineteen-year-old young man taller than all of us, skin as light as milk, hair as straight as ears of corn, standing with fists on his hips, a passable imitation of Mussolini, while he was telling our father that he didn't feel like studying.

Giulia had enrolled in literature, a real nerd. The teachers had advised her that if she chose that subject, one day she would become a professor. While our parents believed it was a vocation that had come to her from beyond, Fabrizio and I knew that such advice would make no difference to her life. At the time she was engaged to a gymnast before she decided to dump him when she met Sebastiano. Giulia was the sort to spend every Saturday night in the disco with her friends. She met Sebastiano there, dancing, maybe tipsy and under the influence of marijuana.

Fabrizio didn't want to know about certain junk, he would look at her white well-aligned teeth in the mirror telling Giulia that if she didn't stop smoking in a few years, she would lose that family value. She showed him the middle finger and then, in her short skirt, left the house without saying goodbye.

In high school, I tried to set up a rock band but I failed miserably. I still have my first guitar at home, it reminds me that if you don't commit to something, you don't get anywhere. I only have dim memories of what I used to get up to with my friends, but I do recall that there were times when we enjoyed joints, porn, outings in Milan, first make-outs and the choices that separate.

I met Lisa after the diploma exams.

One night, I went with my friends to get drunk, screaming into the night that school was shit and we were finally free. But we weren't, I mean we weren't free; in fact, freedom was about to be ripped from under our noses without warning, just like the first beard or white hair. We joined other friends at a birthday party and Lisa was there too. I threw up on the floor after drinking half the cans and open bottles of wine on the buffet table, and she was kind enough to help me stand. I remember Umberto slapping me in front of everyone saying that I had gone too far, that I was an asshole, that you don't mess around in other people's houses. I don't remember much about that night, but they did, Umberto and Lisa, I never forgot them. She sat me down and held me against the backrest. Her hands pulled up my head or helped my back to bend over for another gag. Before I left, I apologized to her, and told her to accept at least one coffee. And so she did.

I always thought she came into my life to rescue me, to support me, just like she did that night without knowing who I was or why I was there. Some people are just kind. They are born that way, neither drama nor time change them, and I hope God blesses them all wherever they are, whatever they're doing, alive or dead.

Her friends didn't want her to see me, they said men took advantage of her. I thought I wasn't like those men, but I ended up being just like them. If I had been more lucid, if I had understood my weaknesses earlier, I would have let her go so that another heart could enjoy her kindness.

But things change. They always change.

5

The tape has Losco's instructions. I send it back and wait for the rustling to become a voice.

"*Are you ready for it?*"

"*Yes.*"

"So, this is what you need to know. At first, reality will seem brighter. You'll feel like you're in a high-definition movie. Every single colour will shine like you're near a star.

"At stage two, things in the world will want to communicate with you, a leaf, a branch on the ground, or even a spider weaving its web behind the bookshelf. Mother Nature will look for a way to talk to you like you've never felt before.

"During the third stage, you will hear people's thoughts, but it will be difficult for you to understand what is really happening. Then reality and dream will be one, you won't be able to distinguish one from the other. Time and space cancel each other out, hours seem like days and days seem like months."

I'm there with Losco. Observing him hesitate, I ask if there is a further stage. Losco stares into my eyes but, at the same time, I have the feeling that he goes beyond by penetrating me with his gaze. It is tense. Although I don't understand him, I realise that he has already tried, that he knows everything.

I should have felt that impalpable sadness pervading his words, his gestures, the way he treats others, but it was elusive.

There is only one thing I want to know, I have no interest in anything else.

Losco avoids my question.

"I bought a few litres of water. If you need more, it's in the utility room."

"Why?"

"You'll find out soon enough."

"But there are six mushrooms."

"One is for me."

I must have looked at the label on the bottle in the middle of the table, he had only bought one type, so I asked him why. I thought it was funny to think there was a link but, as a scientist, I knew it was not just a coincidence.

"Did you get the cheapest one?"

"No, don't you remember, don't you? It was a while ago, you said our heart beats at a ratio of one sodium to seven potassium. The kidneys... wait..."

"One to five for kidneys, I mean."

"Yes, that's right. You may not realize it, but this information can save your life."

"How?"

"Have you ever looked at the ratio of sodium to

potassium in water?"

"Sure, at the lab, we were doing tests..."

"All is one."

"What is this?"

"You see, people study and then they don't understand shit. They just think about using their knowledge to get a job but they don't get it. It's absurd not to take what you've studied."

"Get to the point." I sound impatient, I never liked to be questioned, after all, I am the one with a degree in biology.

"You'll find out the point when you pass stage five."

We've shared other things with each other but the tape didn't record them, Losco pressed the stop button telling me that *it isn't necessary*, that *we are digressing, because only the rules matter.*

The rules mean gallons of water.

"What if I don't drink enough?"

Every time I listen to this piece, the rustle of the tape sounds like the pureness of Losco's silence. His face is impassive as he studies my eyes, while contriving an answer he can't give me. He keeps silent and after shrugs his shoulders like dogs shake their torso to wash away the water.

The evening comes down and I'm cold, so I grab the blanket sitting on the bed and wrap it around my neck. Aunt warned me that it would be better to come here in late spring but my psychoanalyst invited me to keep this diary so that I could collect my ideas. He says that writing helps to clarify things, that sometimes noting down what we have faced is useful to observe it from a new perspective.

I see details, things that when I was in Bournemouth with Losco I quickly forgot. There are his slender white fingers pouring water into my crystal glass, like a loving father, attentive to my needs. Back to *our days at the University*, Losco often thought to himself. We were friends, but he was not the type who listened to people's worries, in his head there was no room for other concerns. Yet his way of being on Socials, spying the lives of strangers, seemed to me precisely a way to pay attention to things in the world. He called it *the surface*.

"Social networks are what the iceberg shows us."

"What do you mean?"

"Do you know the story of the first man who saw an iceberg?"

I shook my head, amused. It was supposed to be the summer just before he left. Sitting in a pub watching a football match I had little interest in.

"Okay, we got three men in a boat. At one point one of the three spots a mountain of ice and exclaims *it's a mountain of ice*. When they come home, they say they saw an iceberg, which was only ice and it was floating on the water."

"Exactly what it does."

"Exactly what it looks like. In fact, what you can see of an iceberg is just the top. These are the socials. If you have the courage to dive, to descend below the surface, you realize that the iceberg is more than it shows."

Losco wasn't a philosopher, and I knew that those few pearls he pulled out of his pocket found a real place in his thoughts. That's why he had decided to leave, it was his way of descending below the icy water that often frightens. Looking at the tip of the iceberg was no longer an option: there was something else and he wanted to discover it.

Look, the last light before dusk is a reddish line beyond the horizon where the sea meets the sky. The purple and black clouds above the crest of the last sun, my tip of the iceberg right now.

Losco's voice again.

"One question."

"Right."

"You must confess now. Ask yourself how far you want to go."

"As far as I can."

"That's a good answer, my friend."

He gives me the first mushroom. I swallow it.

If it weren't for the sweetness of the honey, it would have a savage taste, something like chewed bark taken from the damp earth at the foot of a tree, or inferior quality tobacco.

Then I swallow the others, one at a time.

"Now, the rules."

"Rules?" My voice snaps between my teeth. I want to shove two fingers down my throat, but I think it's too late.

"No smoking. No booze. Sex is forbidden after the third stage. And above all, lie, always lie."

"What does lying mean? What should I lie about?"

"From the third stage, all relations with the outside world must cease. You will turn off your cell phone, we will disconnect the internet. It'll just be you and me. And if anyone comes to the door, send them away, whoever they are. Lie. Pretend you're sick."

"Sounds complicated."

"It is what it is. You must drink a lot of water. Water will be the one thing you can't do without, I promise you. And now we're going out, we're having a party. I've got one, too. I won't go any further, I swear. I'm doing this to be near you. Do you understand?"

He looks at me seriously; Losco's always been a little over the top.

6

Let's go back.

My sigh seems to sink the last slice of sunshine below the horizon of the sea. Sanremo is a flower that gathers its petals before a new dawn. I live in the Russian area. I walked a long way this morning, arrived hungry at a *pizzeria* and then slept for three hours. When I woke up, I dragged the coffee table from the living room onto the balcony of my room. The desk was too big.

I feel the cold pinching my fingertips, so I tap them on the wooden base to better endure February. Sometimes you just need to breathe.

When thoughts don't seem to clarify, I like to be out in the open-air.

I have some headphones so as not to disturb the quiet outside: people retiring in the heated living rooms sitting to dinner or in front of the television; I put them on my legs because now there is little to hear, just a bit of unintelligible ending.

When I got to Bournemouth, I found out that Losco had rented an entire apartment.

"The agency wouldn't give it to me."

"How come? And why did you choose this one?"

"For the view of the sea. Manor Road is the best area."

"You spent a fortune, I guess."

"What I spent doesn't matter."

We were on the ninth floor. From the central salon window you could see the trees, two tall buildings and the sea. The owner had moved abroad and was looking for someone to take at least one room. Losco had offered to pay for a whole month for just two people. At least that's what he made me believe.

I arrived late in the afternoon. In the luggage there was some change, a couple of books, a toothbrush and my passport.

"Don't carry so much stuff. If you need anything, we'll find it here," had been his comment. As a precaution, however, I had brought three pairs of boxers, socks, a white shirt and at least five T-shirts.

"I'll introduce you to some girls when you come."

That was the reason why I went looking for condoms, stayed for a long time in the dedicated department of the supermarket and, after a while, abandoned the idea of buying them. Losco must have thought of that too but I was embarrassed to ask him. The idea of having sexual intercourse made me nervous.

After Lisa, depression had brought me to my knees. Fabrizio had introduced me to a friend of his, Chiara; we went out a couple of times but, the last night, I didn't have the strength to go through with it. Despite her attractiveness and charm, I left her naked on the bed, turning my back on her while I put my shoes back on and whispering that I was sorry.

Fabrizio called me an idiot, but he understood.

"You can't make a mistake with someone like her."

Giulia had sketched a smile and then hugged me. "I get you."

"Anyway, Erica talked to him."

Erica was Fabrizio's new girlfriend.

"What did she say?" I was curious, though I felt like a complete imbecile.

"That you're cute, it can happen. If you'd like to call Chiara back, she'd like to go out with you. Don't beat yourself up too much. Enjoy life."

Giulia had kicked Fabrizio out, calling him *insensitive*, but I was grateful to him. The next day I spoke to Losco on the phone, and if I went to Bournemouth, it is also thanks to Fabrizio and Chiara.

Giulia didn't want me to leave, to tell the truth: she didn't want me to go so far away.

"If you need me, I can't reach you."

Mattia was two years old. I thought he had grown up quickly and would soon start articulating complex sentences, developing ideas and making decisions. And that would have meant entering into the adult world. For a moment, I didn't envy him. I told him mentally never to grow up.

"I'll be fine, I promise."

"But call me if you need me. I'm always there."

We were at home that day, our parents' house. Mom was cooking *lasagna* and Dad was trying to fix a broken chair. He must have asked for our help ten times but nobody listened to him.

A few days later, Sebastiano and Giulia took me to Malpensa airport. She shed a few tears and he, in a soft tone of voice, told me to relax, not to think about it too much.

"Thank you, I will."

I never saw them again.

7

I am woozy about the idea of going home after what I've learned.

The tape starts up again right there. I pick up the headphones and listen.

"Please, breathe now." This is Losco.

There is a void, and it is the void of my words.

"I know what you want to know."

I must have stared intensely at him for a few seconds before he said: "It's only Tuesday."

I let the recording run and close my eyes. It's like sailing in the middle of a storm-swept ocean: you want to vomit but you can't, you try to anchor yourself to something to avoid being thrown in every direction but you keep hitting what's around you, and the waves are frozen, they have blades that you can't remove - once they penetrate, they stay in.

"You're gonna need a psychologist. My advice is to get some rest."

I was advised that a stranger who lived in Marche, worked as a nurse, had skills but Losco never specified what kind.

I left for Marche but first I called Fabrizio to ask him for a favour.

8

Bournemouth has the best seafront on the English coast.

It was September.

There were still tourists, mostly from the east, families of dark-skinned Indians and Spanish grilling on the beach. I also met many students, including Italians, very young people who had just turned eighteen. I was surprised but Losco explained that it was not at all surprising that every year thousands of young people came from abroad, some to study, some to look for a job or just for a limited experience and maybe to learn a foreign language. I felt all the weight of my thirty years.

He showed me around the town. Even though I had my suitcase, we walked for almost an hour. I saw the Ferris wheel and then we walked along the seafront. I was thrilled to see families, students and people of all ages mingle on that curved string of beach similar to an endless hyperbole.

For a moment, I was truly able to forget the past.

We went up to the apartment. Losco had prepared an English style dinner. He warmed it up in the oven and we ate early. He said I shouldn't weigh myself down, that the evening would be very long.

"I thought it was tomorrow."

He shook his head and said, "I have to be there at 9:00. I'll play till midnight, and then we'll come back."

"Right away?"

He showed me my room and pointed to his, which was a double bedroom adjacent to the living room.

"Settle down and then let's eat."

I sat on the bed, greeted by the warmth of my new room. I could hear Losco dealing with the pots and pans, making our meal; I closed my eyes, breathed deeply, trying not to drown in the abyss that for six months had done nothing but drag me down. I thought I was doing something crazy, that I wouldn't find an answer or a cure for my sufferings. I sat on the edge, forgot the suitcase at my feet, no interest in opening it, no interest in leaving that flat. It seemed to me that having dinner and watching a movie were all that I needed, but Losco had planned everything.

When I decided to get up, to get out of my darkness, I thought of something else that I had to rely on, that whatever happened, at least for a while, it would take me away from the pain I was feeling.

Pain is a terrible thing; no matter what you suffer from, it tears you apart; it doesn't let you eat or sleep, it confuses your mind, it takes you into crevices so dark that they are black holes.

Someone says *let go of your past,* but you can't do it. The past builds us up, it follows like a shadow or a dog on a leash, it's the way we look back that determines our success or failure. Sitting on the edge of the bed, I felt I was falling, that there was a double gravity on my shoulders, something that pushed my body down without any possibility of opposing it.

I didn't want to show Losco my fragility, I presented myself with the best smile and the full willingness to follow his little psychedelic experiment. I was curious to understand more. If he had asked me a few years earlier, I would probably never have come to England, but, as my father used to say, *necessity mobilizes man:* it mobilized me too.

I was a meteorite ready to hit the bottom of the abyss with a thud.

On my plate are potatoes, green peas, pieces of jackfruit and a kind of salted pastry whose name escapes me, served with gravy sauce.

Losco is in a good mood. I've never seen him so excited about anything. Even though I recognize him as an old friend, I feel like I am talking to someone who just looks like him. He speaks fast, has a lot of ideas and is enthusiastic about the life he is leading.

"Don't you miss Italy?"

"I don't know. But I'd never go back."

"I know."

"No, you don't know that yet. There I felt oppressed, obsessed, and lacking in ideas. Not that England is better; people spend most of their time in pubs or talking bullshit, but at least if you have a good idea, you can get it done faster."

"And that's what you did?"

"That's what I tried to do. When I got here, I wasn't quite sure what to do. I worked as a waiter to learn English, tried drugs, spent evenings drinking until I threw up, until I found myself with a used deck in my room. I must have been really drunk that day. Someone asked me if I was interested in buying it, and laughing like a madman, I answered that I was interested but I had no clue what to do with it."

"And how did you learn?"

"Dragos, as you know."

Yes, I remember. Dragos was a Romanian who grew up in London. They had become friends, perhaps more than we were. But Losco never confessed much, and even then he didn't seem to want to tell me anything else.

"He helped me make friends. If you live abroad, if you ever decide to do that, remember to make friends."

"Romanians, I guess."

"Romanians, Italians, Spanish and Indians. A small community of people all living together in shabby houses, snorting cocaine from morning to night," then he looks at me and as if to justify himself adds: "Life was hard, someone had more than one job. We paid rent and bills to live on the edge; evenings, after all, were our way of escaping, not to think about how heavy and complicated life was."

"Do you think that helped?"

"What?"

"I mean, snorting that stuff."

He laughs. He laughs so much that he almost chokes on his potato.

"Not at all, it was like a palliative, or if you want a distraction. Cocaine will cheer you up for a while and then you need more, but you had to do it to get through the day, coffee often wasn't enough. Don't think everybody did it. Some people couldn't because of the work they did, maybe they were waiting until the weekend to get high."

"Why did you do it? I mean, living abroad and then living on the edge. It doesn't make sense."

"Nothing makes sense, we'll make sense of it. Do you think your life is normal?"

"I think so, or at least I thought so."

Here's the sadness again. I grabbed a glass of water and took a sip.

"You did the same?"

"No. I mean, just for a while, because I didn't know what to do. Dragos, though, suggested staying away from it, so he taught me how to use the deck. At first, I did it as a hobby, but then I followed him on nights and it became a second job."

"How did that make you feel?"

He stands up straight by filling his lungs with air; oxygen serves to tidy his memories, to transport them from the arteries to his brain. It's as if I could see their path and understand what makes sense of our days; it's as if your whole body is playing in unison. With one voice. I didn't know what it meant, I'd never felt it, but Losco showed it to me with his earnest, proud and accomplished presence.

"Committed. It kept me off from getting drunk, and then I made friends. I kept my mind occupied."

"But it still wasn't enough, right?"

I knew it. He told me about it on the phone, trying to convince me to do the experiment.

"We all need something to believe in, and I believed that by keeping my mind occupied I could get rid of the cobwebs of the past, but I didn't."

One day he had gone too far, a mix of cocktails, someone had poured drugs into his glass and he had plunged back into the tunnel of depression. That's what he called it: the tunnel of depression. Dragos was no longer with him, they had lived in Bournemouth for a while and then he'd left for London on tour.

"You've been lonely."

He shrugs his shoulders; he won't tell me, but I can imagine it. For a few years they had been friends, they had lived together, played together, maybe shared sexual experiences too. I didn't know for sure but I understood that there must have been a strong bond between them.

"I thought it wouldn't hurt me for once, I was sober for a couple of years by that time."

Demons come back if you let your guard down, he told me on the phone.

"Then I met Luca, as you know. The psychologist.

53

Remember, I told you about him?"

Yeah. The same psychologist who works as a nurse who suggested to keep this diary, not to forget.

Luca had come to visit his son who was studying at a university in Bournemouth.

"The first time I saw him," Losco tells me, "he was on the seafront. He heard me talking on the phone in Italian, and when I hung up, he approached me. He didn't immediately tell me what he was doing in life, only spoke about his son, a kind of language genius. He was proud of him because in his family no one could speak any foreign language."

"And how did you get to the mushrooms?"

"At one point I told him I was having trouble sleeping, that I had back pain because of the time I was spending with the decks. He gave me some tips and said the pain I was feeling was related to unresolved things."

"Unresolved things?"

"Something I hadn't faced or overcome from the past. That's how it all started. By chance, I asked him how it was possible to heal from certain traumas, and he told me that the mind can be our worst enemy and that sometimes we need to be guided."

"He drove you to drugs. That's not very comforting."

"Soon, you'll understand."

"You really think they can help me?"

"They will."

9

The beach at Sanremo appears grey. It talks to me, prints frames in my mind, memories of that night. The African sand. Girls in bikinis, beers pressed inside their handbags, the footprints of those who chased each other or stopped for a long chat. There is a bonfire, a stand and Losco for the opening night. The guys with cocktails in their hands in front of the deck are screaming with euphoria. And a graceful student is watching me talk to Losco while I'm next to him pretending to be an assistant, making me feel important. I finally meet her. Lauren. Lu for friends. She knows Losco, but she actually uses him to get some free passes.

"She's good. Don't fall in love with her. Just have fun."

"How old is she?"

"Didn't you ask her?"

"No."

"Twenty-two. She's a college student."

"So pretty."

"You're not the only one who thinks that."
"Have you been with her?"
"No."

10

I go back, before the beach there is the time of recording.

Drink water. Lots of water.

If I didn't drink enough, I could lose control of my hallucinations. Not that I knew what it meant, but the idea scared me.

We've eaten a light meal to slow the fungus' effect.

Losco didn't want the hit to come all at once.

"There's time for the *grand finale.*"

I ate five of them, the sixth one swallowed by Losco. We used honey, a type from Madagascar. He told me that it is the combination of this unique honey and the mushrooms that increase the hallucinogenic effect.

"Will I see aliens?"

"You'll see what you need to see."

When I went out to join him at the beach, I was already nervous. Losco had kept telling me to relax, that I would feel a slight sense of nausea and nothing more. I had no idea what to expect, and yet I never hesitated when he offered me them.

I swallowed those mushrooms hoping to find an answer to my pain and I thought that, after all, death would be a relief from a life without love.

Three things pursued me that night. Lauren was the first. Then the plainclothes cop and, at last, Michael Jackson. Yeah, I know it sounds crazy, but this was just the beginning.

Don't know how things are gonna go from here on out. Not sure if I remember right. It took some time to get out of it, back to my natural rhythm. Luca used to make me do a few breathing exercises, said *they helped keep me in the present.*

Luca is a sweet, reserved and intelligent man, I've never met anyone like him. He had a reassuring way of speaking, a warm, loving voice. He used to massage my back, saying it calmed nerves. I thought he was a chiropractor but he told me he knew nothing of that discipline, his technique had been passed down through his family. Grandma read the oil in the glass, I met her twice, at the beginning to know my current state of mind and, at the end, to tell me that things would go well.

I wanted to believe her, and I believed in her.

I close my eyes to remember better. I have to follow Luca's instructions. Breathe, breathe long. I'm finally there, the effect is building. It's like going into a waking dream, watching the past like a ghost. This is how I see myself now, in Bournemouth, with Losco walking with hands in his pocket and the Ferris wheel that glitters as it rotates.

I press the red button.

Sentient

1

Bournemouth. England.

Here's Losco. He smiles. Strange to see him again after all these years. I can't tell you how long it's been since I last looked at his face, heard his voice so close.

My head's not working now, it's often heavy, often absent. The visits to the hospital didn't help me get out of the fog. I forget things. Sometimes they are in dreams, but in the morning it's all gone again. I've lost my cell phone, car keys, and once I couldn't remember the way home. I got better, though not better enough. They told me it would pass, that it's a shock, not a tumour.

Rehab gave me back some memories, incomplete things. At the beginning, I was struggling to recognize my parents. It took me a few days to go from fear of not knowing who I had next to me to knowing that those faces were my beloved family. First Mom, then my sister and finally Dad and Fabrizio. With Fabrizio I started laughing. He was frustrated that I couldn't remember the shit we did together; the first things I remembered about him were the quarrels with Giulia. That's why I laughed.

They showed me photos, videos, messages. The memories came at once, like obvious things that were on the tip of your tongue and suddenly re-emerge. After ten days, I was able to remember my whole life.

Or almost.

She didn't get in. There was a painful emptiness, a hidden certainty that didn't emerge from the bowels where something of me had pushed her back like a dirty creature. My family, especially Giulia, talked about Lisa to help me fill that void, introduce her back into my life. So I started dreaming about her but I also had flashes during the day, partial access to her figure, like details you can never decipher.

Then I heard music. The music, the notes of a melodic piano meant that something about her was re-emerging from the recesses of my mind. I felt anxiety and despair. I wondered if this time I'd be able to see her face. But to this day, it's something I miss.

C. A minor. F. G. I know the notes, if I had a piano I could play them.

Losco has light skin, a suggestion of a beard that never grows so much. Even in university it wasn't much, sparse under the chin and along the jaws, nothing compared to mine. I have to shave at least once a week if I don't want to risk looking like a brown bear. For years I shaved properly, partly for work, partly from Dad's example; he claimed that shaving was a sign of respect for the people we met.

"Welcome," he says, hugging me. "I'll help you, give it to me."

He takes my trolley, I let it go. I put some clothes inside it, my laptop because I often don't sleep and watch a couple of movies as a sedative. I usually read at least one book a month but it hasn't been like that lately. At home, I mean the one I shared with my ex, we had a collection of books from Harry Potter to Game of Thrones. Harry Potter and Mazzantini's books were hers, they were on the shelves of a small bookshop. Mine were in the middle, a skimpy collection from Ammaniti to Stephen King. Among the few memories I keep, there is a discussion about Faletti's I Kill, she refused to read it because she considered it violent. I told her that no one in Italy had ever written such an intriguing thriller and that she would certainly like it.

"I don't want to read it. The title makes me shiver."

I hear her voice saying it, I see her hands in a hurry pushing that book away and forcing me to put it back on the shelf. Then, as always, I turn around and see her back, hair amassed behind her neck, a few rebellious tufts caressing her shoulders.

All I catch is her slowness.

"How was the trip? Are you alright?"

I'm going after him. The air is tepid, in its slight movement among the people, I imagine it as a snake holding back the heat of the sun. It passes between us. I can smell Losco's deodorant, it's different from how I remembered it. Other scents arrive, the smog of the taxis lined up on our left and something similar to the wort of beer sticking to the asphalt.

"Why didn't you tell me the trains split up here?"

"I'm sorry, I forgot. I usually take the National Express."

"How come?"

"I once had an appointment in London," he tells me as we cross the street to line the shopping centre car park above us. "They were waiting for me at noon. I took it easy, woke up late because I'd been to a party the night before and was still hungover." I can see his back, he's just a couple of steps ahead of me. "I'll keep it short, they cancelled all the trains and I had to take a taxi to Southampton station. It wasn't the first time there were delays or cancellations, so I tried National Express afterwards. Much more reliable, I assure you."

"Is it cheap?"

"I'll show you later. I suggest you book a ride with them. At least you're certain not to miss your flight back."

There is a lot of movement around, on the left, above the road that skirts the park we are crossing, I see the Odeon. Losco tells me that on Mondays he often goes there; the ticket costs less and it is an excuse not to feel too lonely after the weekend evenings.

Sitting in a garden in the main park, some youths laugh, play football, chase each other, let their pets make friends with strangers.

We dig the path with our shadows and arrive at a fork in the road, through the branches of the trees I notice a big Ferris wheel and the salty breath of the sea. Lots of people are converging in that direction.

"Sorry to take you for a longer ride, but it's the best time of the day."

"For whom?"

"For me, of course."

He smiles at me. I nod.

He tells me about his life in Bournemouth. He does it in stages, as if he wants me to breathe in the atmosphere without being distracted by anything else. I thank him. Walking sometimes helps me handle my headaches.

Finally, there it is, the sea. I think it's the only thing in the world that makes me forget everything else simply by looking at it, a magnet for peace.

"It's not *Capo Vaticano*, but the beach is wide, we can come for a swim tomorrow. Let's grill some vegetables, Halloumi..."

"What are those?"

"It's cheese. Then I'll show you."

"Tell me the truth, what's the food like here?"

"English cuisine is very protein-rich, there's no real diet. Fish and fries. In the morning you have breakfast and in the evening you have a snack. But don't worry, there are European or Asian restaurants. Do you like spicy?"

"Yes," and then I remember that she never wanted too much of it, Lisa scolded me saying that when I grew up I'd have arthritis problems. I asked her how she knew as I'd never heard anything so stupid.

"I read it somewhere."

"Where?"

"No, maybe I heard that."

"Are you okay?" Losco brings me back. "What were you saying?"

"Sorry, I just remembered something."

"About what?"

"I'm not sure."

"Was it important?"

"No, I guess not."

I'm lying. I don't want to talk about it. But maybe Losco is right, this little holiday could help me to sort things, to find some peace and, possibly, with peace even memories.

"They recently opened an Italian restaurant that makes the best pizza in Bournemouth. I'll take you there before you leave."

"Alright."

The sea has our reflection.

Giulia used to tell me about our reckless weekends, to help me shed light; we used to talk about this, to *shed light*. I often tried to remember, it was like hitting a brick wall made of darkness. I told Giulia, I told her what I saw, and from that moment on our idea to fight that darkness with light was born. Her voice guided me into the unknown.

When I still didn't know anything about the accident,

she defended me. It was the days after my hospitalisation, I spent most of my time sitting in my bed at my parents' house. If I wasn't asleep in my room, I'd sit in the living room watching Netflix movies at low volume. I'd get a lot of sleep, sometimes 15 hours. I woke up every three hours because of the headache and the pain that came from the bruises I suffered during the accident.

On the third day, I went out to take the rubbish out and two people approached me. A woman was in tears observing me sternly. I thought I knew her husband, a compact little man, hunched up in his brown jacket, bald in the middle of his head. He, instead, looked at me with sorrow. The man with the kind and intelligent face held back what I thought should be his wife. He asked her to behave herself, not to exaggerate.

At first, her words of hatred didn't reach my brain, she was screaming, she had eyes as red as hell and the death-wish of a murderer. I dropped the black bag at my feet and stared at her motionless in my square metre of space.

Who were they?

There was an idea, a hidden knowledge that sometimes takes a few minutes to reveal itself, like when you meet someone you haven't seen in years and you stutter trying to remember their name.

"You killed her."

It was the only sentence I brought home after Giulia ran in my direction and yanked me back in.

We locked ourselves in.

I couldn't get the image of that tiny woman who hated me out of my head.

Giulia was crying too. And she trembled. She sat next to me on the sofa, hugging me. I didn't know what to do or what to say.

"*Why?*"

The only words that could come out of my lips.

We all want to know why. It's a subconscious question.

Giulia didn't want to tell me, she said it was too soon, so I believed her. That night I didn't sleep, I had breakfast at five in the morning and then I asked Mom and Dad to explain.

"Your sister wants to tell you," my mum told me.

I remember the last few months well. It's the before that isn't there.

Giulia started telling me about our eccentric dates.

We drove to the beaches of Liguria or Romagna. We weren't interested in swimming but we wanted the sea to be our backdrop. I watched my sister gesturing, drinking her umpteenth coffee, looking after Matteo to feed some of his whims while she spoke to me.

"I knew it was her."

"You didn't say anything to her afterwards, did you?" Losco is concerned about my sister. Maybe he thinks I've become neurotic or impatient. I ask him.

"No, no, but you have a quick temper."

Let's laugh.

We're having dinner, talking about mushrooms. He

explains how they work. Then, maybe out of some guilt still lurking, he wants to make sure I don't have a row with my sister.

"Giulia was right to tell you. I was closing off. I didn't want to see anyone else."

"How come?"

I'm digging with the spoon on my plate, pulling up one of the last bits of potatoes.

"I didn't want to remember."

"I don't understand."

"I know."

"Your sister said the same thing to me. But she thought someone distant, someone like me, could be useful to you."

I nod. I'd like to say something, but I hesitate.

"Have you talked about anything else?"

"Yes, but I shouldn't tell you."

"Looks like you two had a long talk. I didn't know that."

"I know."

"Really funny, you copy my style now?"

Losco giggles and then says: "She was feeling a little guilty, that's all."

"And for what?"

"She thought it was her fault. Because of suicide."

"I'm not sure I quite understand. She had nothing to do with it."

In the silence between us, I suddenly understand. She felt guilty because she believed that by helping me to bring my memory back, she had driven me to attempt suicide. To forget again.

"I can tell by your expression that you understand why."

Yes, I nod.

"I'll call her later. I..."

"She didn't want to burden you with that, too. And, God, now I feel guilty."

"You don't have to. I'm fine. I'm sorry Giulia thought that all this time, she must have suffered a lot."

"I hardly know your sister. I may have seen her a couple of times in all our friendship."

"Do you remember her?"

"Very pretty. I remember we picked her up outside a club once. I think someone had a flat tyre and she asked you to take her home. Maybe she had a fight with some guys. I don't remember."

"They had broken up. Giulia put the hole in his car tyre."

Losco laughs. He claps his hand on the table to show off his surprise.

"But he never knew," I admit, adding fire to his incredulity.

"What a girl!"

"She's always been determined."

"The second time, we were in college. She had come to see you. She was hanging out with her friends and we laughed at the way they chewed gum and looked like playboy pussies."

Suddenly Losco has put me in a good mood. I don't know what, maybe some details, but watching

Bournemouth from this window gives me good vibes. It's like the city is a medley of the places I've lived in for the last ten years.

"Do you remember it?"

"Not very well."

"It wasn't important. I only remember because of her friends."

"I bet you wanted to bang them?"

"I did, yeah."

"I'm sorry you never knew her well but, at the time, Giulia was causing trouble at home. She didn't want to study and spent most of her allowance on women's stuff."

"Did she make it?"

"University?"

"Yes."

"When you met her, she was still in high school. She scored one hundred, but university didn't suit her. Then she got engaged to some instructor, a very young personal trainer. She was madly in love with him. But then it ended. One day she woke up and realised she didn't love him after all."

"It affected you, didn't it? Why?"

I shake my head. I feel a twinge of pain coming out of my chest, but I have no clue about that.

"Do you want to change the subject?"

"No. I want to understand."

"You'll understand," he says as he gets up and takes the dishes away.

"I'll help you wash them."

"I'll wash and you dry, so we can take a break from talking."

"No, really, there's no problem."

Then Losco turns around and comes close. I can hear his breath.

"No trains are running here. I'll take care of you."

"Thank you."

With his free hand he pats my arm. "Come on."

Losco gets ready. I, instead, get devoured by torment. I have a call, the image of Giulia with Matteo in her arms comes up on the screen of my smartphone.

And then I'd promised to call her.

"Hi, how are you?"

Her voice. She took care of me and I can't bear to make her suffer.

Matteo asks who she's talking to.

"It's Uncle, love. Do you want to say something to him?"

That makes me smile.

"Pass me to Matteo," I say.

"Uncle?"

"Hey, little boy, how are you?"

I'm sitting on the bed in my room. I should really be putting on my best shirt and, maybe, even shave and relax with a hot shower, but I'm thinking of those who have filled the dark and painful days of my life.

"I'm fine, and you? Is there sea where you are now?"

I tell him *there is.*

"Is it as good as Punta Ala's?"

We were there last year, in September after the Covid-19 wave. Sebastiano's parents have a holiday-home over there, in a private residence. The house had a large perimeter garden, a swimming pool and, from the tower, we watched the moon with a telescope. It's a recent memory, it comes to my mind like a flash. Lisa and I were in the tower, I know. I can see it. I look for her hands, mine and hers that overlap in a game of magic, like magicians handling a deck of cards. Her brief laughter echoing around us tells me to stop, that I'm stupid, that she wants to see the moon. I have her hair on my face. I tighten my hold around her waist while she sinks her eyes into the refractors. The light from there bounces off and catches her. I envy that starlight that knows something about her that I don't know anymore. That's why I tickle her hips, I caress her hands to catch her attention. I'm jealous of the starlight. It's an unconscious feeling that I'm really not aware of. I want to play, I want to make that moment deep, laughing, spectacular.

"It's beautiful here, baby. Someday I'll bring you here," I say to Mattia.

That must have been our last happy moment together, I can't remember any more after that. Returning from Punta Ala, the monotony swallowed us up like an appetizing dish, devoured with the same frenzy as a hungry animal. Our carcasses, finally, exposed to the sun, were torn to pieces by vultures, things that were not real but that dwelt in us.

"How are you?" Giulia again.

"I am well. I like it here. Thanks for calling Losco."

"You're welcome, even though I was hoping you didn't know."

"Let me tell you something."

"Wait a minute, I'm gonna ask Sebastian if he can keep Matteo."

I'll wait, sure. I'm going to leave the room and head into the living room. From the large window, the sea looks like a painting; the seagull flying in the space that separates us makes it real.

"So the trip went well?"

"Yep."

"What did you want to tell me?"

I'll think about it. Losco comes out of his room, goes to the bathroom and tells me he's almost ready.

"I'll call you tomorrow. We're on our way out."

"But what did you want to tell me?"

"That you're the best person I've ever met."

"You've never said that to me before."

"I know, I'm sorry. Pride. I gotta go now. I'll call you tomorrow."

"Okay. What are you doing tonight?"

"Losco plays on the beach. We'll stay out for a couple of hours and then come back."

"Nice. Have fun."

I end the call.

Losco is behind me, smelling good, wearing an open shirt, sandals, gel on hair.

"You're not ready."

"I know."

"I'm going down. You have a shower, make yourself look good. There'll be a lot of people there. You can make friends."

"Okay."

"I'll be at the beach. Go down the zigzag and follow the music. I'm right down there. Come on, don't hang about. I want you ready in 20 minutes."

"Alright."

"Open your hand."

"Why?"

Then he shows them to me. That's five.

"We'll limit ourselves to four if you want."

"No," I say. I said it in a hurry as if I didn't want him to overthink, to change his mind.

I feel stupid taking drugs, hoping they can heal me and show me Lisa's face.

Losco promised to take care of me, and I decided to trust him.

"Come to the kitchen."

Show me the honey pot. There's no label. The stopper is wide and, around the neck of the cylinder, there's a hemp rope. Homemade stuff, I guess. There's a strong aroma of sweet but also wild fragrance.

"Is it good?"

"Very much, but it has psychotropic properties."

"What does that mean?"

"It was worked by shamans."

"Are there shamans down here?"

"A few. Do you know Castaneda?"

"No. But I think I've heard about him. Was he a real writer?"

"Yes. He met a shaman. He was his pupil for years. At first, to help him understand reality, this shaman made him take special mushrooms."

"And what happened?"

"He could see the world as sorcerers did."

"Sounds like a commercial thing. Is this story true?"

"I've got a couple of books over there," and with a twist of the head, he points to his room, "maybe you can do some reading whilst you're here."

"Maybe, yes. I haven't read for a while."

"Taste it."

With a stick a little bigger than a toothpick, he lifts a smattering of honey towards me.

"It's quite delicious," I admit, swallowing. "But it's also very dense and has a bitter aftertaste. But it's palatable, really."

"Now send these down, too. Chew them well, you have to make mush in your mouth first."

"Alright."

He pours those into my hand, and I look at them as if they are precious nuggets. I beg them to give me some answers but right after I feel like an idiot, someone unable to pull through with his own strength, a weakling, a beggar, at my wit's end. I don't tell Losco, and I don't know if his calm and intelligent expression indicates that he's picked up my thoughts.

"Life is hard for everyone. We are luckier than others, but things have happened to us that we never wanted to know. Listen to me, I've been through this before you and I thought nothing could help me."

"This helped you, didn't it?"

"Yes. There are shadows you can't wipe away. Sometimes we need guidance."

"Like Castaneda?"

"Yes. He was sceptical at first, didn't believe in the world of warlocks, only believed what he saw."

"And how did it end?"

"He has written more than ten books and become famous."

We laugh.

"Alright, go. It's time."

"How long will it take for them to kick in?"

"Within an hour or so. You'll begin to notice that reality is more vivid. But first, you'll have to put up with a feeling of nausea."

"I'm used to that."

"Not a good thing, sorry."

I pluck up the courage and eat them.

"Chew them well. Don't rush to swallow."

"Actually, they don't taste as good as I thought."

"Help yourself to this."

He gives me some more honey, I suck it greedily.

"I'm going now, I'm late. I'll see you soon."

But in 20 minutes I'm not ready. It takes 40, twice as long. This is typical of my life; everything I do or say costs me twice as much, and the same applies to the time it takes me to do things, to think, to resurrect a memory.

Fabrizio wanted me to follow him to the gym. He had a voucher, a week's trial and a one-year membership for two hundred euros. A bargain. Yeah, he thought it was. Before Chiara, I followed him in his obsession with physique. He used to lift a hundred kilos in an exercise called deadlift. The name immediately put me off and he apologised. I preferred running, yes, running made me sweat, gave me a pleasure that not even food could give me anymore. It was as if the sweat washed away some of my fears. I joined a club but after two weeks I quit, preferring the presence of Giulia and her calm voice to the mess of social activities.

Fabrizio was just trying to help me but his insistence to reintroduce me into society ended with my escape. It wasn't the right time.

Even when I saw Losco's call a week ago, answering him seemed to me an act of terrorism against my privacy.

Evidently my siblings thought that my escape had to have an end or a limit.

I avert my eyes from the mirror, where I can see myself naked. I put on the bathrobe that Losco gave me and sit in the living room. The light has dimmed but it won't be dark until 9:30 pm. I have less than an hour.

Headaches. Nausea. I haven't had both together for at least a couple of months, so I wonder what I'm afraid of.

I try a meditation that Giulia taught me. I close my eyes and breathe deeply. I have to concentrate on my breathing and bring my full attention to its flow. It was something she had studied after giving birth to deal with Mattia. I never asked Giulia if she felt it was too early to be a mother. I've never asked her many things, and the fact that she feels guilty for my mistake tears me apart.

I try not to think about it, but it's a rumble of thunder that keeps ringing in my head.

"Idiot."

Yes, I am.

I focused all my attention on myself, a black hole hungry for light; Gulia's light. Now I'm wondering if going by her three times a week, invading their privacy, hadn't been too much. She certainly never gave me cause to worry about it, but Sebastiano was unusually taciturn, he spoke little and when we dined together he kept his eyes on his food. Other times the wine helped him to be less of an asshole, but in those moments I didn't care, I just wanted to feel well.

I used to play with Matteo, draw, watch cartoons on YouTube or listen to him talk about things I never paid attention to. And when I wasn't attentive, Giulia would take him away from me by giving him a colouring book. Then she'd sit on the edge of the bed and ask me what I was thinking. I don't remember my answers. Maybe I never had any.

It was in one of those moments that she taught me to meditate. Then she lent me a book by Eckhart Tolle that I never read. I promised her I'd read it, but I only made it as far as the second page.

All the knowledge in the world didn't matter. But she knew me. She'd known my fickleness since we were kids, now it was just more accentuated.

"Bone-idle," she told me, when I was only ten years old.

That was my mother's way of forcing me to do my homework or helping her set the table when I didn't feel like it. Giulia repeated it, making me nervous. I never dared to argue with her, maybe because that time passed very quickly.

I think she found more stimuli to tease Fabrizio.

That's funny.

"Bone-idle," she said to me one day, after years, making me laugh. "Now I'm going to teach you something." And she did.

I do it more for her than for me. I sit and I concentrate on my breathing. But I don't have to do it for her; I must do it for me. I'm the crazy one, the delusional one, the suicidal one, the one with the bad headaches.

Yes, I am.

I empty my mind.

***

I'm waiting nervously for the elevator. The door opens. From the inside comes the smell of upholstery and perfume, the scent of someone who tonight is at the same party I will attend.

When I'm outside, I follow the echo of music coming from everywhere. I know the way to the zigzag. I pass through a narrow street, bordered by two long fences.

On both sides, beyond the white wood that marks my path, between the cracks in the boards I can see the gardens. The first, on the right, is of a very tall building, perhaps even taller than the one where I am temporarily staying. The other looks like an abandoned house, but Losco must have told me that they are going to do some work there.

The road bends slightly, on the asphalt, at the end of the street, there is a 'no cycling' sign. The fresh air drags the less acrid taste of the sea around me. It swirls around me, ravishing me. I go slowly down the zig-zag, aiming for the beach, breathing deeply.

I'm wearing a shirt, my favourite jeans and white Adidas shoes. I have a hoodie with me because Losco, just before going out, warned me that it was chilly at night.

"Better cover-up."

I follow the music and, when I am over the zig-zag fence, I see a stand with a white tent on the beach. I recognize Losco even though his back is turned. He's at the deck, talking to someone. They seem to know each other.

I try to reach him when I knock the arm of someone I didn't see.

"Excuse me," I say in English.

He's a tall, strong man with a square face, wide, high forehead and short hair. He looks like something out of a detective movie. He talks, but I don't understand, so I apologize again and leave.

"Hey, kid."

I turn around, a little uncomfortable. What do you want? I know English, but there are some accents I can't really understand. He seems to speak with the slightest movement of his lips, as if he's whispering.

"Yes?"

"Do you have a cigarette?"

I shake my head. "No. I don't smoke."

"You got stuff?"

"Excuse me?"

I take a step back.

"Where are you from?"

"I'm Italian. Excuse me, but I have to go now."

I don't wait for him to answer as I head to Losco's deck with my head down. I think he must have been looking for drugs or something, as if he knew I'd taken some. After all, he stopped me, not other people walking on the beach.

I look if he's still there, to see if he stopped anybody else, but I can't see him as the crowd has swallowed him up.

"You did it."

"What's up?"

"Good. Meet Thomas."

I shake his hand. He asks me what part of Italy I am from.

"Milan." Lie. Even if I told him the name of my real home town, he'd have no idea. Milan is more straightforward, it's the fashion capital.

"Have you known each other long?" he asks.

Losco explains that it's been at least ten years. "We went to university together."

Thomas nods, following the dialogue as he touches keys on the console.

"Do you want to move here?"

"No."

"They all say that, then they come back."

Thomas is taller than all of us. He has reddish hair, has brawny, geometric tattoos on his arms and the writing NOPE on the phalanges of his right hand.

"I am Irish. From the north."

Now I understand why it's so hard to understand. It makes no difference to Losco, his English is perfect, soft, fluent. I envy him. I have confused memories about our phone calls, but living in a cosmopolitan city like London has made him able to interact with the whole world, with all kinds of accents.

"How do you two know each other?"

I'm asking Losco, but it's Thomas who answers.

"Mutual friends. Then we started playing on the radio on Thursday nights. We've been working two one-hour shifts. I usually take the second hour."

"I didn't know that."

"You don't remember," adds Losco.

Maybe he's right. Lisa's not the only thing I struggle to remember, but unlike the rest I can access with the slightest effort.

She just doesn't come back. A ghost I only know the shape of.

"Do you like house music?"

"I don't know."

"What kind of music do you like?"

"Italian music."

"I know a couple of songs," he confesses. "Gloria. Is that right?"

"Yes. Umberto Tozzi. *Bravo*."

Thomas nods, happy, then brings up the volume of the remix he was playing.

I ask Losco when he's going to start.

"Now. Five minutes. How are you?"

"I guess well."

"Nausea?"

"It's passed. Why are you making that face?"

"I don't know."

"Is something wrong?"

"I think it's perfect."

"What?"

"This moment. Come on, stand over there and dance a little."

"No, I can't."

"Is there a song you like? But not Italian."

"I have to think about it."

"I'll look at you and then I'll tell you what your song is."

It's Losco's turn.

I get two beers and then place one next to the deck.

I feel uncomfortable, but to make myself stay, I let the crowd take over this rock-hard boy. That's how I feel, and maybe that's how I've felt the last few years. I watch carefree young people dancing around me, girls in their daringly short dresses, doused in perfume as well as the smells of alcohol and cigarettes.

I was once young too, I used to be so much a part of this kind of set, to be in it, like wine in a bottle, and flesh inside skin.

I sip the beer, Losco says it will loosen me up a little. He warns me not to go overboard though, in order to keep high from the drug.

Just one, I promise.

I don't know when it happened but my head seems wider as if it could also contain the sky, and then my thoughts are less hazy. I wonder if it's because of the mushrooms or if it's half the beer I've already drunk.

"Excuse me."

I bump into a girl. She has blonde hair like Giulia and, for a moment, I thought it was her.

"It doesn't matter," she answers, showing me a white smile, her lips kissed red and an aperitif squeezed in her right hand.

"I'm not a very good dancer."

She laughs, squints like a Japanese anime without saying anything.

Out of embarrassment I turn around. I decide to move near the deck to stay in my comfort zone; after all, I'm not here to pick up.

"Do you know *en bi*?"

Surprised, I look confused at the faces around me as if a presence was speaking in the crowd.

"Who?"

Her hand points to Losco. En Bi stands for NB, New Babylon.

"Yes," I answer, burning with embarrassment. I hope she doesn't see it, but I'm sure my face has the same colour as a pepper. "We're friends. Old friends. And you know him?"

"Yeah. I mean, not well, but yes, of course."

"Do you like his music?"

Laughing back, she says: "He lets me in for free."

I don't know what to say. Her answer seems so silly to me that it deserves nothing more, but at least she was genuine. And then, she stares at me intensely.

I tell her my name and she introduces herself as Lauren Parker.

"Are you here to study?"

Losco had mentioned to me that I would meet a lot of students in Bournemouth because of its many universities, so I knew I could not be wrong if I asked her about that.

"I study chiropractic, but my family lives in Greece. I grew up in London. And you? From the accent, I'd say you're Italian like N.B., right?"

"True."

"I like Italians."

"Have you ever been to Italy?"

"Yeah, a couple of times. In the south. Beautiful place."

"Do you remember where?"

"Amalfi coast. Years ago, I was still in college. A

family vacation. Look, I've got to get back to my friends, but don't disappear, I'll come back and see you."

"Okay. I'll wait for you."

"Gimme your phone, please."

Doing as she tells me, I pass it on to her without thinking much. She's like a magnet who's found her pole.

"Okay. I've got your number."

"Thank you."

I watch her leave, and as she goes, as I look her back disappears into the fray. A memory comes up, something I feel profoundly ashamed of, and I hate myself for daring to flirt with a new girl. I drink my beer all the way to the foam on the bottom.

Losco with one hand beckons me to join him at the deck, and I'm happy to get out of the jaws of that young woman, for whom everything is simple, beautiful and untroubled.

"So you met Lauren?"

"She knows you."

"Yes. She's very social, makes friends easily."

Sarcastic, I know Losco and I know when he is being that way. "What do you mean she makes friends easily? Have you slept with her?"

"No. She's a nice girl."

"Are you warning me to stay away?"

He shakes his head and, while handling the deck, answers: "You are free. Be free. But remember the rules."

"No women."

"It's okay now, don't worry, enjoy this moment while we're out in the open. Anyway, I've found your song. Get on the track and I'll play it for you."

"I certainly don't know it."

"Get my phone, there's an app that recognizes songs. Open the app and share the song on WhatsApp."

I move in front of the deck, a few metres back, looking for Lauren, but she's not there. I open the app. I like Losco's music. I like that song. The girls slowed down their movements, clapped their hands to the rhythm of the bass. They know every word. At the chorus, we're all swinging like lonely swings. The shame is lost. The music, this song, and maybe the new reality that I'm about to get to know, have dissolved it or pushed it back where we usually hide things we don't need anymore: cellars, closets. The shame is still there, but that door is closed. For a while.

Duke Dumont. Ocean drive.

I share the song on WhatsApp and then put my phone away. I raise my hands to heaven at the second chorus, laughing along with other laughter, which is unknown and divinely beautiful. It's all too good now. My head is bigger than the universe, and my eyelashes, when they blink, are raised in the raging winds.

Finally, the song fades into silence. I know for sure that it has left a void in all of us.

Losco plays another piece of his, less melodic, faster.

The nausea pushes me through the crowd and heads for the shore. I realize that the light is gone; the night walks all over the horizon descending slowly down to us. I can't throw up. I try to help myself with my fingers but it doesn't work. My instinct is to ask Losco for help but then I hear his words in my ears: *be calm*.

The ecstasy has given way to nervousness. I walk, I think it will do me good. I go towards the Bournemouth Pier. It will be a mile or maybe more, but its vision comforts me, it is like a safe destination. On the shoreline I'm not alone, there are couples, groups of three chatting while drinking beer and dogs off leads playing with other dogs.

The music slips behind me, even the way it slows down, fading with the distance, which comforts me. It's as if things must have their own place, a margin, a limit, so that others further away can find some space.

2

Which hurts more, the truth or the illusion of it?

I'm not sure, but there's something in front of me. A big bird. It's shrouded in darkness, but from the size of it, I think it's a seagull. There are lots of them in Bournemouth. In the past, these animals flew over the sea, daring to get to the beach but no further. Now, for food, they go into the cities. Their contact with humans has tamed them, made them somehow more social. They are not yet at the level of dogs or cows, whose artificial domestication has made them friendly. Seagulls' response to stress is still very high: if you get too close, they fly away and in some cases they can even attack you.

Saber, this seagull that seems to be struggling to fly, gropes the backwash in search of something. People walk past him regardless of his presence and he keeps jumping around as if...

I'm so close. I can see him better. The faint light from

Losco's deck reaches this part of the beach and shows him off.

For study purposes, I once read a book on how to rescue birds. It has a broken wing. What I don't understand is how it managed to break it. Maybe it collided with one of his peers, some kind of aerial brawl. Or maybe someone in the crowd beat him up.

The undertow sounds sweet and goes deep into me. The lights on the street lamps are warm, animated by good nature. I take off my shoes to feel the fresh sand under my feet; I put them in the water and it's like being immersed up to my neck.

Saber stares at me. He moves his head in jerks and scrutinizes my movements with a sideways glance from one eye.

"I don't want to hurt you."

I sit on my calves, three steps away from him. He is attractive. The hallucinogenic effect must have expanded the receptors hidden in my eyes. Saber is a high-resolution object, a four-dimensional reality lifted to the power of 3D, something that I can only explain by jabbering about nonsense.

"What can I do for you?"

Saber backs off and moves along the shore, looking for the concrete jetty that stretches into the sea. In the afternoon, walking with Losco along the beach, I noticed the seagulls gathering up there aiming for the best of both worlds: to be close to passers-by and the water. I raise my head to the sky, a useless gesture because I know that there are no seagulls around, they will be on the edge of the crowd, in the less used beach areas. The night heightens their response to stress.

I get up thinking about Losco.

"I'll be right back."

Saber seems to understand, I'm sure I saw him wink.

I'm running to Losco. He's no longer the DJ; Thomas has taken his place at the deck.

"I was coming for you," he says when he sees me.

"You finished so soon?"

"I was worried about you. I asked Thomas to replace me."

"I'm sorry."

"What's up?"

I'd tell him about the seagull right away, but the way he's looking at my pupils is starting to worry me.

"Why? What's wrong with me?"

"Now you can see every detail of my face. If I smile, you can see distinctly all the muscles that lift my mouth."

I see them.

"Well? How does it look?"

"Weird but interesting. It's a high-definition film but, at the same time, it's as if each shape is walking on several dimensions. There's a contrast between your image and the background."

"At home I'll show you..."

"But first you have to come with me, there's something I want to show you. Can you help me?"

"What have you done?"

"Come on."

It's a lucid drunkenness that I don't control; it drags me, excites me, intoxicates me with new energy. Feeling somewhat disarmed, I observe the shapes of the faces that come up to me, the details that the brain usually leaves out. This time the eye catches them and the mind memorizes them. There are two divergent speeds, one slower that shows me even the most imperceptible movements of a person's face, and the other that makes the ripples of the sea frenetic images in continuous sequence.

"Do you see it?"
"What?"
"Saber."
"You mean, the seagull?"
"Yes, Saber."
"What does Saber mean?"
"It's a character from a Japanese anime."
"What? I mean, what am I supposed to do with this?"
"His name is Saber. Can't you see he's hurt?"
"What do you want me to do?"
"Isn't there a number to call? Like some kind of English animal shelter?"
"At this hour, I doubt that those services are open."
"Can we leave a message?"

Losco doesn't have time to answer. We both turn to a figure who seems to emerge from the shadows of the night. I recognize him. He's the same guy who stopped me a couple of hours ago asking about drugs.

"Can I help you?"

Losco seems to look away so I feel compelled to answer him. "It won't fly."

The stranger nods, takes one look at the seagull and whispers something I don't get.

"Do you know what to do?"

"Did you do this?"

"No."

I look for Losco's approval but he doesn't respond, he's looking for something else and does not seem at all interested in what's going on.

"I'm a police officer. What's your name?"

I tell him my name and add that I'm in Bournemouth as a tourist.

"Is there anything you can do?"

"There's nothing we can do. He will die."

I can't remember how to say *veterinario* in English, so I ask Losco.

"There is no specific service for these animals. They're not like cats and dogs," adds the policeman seriously. "Tell me the truth, did you kick him?"

"No," I protest for the umpteenth time.

Then Losco pulls me by the shirt, telling me *it's time to go*.

"Where do you live?"

"Up here on Manor Road."

I force Losco to reveal where we live, but he's not happy to share that information.

"I'll keep you in the loop. I'll call a vet tomorrow."

"Thank you very much."

Losco takes me by the arm. I look at Saber for the last time knowing that I will probably never see him again, but I also notice the investigating eyes of the policeman. They undress me, they know my thoughts and what I did. So I turn around, listening to Losco reproach me for having too much confidence in strangers.

"But he was a cop."

"Yes, my grandfather too."

"You don't believe him?"

"Did you happen to see the badge?"

"No. But what do we do now?"

"Give me five minutes, then we'll go up."

"Why? It's so nice out here?"

He stops in front of me, plants his eyes in mine and says: "It's coming."

"What?"

"The wave. And when it comes, you'd better have plenty of water and a safe place to stay."

"You're scaring me."

"It'll be great, I promise."

I'm already euphoric and yet I keep thinking about Saber. He's over there, hidden by the concrete wall that separates the two beaches. And then I have to have a stupid smile on my face, one of those disco smiles, one of those disco nights that I no longer remember.

I laugh, hiding that fun with one hand. I would like something to drink but Losco's been very firm: *no more alcohol.*

"Alright."

I decide to check in again on Saber to make sure he's ok, but somebody's pulling my shirt sleeve. I recognize those eyes - Lauren. She's got a better smile than me. I think she must have taken something too. I don't know about drugs, I couldn't tell. Sebastian used to make us smoke a little weed, but that's all. There was a moment when Giulia was determined to break up with him after she found out he sometimes did cocaine with some of his old friends. She didn't like that shit. I remember, yes, and I also remember Lisa asking me to stop those trips, to focus on our future.

We had a little piece of that future, but not all of it.

"Hey. Where you going?" asks Lauren.

I'm about to tell her the truth but it would be too difficult to explain the situation. I want to laugh, I want to look at those bright but dark eyes of hers that stare at me hungrily.

"I'm waiting for my friend."

"What are you doing later on?"

I don't know if it's time to lie, but that's what Losco advised me to do, no matter what. Lie.

"We have an important commitment. We have to go somewhere."

She's disappointed, she makes a strange noise, like a missile going from roar to buzz.

I'm sorry.

"I wanted to introduce you to my friends?"

I resist but I would like to confess, tell her everything, tell her it's a blast, describe how her face is now so full of details, how bewitching her smile is. I must resist this temptation that excites me.

"We can't stay, I'm sorry. But how about meeting later or tomorrow?"

"Where do you live?"

I tell her my address.

I realize I fucked up, but I can't turn back. Losco said no women, no sex, and I left her the goddamn address just thinking about sex.

"Look, what did you take?" she asks, whispering and approaching me.

"Ask Losco, I've never felt anything like this before."

"Sounds interesting. Can you get it for me?"

"I think so, but I have to ask him."

"I'll do it, don't worry. So we'll be in touch?"

"Yes."

She caresses my face and then she goes off and turns her seductive back on me.

I hope I haven't screwed this up.

Losco's still talking to Thomas. Sounds important.

I walk away from the crowd and look at the sea. A reflected moon shines golden on the water where I can even count the slight ripples of the waves. It's all wonderful. That light is marvellous, it throws itself on my face and it's as if golden hands slide down from iridescent blades to touch me.

Someone bumps into me, shifts my attention back to the sea. I don't care who it was, I want to find those fairy hands. But then the music goes down and I feel like I hear familiar notes, it's a piano, a sweet piano. Other hands appear in my memory, they're Lisa's. It's just a flash, a photo-story snapshot.

I must be hallucinating because the one who crossed my sight, walking barefoot on the shore dressed in a red jacket and pants of the same strange colour, cannot be who I think he is. It's the same image we had in the room. He was Lisa's idol. We used to listen to his songs in the car, and I often asked her if we could put on something else. That memory is atrocious, so much so that my heart beats so hard that I feel as though it's going to break through my chest.

I want to reach him. Maybe it's just someone who looks like him. Perhaps it's this drug that's projecting into reality things that are in my head.

Losco's right, and if he is, then he can help me.

I'd forgotten that poster, I'd forgotten Michael and his inimitable red jacket with black borders from when he was still enjoying the success of Thriller. That boy who looks so much like him is advancing into the night, moving away from us; I think I've made a mistake, I've confused red with black and mistaken the bandana I see on his head for his curly dark hair.

C. A minor. F. G.

My hands, meanwhile, without knowing anything, are moving their fingers in the void, like looking for the keys of an imaginary piano or instrument. They play in the air. They play music that's in my mind, as if there were invisible wires connected to my fingers. And I remain like that, suspended in limbo without understanding, that looking at my hands now makes no sense, because they are there but they are no longer mine. They are the ones I have forgotten, the ones I have betrayed, the same ones I have caressed with different moods for years. And the sweet clangour of the sea, dragging its backwash to my feet, is the background of this heart-breaking melody.

I let my arms fall on my hips but it is not a surrender of pain, it is rather a determination to know these wonders. So I forget Michael. I forget the song and her hands on top of mine. There is only the movement of the sea. It's all the same as before. It's real now. There's no reason to leave. I could be at its feet for hours. The movements of this cleansing water vibrate with my whole being. I wonder how the moon can stay up there without ever moving. It seems as if everything has been set as a theatrical scene.

I wonder what would happen if I tried to draw the curtain back.

Losco calls me.

"Let's go. It's late."

"What time is it?"

"Sorry, it took me almost an hour."

I'm surprised. "It hasn't even been ten minutes."

"I know. That's why we have to hurry."

"Before the wave comes?"

"Yes. Before the wave."

3

Losco has a Vishnu poster I've never seen in my life. I only notice it now as I undress. It's on the wall above the desk. A divine figure wrapped in his mystical shroud. He has a calm face, lips relaxed, large eyes slightly squashed at the sides. He holds with his four hands objects that look like archaic weapons or religious utensils. I don't know for sure, after all, I never even knew much about my own faith.

Losco asked me to hurry up, to dress comfortably because we have to sit for a few hours.

Before the wave comes.

I'm wearing gym pants and a white T-shirt bought on Ecosia, the search engine I use instead of Google. I started using it before the accident because of an ecologist colleague of mine. He says that I can plant trees effortlessly, plus save the planet. I don't believe it, but the service is the same as Google. I've even installed Ecosia on my laptop.

I stop in front of the strange figure of Vishnu. It's as if it shines inside me. A god inside. A carrying force that has chosen me as a hidden dwelling, maybe to rest, maybe to enlighten me.

Lisa had also installed Ecosia on her devices. I sharpened her image of her back sitting at the living room desk. She didn't sit there often, I used it for work. She was looking for songs. That last year she had decided to learn a song and take it to the show at the music school she had enrolled in.

Why would she do that?

Why did she enroll?

Losco calls me; he was right. Things have started to communicate with me - I realized it with Saber. I think about him and I'm sorry. And now I have the impression that Vishnu really wants to get out of his frame and sink into my soul.

Losco has distributed the bottles of water throughout the house. They stand on the edge of the spaces and look like many little men waiting for something. The water inside moves like jellyfish, floating gently and giving me some peace.

"Come with me," says Losco, taking me away from my catharsis. But as I turn my attention away from them, I notice my face in the bathroom mirror.

"I'll be right there," I tell him.

Losco nods, asks me to hurry up, that I'll find him sitting in the living room.

I close the door behind me. Approaching the mirror, there's a sparkle in my eyes that attracts me. I can see every layer, filter, passage or construction that makes up the retina or the sclera or the colour of these two unknown globes whose black edges flow like an escalator conveyor belt.

With my fingers I feel the skin just below the lashes. It is soft and elastic, free from any hint of wrinkle or furrow. It is perfect. I wonder if it is just the hallucinogenic effect or the ability of these mushrooms to make me so young. I see myself as twenty again, in the best years of my life, in the heart of my relationship with Lisa.

I ache for those days again and feel an overwhelming desire. And I advance, I get closer to my reflection, looking for myself in that double image that now is a young university boy ready to dive into new adventures. There's something in my irises, it's as if I were watching a movie, a film flowing, showing me buried truths.

I had to forget.

Twice, I've been told. A rare case, something that happens once every hundred years.

I'm not sure it was true.

I get so close to the mirror that I touch it with the tip of my nose. I focus and it's incredible how fast my eyes can do it. Then I move aside and play the finger game. I place it three feet away from my face and I approach it, slowly. I keep seeing the finger, sharp. I see him and the rest in the background as clearly as the closest things. It's like having a thousand eyes and new colours to discover.

I want to see that film. I look for myself again in those irises. I do it because the emotion is overwhelming; it supports me, it dares me to do things that from another point of view would be considered crazy.

I pull the skin underneath my left eye downwards, the red veins recede, like streams of water that dry in the sun and retreat into the dark corners. They fall back into the white of the sclera.

I want the film.

I want us.

At the same time, I want to enjoy this feeling that seems to open up the centre of my chest.

I look for the images that I had glimpsed just before, imprinted in the reticles of the iris. In iridology, the lower part is dedicated to the kidneys. Going up, clockwise, there are liver, heart, lungs and spleen/pancreas.

I took a course. It was a long time ago, maybe before or shortly after I graduated. I wanted to explore the human body. I was fascinated by its function and nuances. Lisa had spurred me on, saying she was proud to have such an intelligent boyfriend. It fueled my ego. I took those classes with a friend, Umberto. Laughing to myself, I recall how Umberto slapped me the first time I got drunk. After college, though, he started drinking too. At first, it was a purely intellectual friendship - we both had a passion for science - then it became something else. The memory drags me away from my own reflection.

Losco calls me.

"I'm coming."

I keep thinking about that course.

The filaments of my left iris reduced because of my

dilated pupil. It's as if I am observing myself with a microscope: as I approach every detail becomes clearer, expands. I am an atom that explores the entirety of itself.

I wonder what's in the other one. I focus my right eye, in a flash I hear those notes, a music that seems unforgettable, that gives me her hands and skin but not her face. The notes build something of Lisa. And there she is, I am sure, in there, an image squashed between the outer edge of the pupil and the sclera. The seated image of Lisa.

The filaments that colour my eyes bring her to life. She is pushing her fingers on a keyboard without music, because the music comes from outside, as if it is playing behind me.

So I turn around and find the patient and understanding figure of Losco asking me to follow him, that the time has come.

"How can this happen?"

"You are in an altered state, your senses are altered. Things want to communicate with you. They want to make you see what you need."

"I want to see her."

"Come with me."

I follow him.

Before I come out of the bathroom and turn off the light, I turn my attention back to the young boy in the mirror. I would like to ask Losco if he can see what I see, if I am the one the mirror shows me but I don't. I follow him into the living room.

"Let's sit on the floor. Take that cushion if you like."

I take a cushion from the sofa and put it on the floor. I sit on it, mimicking Losco. I laugh because the water has created a perimeter around us and the little waves inside them are dancing in unison. Shimmering. Harmonious.

"Beautiful, isn't it?"

"Yes. Do you see it too?"

"I see. But I've experienced it before."

"In short, you won't go any further."

"No. I'll stay here with you. Always. I'll guide you. And when you come back, after the mother wave, you'll find me exactly where we are now, but it'll be a little different."

"How different?"

Smile a little. "You'll find out."

"It's gonna hurt."

"It will do its job. There's no going back from here, my friend."

"I don't think I want to go back anymore." I'm serious. The past I persist in forgetting has the features of a pained body three times mine.

"You must accept the events."

I nod. "What should I do?"

Losco crosses his legs and joins the index finger and thumb of his hands in the form of the Buddha that was painted in the picture hanging on one of the walls of the room.

"Do as I do and follow my voice."

"Alright."

It's an uncomfortable position. I recall a moment when Lisa and Giulia were discussing Yoga. They wanted to take a course, did the first free trial session, but after that stopped going.

Why?

Left eye. From the kidney belt, going up counterclockwise, the eye shows us the healthy state of the spleen and pancreas, then the lungs and...

"Now, close your eyes."

I had already closed them, I had closed them to think of my eye, of what I had seen, of its forms that created other forms, perhaps my most hidden memories. Possibly they are right there behind my tired irises or hyper-dilated pupils.

Orthosympathetic, the pupil dilated. Parasympathetic, pupil narrowing.

"Follow my voice."

He says that because he must have heard me laughing to myself under my breath. I'm a naughty little boy.

"Bring your concentration to your breath now. Do it. Don't let your mind wander. Things talk to you, but they're like people who are all talking at the same time, wanting to say something to you. We have to shut them up, make them talk one by one harmoniously. Before the mother wave comes."

I'll try. It's hard. Hard to be in this position with your butt sitting on a flat, uncomfortable cushion.

"Breathe in. While you're doing it, think you can inhale this room with all its stuff."

I'm laughing. I'm not stopping.

"I'm sorry."

Losco laughs too. "Don't worry, I know it's weird."

"I'll do it."

"Now. Inhale."

And it's the moment. I can hear those notes coming from a piano, I dragged them from the bathroom all the way here and like submerged ramparts rising up from the waters of a dried-up lake, they flood inside my head. I see her in my right iris. Her hands, her pose. Lisa, in fact, is sitting in our living room. I'm watching TV with my headphones on, listening to the documentary on the destruction of coral reefs. As a scientist, I loved those programmes. I wanted to travel to get to know the world, but then I never did.

Why not?

Another question I can't answer.

At the lab, I was earning pretty well. Not at first, of course, but then things got better. Yes, I'm sure they did. Even if I saved up enough money to buy a new car without a loan, I never went to see the coral reefs I dreamed of. We had a holiday in Egypt. We stayed in the village for a week, sunbathing, going down to the beach, doing a few laps and eating all day. We stayed offshore, in the open sea, we wanted to dive to see the coral reef but I didn't feel well. On the way back, we climbed on a rock and threw ourselves into the sea from several metres up. Lisa ran in front of me and bravely hovered in the air. I hesitated partly because I felt nauseous in the boat and partly because I was cold. However, the real truth was a third factor: the height. It seemed to me an impossible distance to do in free fall.

I breathe in.

Like that memory, my air-filled body seems to move in slow motion. Time slows down.

Lisa called me from below, said I was a wimp, that the water was fresh, bright and, finally, I could see my reef. I wanted to dive, I wanted it with all my heart, but I left that rocky pedestal and made my way down to Lisa on the beach below. She was curled up on the edge of another rock, her body directing me to the fish – gold, purple and who knows how many other colours - swimming between the bottom and the surface. She had skinny shoulders. She was wearing a distinct swimsuit, a bright colour, maybe yellow. Her mother gave it to her and Lisa decided to wear it to please her. We sent her a picture of us on the shore. Lisa didn't like it. She said it made her feel old or like a schoolgirl. But she was glad to make other people happy.

This memory shakes as I reach Lisa at the rock to see her face. I want to look at her face, not the fish. The fish can wait. She, on the other hand, has no more time. Everything moves under the pressure of a multi-dimensional earthquake, like when you agitate the water in a bottle or your computer screen while watching a movie.

I reach out my hand and try to hold on to Lisa's right shoulder, but the suction of my breath is dragging away this beautiful dream too.

I don't want to leave you anymore, my sweet love.

I don't want to leave you alone, not even for a moment.

So, I think if I breathe out now, I'll be there with her again. But even when the room has been sucked into my nostrils, my lungs have been filled with her and my hopes have been pushed to the limit of endurance, I simply cannot bring myself to exhale.

"Have sweet dreams, my friend."

The Mushroom Effect

1

Who am I? Who are you?
Is death a sweet rest or an endless nightmare?

Open your eyes.
How long has it been?
I don't know. It's easy to see the differences now. It's broad daylight. A delicate light falls gently into the room through the big window. Time, though, is something I'm not aware of.
How do I look?
Losco is not here.
The bottles he scattered everywhere and seemed to be connected by a single inland sea, are gone. Losco must have put them back in the closet.
My legs are sore from the unusual position. I must have fallen asleep like the Buddha in the picture, a kind of trance. I think Losco hypnotized me.
From the outside, there's a silence broken at times by the chirp of birds. That's all there is. This hollow sound seduces; it is vast, deep, in it all things sleep, and yet it is

so easy to break.

The silence is a Buddha sitting under a fig tree.

I wait for steps to break this mystical atmosphere. I remember that Losco snored and so I stretch my hearing in the hope of catching his clumsy breath, but there is nothing there.

Carefully I step out and I head to his room, just outside the living room. I enter, trying to open the door as quietly as possible. There's a pleasant light filtering through the curtains roughly at the end of the room. A bundle of sunshine has slipped into a crevice by climbing down to the core of the bed. I observe Losco's absence and imagine that those dots floating in the light are pieces of him coming back to life.

The effect of the mushrooms must have influenced me: I think of things that have never before been in my head.

Maybe I'm wrong.

A couple of Castaneda's books are laid on the bedside table.

In my senior year of college, I was obsessed with science fiction. I wanted to write about it. Lisa thought it was a good idea, that I could publish it. She said her mother had a cousin who worked in the Press Office of a major publishing house. All I can see of us is my laptop on in a dark bedroom. She and I are lying down, the blankets reach up to our chest and I'm showing her the first chapter, which I wrote in the library right after lunch. A malfunctioning alien spacecraft had landed near an isolated village. We play with our hands and the light on my screen, projecting non-existent things, pretending they're real, sometimes giving names to those shapes.

It was something we used to do towards the end of university, then we stopped. Lisa had started staying at my house a lot, we'd have dinner and then we'd run into the room and make love.

I've often wondered if we were a happy couple. Of course, I still don't have the answers I'm looking for, but at least there's something I can smile about.

I look around. I don't think Losco slept on the bed as the blankets are well smoothed, the pillows are lined up and the room smells like lavender. I don't see any misplaced objects or the typical boys' mess.

Fabrizio would leave his things around the whole room. Mum would pick them up and tidy them up carefully. I, on the other hand, always tried to be as tidy as possible. Unfortunately, we shared the same room and often my order wasn't enough. Lisa would only sleep over when we knew for sure that my brother was coming home late. Sometimes Fabrizio didn't show up for two or three days. At that time, while I was writing the book, he had met a model and often stayed with her. He said she lived in a loft in Milan. Giulia didn't believe him, but I was just grateful to be able to share a bed with Lisa.

I never finished my novel, but I know where it is. I printed the first hundred pages for this alleged editorial contact to read, but we never got an answer. At the time, I didn't care. The eagerness to write was annihilated by the pressures of the last exams, the projects with Lisa and perhaps something else I have no memory of.

Youth.

Six or seven years ago.

I'm thirsty. There is some milk in the fridge, a carton of mixed juice and coke. I pick the juice and gulp it down.

Losco warned me I'd get thirsty. He says it's to replenish the fluids and slow down the hallucinations. What would happen if I didn't drink enough? If my intuition isn't wrong, I suppose my heart would suffer a fair bit.

I take the juice bottle with me and go to the bathroom. I'm halfway down the hall when I hear the sound of the intercom. I think of Losco, maybe he went out for a walk or to buy something. I didn't check my phone. I have no idea what time it is. Judging from the daylight, It's probably no later than seven in the morning. I'm not tired or sleepy. I need to urinate, take a shower and grab a bite to eat.

I'll ask Losco if we can visit Bournemouth, or better, take a dip in the sea or, anyway, stay out as long as possible.

"Losco?"

There is interference, the sounds the receiver makes are irregular, biting. I put it down, but right after that it's still ringing.

"Losco, is that you?"

No one's answering. I press the green button, I don't want someone stuck out because of me. Losco says *it's a*

The urine is white. I didn't eat a lot of protein yesterday, I didn't even eat saturated fat; Losco's peas and potatoes were a light dinner. I drank a beer but it seems my body refuses to expel it.

I wash my hands and stare at myself in the mirror. I am like last night just before sitting in the living room with Losco, a young man with white skin who is starting university. How this is possible, I really don't understand it, and yet I am sure that the hallucinogenic effect has almost wholly waned.

A feeling of well-being and joy pervades me, a sort of deep and positive melancholy. I'm a super-man.

When I approach the mirror to look at the right iris, my image splits, blurring. I try again but the result is the same. I'm sorry I couldn't taste this magic produced by mushrooms long enough to understand it. I'll ask Losco for some more. Maybe I fell asleep too soon. Perhaps the fatigue from my journey did not allow me to stay awake for long enough, yet during the beach party I felt more alive than ever.

Losco was inscrutable. For sure the experience with mushrooms helped me to see things I couldn't remember anymore, but it wasn't enough to give me what my mind keeps hiding.

There's knocking on the door, two well-aimed shots.

I dry my hands and, in small steps, I arrive in front of the door. Through the peephole I see the man from the beach. He's in an official uniform now, but his gruff face hasn't changed.

He looks even more annoyed than last night.

What's he doing here?

Saber.

I wonder, *how he's doing?*

The man hesitates then hits the door again. I'm opening. His silence is only moved by his eyes dancing on me. He recognized me instantly, but I'm sure he's looking for something else.

"Good morning. May I help you?"

"Remember me, kid?"

"Yes."

The man speaks fast, out loud. I just hope I understand everything he says. He's far more robust than I remember.

"Are you alone?" he asks.

He looks for Losco behind me. His movement spreads its essence which is bitter, penetrating, a mixture of cigarettes and whisky, the same smell as Umberto's at the end of our soirée. I'm sure it's a recent memory, no more than a couple of years ago. It seems such a strange thing to me that I cannot give any word.

"Do you live here?"

"No. I'm staying with a friend."

"Do you have any ID?"

"Yes. You want me to..."

He raises his hand to gesture that it's not necessary to show any ID, that it doesn't matter.

"What can I do for you?"

"We put that seagull down. Do you remember it?"

"Saber. Yes. But why?"

"A seagull that cannot fly is already dead."

I'm not sure I grasped the full meaning of his sentence but, deep down, I already knew that answer. Without wings, he couldn't defend himself, he couldn't hunt and so get food. He would have died anyway.

"I'm sorry."

"The vet said someone hit him."

"You mean, it was a person?"

"That's right. These things don't usually happen around here."

"I'm sorry, I don't know what to say."

He doesn't answer and peeps inside behind me. I know what he's thinking, while I concentrate on him I draw on the last residue of the mushrooms to notice every movement of the muscles on his face. There is a mixture of curiosity, annoyance and bitterness. How those three aspects can live together, I can't explain it, but I see bitterness when the corners of his lips fall down, curiosity in the dilation of the pupils and annoyance in the furrow between the eyebrows. And at the last, he has a quick sigh that lifts his torso and shoulders.

He suspects me.

"I just wanted to let you know that the seagull has been put down. Have a nice day."

"Thank you, sir. You have a good day, too."

I close the door slowly. Through the peephole I can see him standing in front of our flat. He's making notes in a notebook. He doesn't just watch my doorway but even the apartment next door.

I don't care.

My phone is on the table. It's hot. I turn it on as I want to know where Losco is. I need answers. And then we need to book a return ticket. I'm too excited to pay attention to a cop who thinks I kicked a seagull. There's no evidence, and even if he checks the cameras on the beach, he won't find me fooling around with Saber.

Or was it me?

"Come on, move."

What's happening to me? Now I'm getting angry with my phone. Where's my newly found light-heartedness?

It's 6:06. I'm getting three messages. One is from Losco, the other is from my sister and the last one is an unknown number.

Losco
I have work to do. I'll be gone all day.
Remember to drink and stay calm.

Stay calm? What does that mean?

"Where are you?" I text back.

I'm a little disappointed he didn't tell me he was working. I thought this week was some kind of vacation.

Giulia
Mom wants to know how you are and so do I.
Are you okay?

Hi, Giulia. Everything's fine. The place is
nice, but the highlight is the seafront.
You'd like it. It reminds me of when we used
to go down to Rimini at weekends.
Good times.
I'll give you a hug.

Even though I didn't write the name, I know the
other number. It's instinctive, an absolute certainty inside
me: Lauren. She sent it to me ten minutes ago.

Lauren
Hey, there. My friends are asleep. What are
you up to?

I look around like I'm hiding a secret. A lad on his
first date.
"But you are."
Yes, I am. I've spent the last 11 years with Lisa and
only dated two other girls before her. Nothing serious. I
lost my virginity to the second girl, I was 17. I thought it
was love until I found out she liked someone else. He
was a big boy a little older than us, senior year. I saw her
with him soon after.
It's funny, yeah, because a while later I heard they'd
broken up. That same night I got drunk and met Lisa.
Destiny?
How would things have gone if Umberto hadn't told
me that my ex had broken up with the guy she left me

for?

I'm not sure I'm up to a phone conversation. I'll text her.

I just got home.
Where are you?

I hold the phone in my hand, hoping for an instant response. I open her picture on WhatsApp, she's cuddling a black puppy in her lap. In the background there's a white beach, maybe Greece or an exotic resort even further away. She's smiling.

I'm trying to imagine myself over there with her, taking pictures on the beach, going back to our room after dinner and draining in an hour of crazy love-making.

From the reflection of the display, I can see my dumb smile. I want to feel guilty, but I can't. She's a relief. My last adventure with a woman was a disaster. Walking down the aisle, talking about banality, hearing her laughing at my stupid theory about the size of dogs reflecting the size of their owner's attributes. I thought she was sexy, the right price for a meaningless evening. I really thought it didn't have any meaning. I had done it because of my brother's insistence that sexual desire was nothing more than a need arising from the pressure of my hormones. It would be good for me, but after the first exchange of saliva down a *Naviglio* side-street, followed by my announcing that I wanted to get straight to the point, my excitement dissolved like an ice cube under a powerful sun.

We went to hers. She offered me another round of beer but, to keep up the already weak excitement, I dragged her into the room, undressed and laid her on the bed. My erection didn't come. She tried to play with me; I tried to find her exciting but, exhausted, I told her that I felt sick, that I needed to leave, that I was sorry and it wasn't her fault.

Lauren
I was at the pier, but I'm on my way to your place.
Shall we have coffee together?

That's a good idea.

I run to my room, looking for my jeans. I put them on. I open the suitcase. I have my toothbrush, nail clippers and a small folding comb - travel stuff.

It's 23 degrees outside and soon the temperature will rise another four or five.

I choose a T-shirt with Einstein's equation printed on it. I bought it on Redbubble-dot-com just before I left. It looked nice. I had a similar one with the Pi Greek symbol and the first 500 numbers printed on the background. My sister gave it to me. She knew better than anyone else my passion for mathematics; I couldn't have worked in the lab if I hadn't got good enough grades at university. None of my friends had much of a grasp of mathematics. Apart from Umberto, who was a real science enthusiast, the others thought I was some kind of genius.

Losco himself didn't understand that world of numbers, he much preferred to deal with people.

I brush my teeth and wash my armpits. There's some man spray in the cabinet under the sink, so I use it. My hair is messed up but I prefer not to comb it; maybe a more flamboyant look will make me more attractive.

I have the same hair as my father, curly, brown. Giulia said I was the adult version of Finn Wolfard in *Stranger Things*. She and Lisa were always debating on Messenger about the episodes and what the new series would look like. Lisa would never watch an episode if Giulia couldn't. They were waiting for each other.

They loved each other.

Maybe I shouldn't...

Another message comes in. Lauren tells me she's in front of my building.

Yeah. I'll be down in two minutes.

I'm desperate for a gum or something to prolong the freshness of the toothpaste.

I go back to Losco's room and on the bedside table on the left, next to Castaneda's books, I find a small packet of gum already open. I take it.

Lauren is sitting on the low wall that borders the

ramp to the underground car park.

Her legs are crossed, and she is dressed in a horizontal striped T-shirt that I hadn't noticed the night before, and torn high-rise shorts, with a light pink belt.

She looks fresh, kind, alive. I don't know whether it's just my imagination, but her shape seems to fill something deep within my heart and fuels my curiosity as I look at her. She smiles as she admires the stone vase that houses a variety of flowers.

"Hi."

She raises her eyes to me, stretching those thin lips of hers that seem to be elastic and endless.

We embrace each other. I breathe her scent again, clean, stolen from nature, perhaps from those same flowers that she observed with wonder.

"How are you?"

She tells me she's fine and doesn't feel like going home.

"I need coffee."

"I arrived in Bournemouth yesterday. I don't know anywhere here."

Lauren seems unconcerned. She looks for something in her purse: her cell phone. She checks the messages and then tells me that no one will bother us for a while.

"Where are we going?"

"Let's walk. The place opens at 8:00."

It's 6:40 in the morning. I can't remember if I had that energy before I got to Bournemouth; if I had it before this trip. I still think it's the residue of the mushroom effect, a fleeting spike in serotonin around my grey matter. It's holding me up. This challenge doesn't seem to scare me.

We go down along the zigzag to the beach, where there are a couple of men in fluorescent uniforms picking up rubbish discarded on the sand. We walk towards the pier because our Café is near Boscombe, a suburb of Bournemouth.

"It's not a nice area, but the place we're going to is alternative, very nice. You'll like it."

"I trust you."

I feel silly. I keep looking at her shoulders and the liquid movement of her hair that seems to be lifted by little fairies the size of grains of sand.

Sometimes she laughs and I want to tell her that I feel really stupid but maybe she likes me, maybe she finds me interesting. It's like I can feel it. I feel it. Every few seconds she flicks her hair back with one hand to stop it falling over the face.

"I have one more year before I graduate."

"Do you want to go back to Greece, stay with your parents?"

"That's the idea. My father has a chiropractic studio there, but with the current crisis he's thinking it's time to move, maybe Portugal. He has a friend there who could help him out."

"What do you want to do?" I ask.

She shrugs, such a fleeting gesture that if I wasn't flirting with her, I wouldn't notice it.

"I'll tell you next year."

"Alright. Fair enough."

We get to the pier, walking on the bridge. There are some sorts of musical instruments. We try playing some metal tubes with soft-tipped mallets. She enjoys it and if she likes it, I like it too.

"You're very good," she says.

I just got the rhythm right. And then suddenly it goes all weird, so I ask her if we can see the sea from the end of the pier.

"Yes, come on."

She takes me by the hand and drags me to the end of the bridge. I look at her from behind, enchanted by the fluttering of her hair. The gentle wind seems to lift and caress it from below with an invisible hand. We look out over the balustrade and breathe the salty air of Bournemouth.

"What do you do in life?"

"I work in a science lab."

"Yes, sure. Look at your t-shirt!"

I laugh at her remark, feeling a little stupid.

"Are you some kind of mad scientist?"

"No, no, not at all."

"Just kidding. But it's very interesting. What kind of job is it?"

"We analyse water, but we also do other kinds of tests. Mostly we treat food."

"A researcher."

"There is little research in Italy."

"Have you come here just to meet your friend?"

I spit out some nonsense and try to translate simple sentences into English quickly in my mind. I won't tell her the truth for the moment, but I don't want to lie either. If I lie to her now, I'll have to lie to her all the time. Where I come from, they say that *lies have short legs.*

"We hadn't seen each other for years, and then I promised him I'd come here one day. Here I am."

"Don't you have a girlfriend in Italy?"

I can barely smile at her because of the embarrassment, but it would be complicated to explain everything.

"Not anymore. We broke up a few months ago. Do you have a boyfriend?"

"I'm looking around."

"Then I must think I'm lucky to be here with you."

"You are."

"Thanks."

We're close, my arm brushes hers and now I feel my face developing the hue of a clown's nose. So, I pretend I'm getting air to cool my lungs.

"Wouldn't you like to do something else one day?"

I had already thought about that, but my job is the last thing I want to discuss now. I hadn't made much effort to find one anyway. With constant headaches and nausea, my father took on the responsibility of supporting me, even financially if I needed it. Months ago, I admitted that before starting over with a new job, I wanted to take some time off, maybe even a year. My parents agreed but urged me not to shut myself away.

"I'd like to teach." Even though I never really

believed it, it's something I'd discussed with Lisa. She had advised me to do contests or ask my former biology professor.

"In college, you mean?"

"Yes."

"Um, good. I like smart people."

We leave the pier, go up towards the city and head to Boscombe. It's a different area, a district with ethnic shops and charity shops. At the beginning of a wide pedestrian street, there's a McDonald's. We go further on.

Lauren tells me it's the roughest suburb in the city, that there are lots of homeless people and folk with mental problems. I look around but I'm distracted, I don't care. I get the impression that passersby only have eyes for us and I avoid dwelling on their crazy expressions.

I don't want to be there but I let Lauren gently guide me to our destination.

We get there soon. It's a rough, alternative place, with a long counter for the cafeteria and an open kitchen at the end of the room. Café Boscanova. They have a blackboard with the specialties of the day but also a menu for breakfast.

We sit on the bench behind the entrance window.

"I need a cappuccino."

"Yeah, I'll have one, too." I look at the menu and point to what I'd like to eat. "Have you ever tried it?"

"I recommend it. They also make a great breakfast."

"I'm not really hungry, but I'll have this."

A girl comes along, asks us if we just want a drink or food as well. Lauren orders her cappuccino with almond milk and I order my toast with avocado.

I ask her if she has a problem with milk and she says she's a vegetarian.

"Does it bother you?"

"No. How long?"

"Since I was 19. So, let's say three years. I must admit, in the early days, I did eat fish sometimes."

"And you're okay?"

She laughs. "Yes. Very much."

"Sorry. I guess that's the question everyone asks you."

"You mean to ask me if I might die?"

"No, no, absolutely not. My biology professor used to say that by combining cereals and legumes, vegetarians had all the nutrients the human body needs: protein, minerals and vitamins. Then clearly you need green vegetables, bulbs, roots, but I guess you already know all that."

"Glad to hear it from someone who studied biology. You make me feel less crazy."

"Is that how people make you feel?"

"Yes. That's why I say I'm a vegetarian and not vegan."

"So, you're a vegan?"

"Recently I've become one."

"You're not crazy. I mean, I never really thought

about it. I never considered whether it was right or wrong to eat meat."

Lauren sits next to me, and we're arm in arm. She takes my hand and declares: "Could we talk about something else?"

"Alright. Do you come here often? Is this your favourite place?"

"I literally love it, and they make a great cappuccino. You'll see. Besides, you're Italian, you'll be an expert."

"Cappuccino is an Italian word."

"I didn't know that. That's great. Are there any other Italian words you think we might use in England?"

"I don't know. But we use some of yours. Do you want to know which ones?"

"Yes, I do."

"Relax. Break. Fast and food. And... now I can't remember."

"Interesting. Can you wait here a minute? I need the toilet."

"Yeah, go ahead."

Not many people walk at that time but I still have the brutal impression that every passer-by is turning their attention to us. I might even say that I'm their sole focus.

A homeless man is sitting on a cardboard box against the wall of the bank across the street. He's staring at me all the time. A spy. I read somewhere that some drugs can cause obsession; I wonder if that's the case.

A waitress serves me cappuccinos and avocado toast. "Haven't I seen you before?"

I was distracted so I ask her to repeat it. While she was placing our order, I lost sight of the homeless man. The cardboard remains on the ground but there is no trace of the man. Perhaps he turned the corner looking for something else, but I had the distinct impression that he'd simply vanished.

"Are you alright?"

"Yes, sorry. I was looking at something. I've never been here before. This is my first time."

Clumsily I smile at her. She's pretty, smart, maybe the same age as Lauren.

"Are you on vacation? Where are you from?"

"Italy. I came to see a friend."

"Is she your girlfriend?"

"No, we met yesterday. Do you know her?"

"Yes, I do. She comes here often. So have fun."

"Thank you."

The homeless guy is sitting on his cardboard box and he's staring at me again.

"Here I am. Sorry to keep you waiting."

"Don't worry about it."

"What are you doing tonight?"

I try to look at her, but I'm still thinking about that man across the street. Ever since Lauren came back, he's been sleeping on his box, ignoring me. Maybe I'm more tired than I thought. Perhaps I need a drink so I don't risk going crazy.

"I don't know. We don't have a plan."

"Good. I've got one for you, if you like."

"Sure. Go ahead."

Even though one part of my brain is listening to her, the other is frightened and captured by the evil and penetrating gaze of the homeless man who has started to stare at me again. That shining and scary furrow between his eyebrows is a warning, an emotion that is not only external but belongs to something inside me. I don't know. I have to answer Lauren or she'll think I'm still high.

"Do you like the idea?"

It's Tuesday and there's a student night at a club whose name I didn't get. I don't like the idea. I'd rather do something else, but I tell her it's fine. I'm up for it.

"Amazing," she cheers and kisses me on the cheek, which makes me blush. "I need to get some sleep. Then I'll call you so you know what time to be ready. You're not gonna eat that?"

"Yes, I'll eat it. Maybe I need to sleep a few hours too."

We walk to where I live - she didn't want me to escort her home.

"Have you been here before?" I don't really know why I ask; it's just the way she is looking at the top floor, as if she knows something. After all, Losco told me that *she makes friends easily.*

"Yes, last year. A friend lived there."

"What kind of friend?"

As I go up the stairs I take from my pocket the keys that Losco left on the bedside table in my bedroom. A duplicate.

I know. I'm jealous. Lauren has something I can't explain, a kind of freshness and fragility that I'd like to hold onto forever.

"A friend. I guess he doesn't live there anymore, so don't worry."

"Okay. Sure you don't want...?"

"No. See you tonight."

I hug her. She prints a kiss on my cheek, near the side of my right lip. I breathe all of her. Her movement stirs an infinite fragrance of woman, which penetrates me through my nostrils, and I really wish this moment would linger long enough to fully inhale it. Then it passes as quickly as it arose, a gentle gust of light air, of her, of the two of us, strangers to each other but both greedy and waiting, like priests for the moment of prayer, for an act that will perhaps save us or condemn us forever.

Her kiss with the taste of almond cappuccino is a kind of promise, a momentary goodbye, a monk's silence, the assent of the eternal father to the firstborn son. It is the closest thing to the sacred and at the same time to the profane I know. But how all these thoughts come to me are a mystery. It is certainly she who provokes them, as if gestures were enough to define us.

2

I should have insisted on taking her all the way home. An Italian woman would have appreciated it, but we're not in Italy.

I hesitate a moment before going back, I look at the neighbour's door, both the policeman and Lauren might know the owner. Maybe she wasn't honest with me. Compared to mine and the other two doors on the floor, this one has an aged look: the wood is faded brown and, in the corners, it is even white and scratched. There's no umbrella stand or shoe-rack like for the rest of the apartments. I wonder whether it's uninhabited.

Maybe Lauren wasn't lying to me.

I go to take a shower. The toilet's uncomfortable, the brass hand-shower is too low to wash my hair, so I have to lift it up. The tepid water runs down my body and then flows away from me, dividing into millions of particles as it does so.

I can no longer see Lisa in my eyes or the waves in

the plastic bottles moving together, but these drops flowing away from me are quite distinct. Everything slows down, even my heart. I'm afraid. I turn off the shower and wait. I let the last stream fall into the bottom of the bathtub, holding my breath. I still have some soap on my body, but until I am sure that my heart is beating at its natural rhythm, I don't want to do anything else.

I breathe in and out.

It was just a passing feeling.

I still look in my right eye for Lisa, but my image is blurred and doubled again. It's not working.

I left my mobile phone at home on the table. There are messages but nothing from Losco.

Fabrizio:
How are you doing?

I'll answer him later.

Giulia:
We were crazy, but it was a good period.
Do you remember the lighthouse?

A lightning bolt through my mind. It was one of Sebastian's favourite places.

Portofino in Liguria.

We walked from the path of the Kisses of Pareggi to the Lighthouse without stopping.

There is an image at the beginning of the path: two

faces painted red on a transparent board. Lisa joked that they looked like us when we were growing up. She draws their contours with one finger and then, as we walk along the narrow path around the rock, she says that at least every ten metres we should give each other a kiss.

Giulia and Sebastiano were ahead, they didn't hear us, they were more interested in the national flags attached to the fence and the view of the sea.

We had decided that walk was personal, that we should walk taking our time.

Lisa wanted to kiss me.

There were padlocks attached to a safety net and I told her that those people had certainly seen the film from Moccia's book. Lisa had read them both, I knew; they were her first readings as a young girl in junior high school but she didn't care. She took my hands and put them on her hips. I kissed Lisa against the fence, breathing her and the sea in the wind. We giggled.

I wanted to go ahead and see the lighthouse but she insisted on kissing me every ten metres. No, it was ten steps. Then, I went further and she held me back again saying I had to go back to our promised ten steps. And laughing, we did, we counted ten steps and kissed.

We got to the lighthouse an hour late. We didn't answer Giulia and Sebastian's calls, we didn't give a damn.

I can't place us in a moment of our past, it's as if it was yesterday or last month. I remember the sea behind her, between the branches of the trees that lined the road and her hair sliding backwards. I can feel even now that she was on my body.

I have the feeling again that my heart is struggling to beat. I take the fruit juice I left on the shoe rack in the entrance hall and gulp it down. I grab one of the bottles of water from the closet because I like to drink it at room temperature. Giulia and I are similar in that. Fabrizio loved the water from the fridge. He used to drink at least a litre a day and then would go on to his endless cocktails with friends. Dad liked his glass of red wine at every meal but my mother preferred sparkling water. She and my brother were very much alike.

For a time, Lisa and I got into the habit of having a glass of wine with dinner, too. It helped relieve our stress. Then we stopped.

Why?

I'm surprised. No headaches. No nausea. Perhaps they'll come back as soon as the last remnant of it's gone.

I'm drinking.

The last message is from Lauren. She thanks me for the two hours we spent together. I'll send her a smiley face.

See you later.

I sit down to find time to write to Giulia. I would like to tell her about these mushrooms and how in only two days they managed to resurrect memories that I thought I had lost, or were nebulous. Now that fog is less dense, but there are still things I'm struggling to focus on.

I used to kiss Lisa every ten steps but I can't see the whole of her face. She had soft red lips, kept a lip gloss in her purse for every occasion. She didn't like dry lips, she ate little and drank a lot of water.

Lisa never needed the gym even though sometimes, when I came home, I would catch her doing free body exercises. She would work out for a week or two and then she would suddenly quit. She said to herself that she wanted to learn to persevere. She felt she wasn't trying hard enough in life.

That's sad.

I wonder what I did to comfort her. Perhaps I told her it wasn't true, or maybe I kept silent.

The last kiss was hurried as she really wanted to see the sea from the Odero Castle of Portofino and its elegant tower. She wanted someone to take a picture of us. She wanted her mother to know we'd been there. She took a picture of me alone as I approached the tower. I took one of her in return. She didn't want to remember the view without me at her side, but I insisted that her mother would be much happier if she was in the Odero photo than if I were.

She refused. She didn't like the photos alone, said those are the photos you take at funerals. She said one day she'd take one for her grave.

I want to cry but I can't because we were so happy

then.

I'm deleting some emails, job listings that I have no interest in right now.

Giulia convinced me to join the agencies to think about my future.

"Even if you're not interested now, there will be a time when you want to leave again."

Her words.

I did it for her.

Sebastian could put me in a bank or a shipping company, his father has several friends in that world. One day he patted me on the back and told me there was no last resort for us, which was his way of letting me know he'd set me up somewhere.

Currently, the lab is paying for my absence; Roberto, the manager, would like me to go back but, even though I haven't told him yet, I have already made my decision.

There are memories in the lab that I can't shake off.

I fell asleep on the couch. I look at the time on the display. If I'm not mistaken, I've only been here half an hour. I'm thirsty.

***

Tourism is evident in Bournemouth. Lots of people are already lying in the sun, some are walking their dogs or playing volleyball on the beach in their bathing suits. Others run from pier to pier or do exercises in the reserved areas.

The sea is an intense blue, a deep-mature pastel, so much so that even the sunlight struggles to reflect. The dazzles on the water find space in the last stretch before the shoreline.

I take off my shoes and taste the warm sand under my feet. I slalom among people chatting or reading a book. The university boys show their pale and perfect forms, the elderly a little curved on their shoulders amble near the shore, often in pairs or accompanied by their children. And the feeling is the same: I am the centre of attention. Girls turn around as soon as I notice them, even if they are several metres away. Then they get up, showing their sensual attributes, their pale thinness that won't tan, their vivid eyes sparkling, perhaps curious or attracted by something around. The homeless man showed hostility towards me. They, instead, display a sexual interest that alarms me in the same way. The boys ignore me, it's as if they don't even notice the ambiguous attitudes of their fiancées or friends.

Obsession. Paranoia. Is that what I'm suffering from now? The headaches and nausea are gone, but I prefer them to madness.

I push my feet in the sea, turning my back on the rest. I'm confused. On my left, towards the Pier di Boscombe, there is a kind of concrete terrace overlooking the sea. It is free and I reach it walking along the shore, stroking the snout of a black dog on the way and wondering how Saber must have felt whilst dying.

I sit on this cold and wet rock, throwing my feet in the void repeatedly hit by the foam of the waves that crash against the sides of the platform.

I, too, have seen death, and twice. It took a loved one and memories from me. I lost many of them, but I would let them all go just to see Lisa's face again. Just before attempting suicide, I looked at the photos of us that we had diligently slipped into the albums we had bought together. Each album had a name. There was the one in Portofino, with a few photos. There was the one at the lab, the one of Lisa coming to visit me and the business dinners we both attended.

The album of our house, before it was furnished and after.

I remember a picture of us both, Lisa sitting on the shelf of the kitchen and me biting her arm to pull her down. Giulia took that picture. I can see us, I can even see that photo, I know the details but I can barely focus on our faces.

The truth is, in that photo, her hair covers half her face.

After my second hospitalization, my mother, Giulia and I decided to hide our photos. I went to a psychologist to try to recover memories in a natural way. I couldn't resist much, it seemed so simple to him, for me it was terrible. I told myself that if I had become suicidal, it was because what I had done to Lisa could not be easily forgiven.

I'm attracted to a drop of sea on my arm. It's different from the others, slightly larger, spherical, and the interior looks decorated like those Christmas balls that you shake to see the snow strewn everywhere. And as I get closer, I have to pull back. My question about Saber has been answered. He was put to sleep on the beach. There was an old man with a syringe who gave him the injection and then wrapped him in a black garbage bag so he wouldn't be left on the beach.

With one finger I crush the drop of water. I'm starting to get the hang of it.

Losco's voice echoes in my head. Nature wants to talk to me. I understand that. In everything there is memory; water is made of memories. I had read Emoto's studies and observations some time ago. Branded as alternative literature, Umberto and I were fascinated by it.

This is what I have to do: communicate.

If nature around me has memories, perhaps there is also the possibility to reflect them.

Not very scientific from someone like me. I couldn't remember Lisa's lips before I left. I couldn't remember Portofino, nor anything else I've been trying to keep on a leash in my darkness. Or maybe it's just this new sky or this hard sea that relieves my discomfort a little.

Back straight. I close my eyes as Losco advised. I inhale, trying to fill my abdomen. The water is cold and my arms are shaking. Remember, *Francis*, come on. Losco promised it would work.

I exhale. I don't know which senses catch their movement but I have total perception of the hairs on my arms flexing like the ears of rice bent by the wind. Then I breathe in and they raise their heads again. It's not the wind, the air is still and I'm sure it's not blowing from the sea or inland. It's me, it's my body breathing.

I should have learned meditation with Lisa. She had bought an Osho book to read at her leisure. I see her reading sitting on the couch.

I've come home now.

I exhale.

It's been a long day at work. She says hello but I don't look at her. I put my briefcase at the entrance of the living room puffing but glad that the weekend has started.

She's got her head in the book again while she's talking to me. Her hair is covering her face. Her feet are on the sofa, the book resting on the thighs, she's locked in a shell to support herself.

I take a sip of water in the kitchen. I notice the table and the bouquet of flowers in the middle. Spring, I'm sure: the lab was open during lockdown for Covid-19. They have a marked colour, a passionate pink, small, light petals with pronounced stamens. She wanted them for the kitchen, said they made her happy, that azaleas were among her favourite flowers.

Yes, they were.

I inhale.

Because her absolute favourite was almond blossoms. She would confess that to me shortly after.

I complain: I'm hungry, I'm thirsty, but I don't really know what's bothering me.

"Come here on the couch with me. A kiss?"

I don't feel like it.

Why not?

I know why. I didn't sleep well: it was a tough time. But the truth lies elsewhere.

I take off my jacket, unbutton my shirt. It's cool in the flat, the temperature is comfortable. It must be late March or early April.

May is her birthday, but I haven't thought of a gift yet. Last year we went for a weekend in the mountains. It was a spa package, one of those where you do sauna, massages and treatments you prefer. She had tried them all, I only had a facial massage. There was a girl at the spa, named Caterina, whose family was from the south: Catania. While she was applying the mask to remove my blackheads, we talked, we laughed and, just before leaving, I wanted to give her my phone number.

I ask her what she's reading. Lisa does three things: she hands me the book, gives me a hurried kiss on the lips and gets up to go to the bathroom.

"Don't lose my page."

I didn't even look at her face.

It's a manual of spirituality. Apart from Emoto's book and Siddhartha by Herman Hesse, I can't think of any other similar ones I've read.

"You know, I'm a scientist and I don't believe in such

things," I say out loud.

Lisa's laughing.

Right now I'm also laughing because her laughter has entered my head.

She's close.

I exhale.

Lisa responds by saying that if she's not able to do yoga with Giulia, at least when she is at home she can meditate alone, develop self-control.

"If I don't eat something right away, I'll lose *self-control.*"

Then we're in the kitchen. I set the table as she drains the pasta. She tells me about the book, but actually she's planning on taking singing classes.

"Why?"

"So I can become a famous singer and we can buy a house."

I go along with her. "Interesting. Which house would you like?"

"I don't know. As long as it has a garden."

"Dogs? Cats?"

"One dog and three cats."

"I want a fish tank."

"Since when have you liked fish? Besides, you know the cats would eat them."

"You're right. Then I want a bonsai in the garden."

"No."

I don't look at her, but I know she's turned around. I can see her skinny legs through the spaces between the chairs while I pick up a napkin off the floor. A gust of air came through the window and blew it off the table.

"What do you mean no?"

"Then the garden must be big enough for an almond tree."

"Since when have you liked almond trees?"

"You don't know?"

When I get up, she's turned her back again. Lisa puts the spaghetti in the sauce that she's heated up in another pan. I don't tell her anything, I don't know if it's a perfect memory, I don't know if what I see really happened, but what I feel is shame.

I inhale.

Open my eyes now. It's not the sea that wets this sunburnt cheek.

The truth?

I don't remember why she liked almond trees. I don't even know if she ever told me.

3

The neighbour's door is ajar. The owners must have rented it out again.

From the inside someone is moving heavy stuff, and I am sure the umbrella stand and the shoe mat were not there this morning.

I hesitate before going back in and pretend to look for the keys in my pocket, so I get closer to the door. A suitcase keeps the door open just enough to see inside. There's someone there. It's a boy. He's got a brown jacket and is wearing very expensive Oxford shoes. Then he disappears. He looked tall, handsome, maybe a model. I can feel his steps getting closer, so I take the keys out of my pocket and I go back to my apartment.

I check my messages. Still no word from Losco. I'll text him.

Shall I make something for dinner?

I had lunch at a place near the pier in Bournemouth

watching the sea and the seagulls fly over the area in search of food. Without the guidance of someone, my *morale* has dropped, so I decide to wait to hear from Losco and Lauren.

She's probably still asleep.

Hello Fabrizio. I'm fine. I'll call you sometime soon.

I won't. Even though we're brothers, we rarely call each other. One time he had a puncture at Navigli, in Milan, and I had to go pick him up. He was only 19 and Dad had lent him his car to hang out with a girl he'd just met. I was asleep and I left my phone on. He called me because he knew Dad would get mad. I had to wake Umberto up to drive me to Navigli. An odyssey.

Sometimes we still talk about it, he says *I made his evening*.

I now realise that this event triggered two things. First, Fabrizio learned about cars, and when he got another puncture on the same road to Navigli, he came home proudly saying that now he was finally a *free man*. And second, he reconnected me with an old friend from high school: Umberto.

That night we didn't go home.

Lisa did not know anything about it and Giulia was still engaged to her previous boyfriend.

When Umberto suggested the strip club to me, I told him it was risky, that if Lisa *found out*, she would dump me instantly.

Umberto, however, just wanted to take a ride, see what it was without spending a lot of money. I accepted. We took the ring road again and headed to Lambrate. I don't remember the street, but I do remember that we paid twenty euros each and we left drunk. We laughed so much in the car that all we could do was to keep repeating just how hilarious it had been.

Then, luckily, we didn't talk about it anymore.

Fabrizio had been there several times but he had never tried to drag me to one of those places.

"I feel sorry for you, brother," he said, touching my arm. "But you're lucky, you've found someone to love."

At the time, I thought I was lucky too, that's why I avoided seeing Umberto again; that's why I was determined to bury that particular memory.

A few months later a different stage in my life would begin: Lisa and I would follow Giulia and Sebastiano almost everywhere and the sense of guilt I felt fell into a bottomless abyss.

Hot. It's happened again.

I'm sitting at the table in the hall, facing the window. I'm waiting for Losco's response but while I'm checking the phone I can't find any other messages. It's been a while, I'd say at least three hours - a trance or maybe an after-effect of the drug? I don't think it's fully worn off yet. Everything seems calmer, more static, and yet sometimes things behave strangely.

It was certainly strange to see Saber's death in a

droplet of water, so what else could happen?

There's a message coming. Looks like one of those synchronistic events Carl Gustav Jung talks about. It's Lauren. I was just thinking about her.

Lauren
Hey, there. I've just woken up, and I'm super-hungry.
I'm getting up.
Do you *wanna* go out?

Hi. Tell me where and when.

I end the message with a smiley face and send it. Those little yellow faces can give a more carefree tone to the seriousness of digital messaging. I have friends who hate emoticons, they refuse to put any symbol in there, even to be ironic. Umberto is one of them. Sometimes he would try to make me laugh in his texts, but it never worked. He had other qualities though; he was intelligent, charismatic and funny face-to-face. He took life easy, and often said that it was our duty to live our best years to the full.

Now I wonder what happened to them, if it is possible to access a kind of time machine to get those *years* back.

His philosophy ended up sucking me in and overwhelming me.

Lauren again.

Aruba. 6:30.

Another coincidence? It's the same lunchroom.

I don't know if Jung was right, but Lauren certainly has changed my mood.

And then something happens. I get up from my chair and I get closer to the window. I know there's the sea in the background but the street below is shaken by the wind. The branches of the trees are rocking and they remind me of the waves in the plastic bottles the night before. They are instruments playing in unison, children going round and round hand in hand - a harmony I cannot describe.

The trees underneath and those going up to the cliff road all swing in rhythm. Suddenly the world is elastic - a flexible plastic construction - animated and special. I don't know how unusual it is, but this will of nature to communicate with me is frightening.

The trees bend for the last time, their green heads as wide as broccoli pointing south towards Bournemouth Pier, in an explicit statement of destiny. Over there is Aruba.

4

I see her walking along the park road. I notice her mouth, which reminds me of a bright red flower, one that opens to the buzzing of bees.

I don't brush up against her, but instead stay with my hands in the pocket by the Ferris wheel. Between me and her there is a space filled with elements, each one charged with an energy that I can feel, even see. People move in the space between us, sometimes hiding her from view, and when this happens, I feel hatred and want them to disappear.

She's wearing a distinct dark dress, I would say black or possibly midnight blue. Lauren is a snake, she has the shape of things that crawl, that are as flexible as the plastic trees I saw from the window of my apartment. She's made of a substance that denies death and loves life. A substance that, in order not to weaken, must regenerate, change, dress in other clothes. She is the mother of the tardigrades, those indestructible creatures that endure through time, through fire and even through tectonic shifts. She is the first Eve. A primitive hunter would have stamped her on the rock along with the mammoths. The pharaohs would have crowned her. The waters of the Red Sea would have opened for her without disturbing the angels and the firm faith of Moses.

I dare not move, she comes towards me and I feel like the enemy who, exposed, sees the Roman legions descending upon him.

We're hugging. I tell Lauren that she looks wonderful. I throw her a smile.

I'm wearing a pair of jeans and the shirt from the night before. I didn't expect to do much today, but suddenly my life is changing at an unexpected speed. I'm a driver switching from the motorway to Formula 1.

Lauren's smell is as delicate and as soft as I imagine her skin. As she explains to me what she did after she woke up, all I do is smile at her like a fool and stare at the vein on her neck that beats to the rhythm of the heart.

I can't kiss her now.

I breathe in.

They have a vegan burger, served with fries and salad. To make her happy, I'll buy her order and a couple of beers.

"You have no idea how hungry I am."

"You were telling me that we're going to join your friends later, right?"

She talks fast, I often don't understand her and I have

to try to figure out the general meaning of the sentences. I smile and nod. The euphoria I feel makes everything comfortable, even this iron chair I'm sitting on.

We are on the outside, outdoors on the balcony and the pier and the sea are our backdrop. There are still people on the beach, groups of boys playing volleyball or boomerang. On the terrace we are not alone, others are sitting behind us and in front; the room slowly starts to fill up.

Lauren is irrepressible. She asks me questions I can only answer yes or no to.

"Do you have brothers?"

"Yes, I do."

"Sisters?"

"Yes. Just one."

"What's her name?"

"Giulia."

"I have three super protective brothers but they don't live here. Two of them are in London and the eldest has opened a dental practice near Oxford."

That city reminds me of my new neighbour's shoes. I know Oxford shoes well because I had a pair that I used to wear during business dinners or important evenings with Lisa. A shiny sort of shoe that is uncomfortable to wear. Lisa didn't like them and yet I never changed.

"Which of the three is your favourite?"

"David. He's the youngest. We grew up together."

Fabrizio and I are four years apart. Giulia, instead, was born two years after me. She let herself be protected by her brothers until she came of age. After that, she didn't want to know anything about our authority. She would leave the house unannounced and return late. For several years her life had been warming up for the most exhilarating and eventful evenings that were to come. Fabrizio used her as reference. Then, however, Giulia changed, got tired of the evenings, found Sebastiano and a job. She wanted to be independent from Mum and Dad, but I think she was ashamed of not being able to graduate. One day she told me that if she came back, she would at least try to commit to school, but by that time she didn't care.

Meanwhile, the beers arrive with two shots of Jagermeister. The smell is so pungent, it has the ability to awaken something in me.

Lauren distracts me. "Do you know how to do that?"

"No," I'm lying.

"Put a little salt on your hand and then throw down the Jager in one shot. Are you ready?"

"Lemon at the end?"

"Don't you guys have shots?"

"We called it *cicchetto?*"

Lauren laughs. She thinks that name's funny. "Can you say it again, please."

"*Cicchetto.*"

She can't pronounce it right. "I like it. Teach me some more words, okay?"

We down the shot full of excitement and toast to our night. I lick the salt and then throw the Jager down. I don't want to see the memories that emerge as I screw up my eyes with the strength of the alcohol that struggles to blend with the acid and other fluids in my body.

No, I don't want to remember. They are various memories, some pleasant with Lisa, some I'm ashamed of, and one, just one I wish I didn't have to remember.

The last one.

The last one is Lisa drunk. My heart hurts.

Lauren's still distracting me, dragging me away from pain and something even worse than that.

I put lemon between my teeth. Lauren throws her head back saying she thinks my face is hilarious. Alright, if she laughs, that means it can work. I haven't felt like this in a long time.

"It would be good for you to stay here for a while. You'd have a good time. You look so serious."

"With you, I have fun."

She pinches my arm, and tells me I'm crazy. Yes, I am. I'm mad about her. Crazy for her uninhibited gestures, her unstoppable euphoria, her young flesh shaking my old bones. It's as if I had a wild howl within my chest that I want to release - a primordial cry that has been silenced for millennia.

"I'm wondering if you'd like to share some MDMA with me. Would you?"

We sipped our beers. I wish there was Losco to know if that's something I should do. I tell her I'd like to, and so Lauren sends a message to her friend who can do a good price for us.

"Can't wait. Just don't say anything to my friends. Some of them don't approve of this stuff."

155

"And they still have fun?"

"They get off in their own way. They say it's better but I think it's all bullshit. What do you think? You're a scientist, you'll know more than we do."

"Actually, no. I guess it depends on the quantity, though. According to the Lancet, alcohol is the most dangerous drug."

"More than heroin?"

"I'm not sure, but drugs like LSD and MDMA have a lower danger level than alcohol. Again, I think that's true because alcohol has done more harm than these drugs."

"I never thought about it."

"I might be wrong."

Soon our two burgers arrive.

She tells me that her friends sometimes don't call because she's vegan, but that she doesn't really care. In college she's met other people like her, and so Lauren found an escape there.

"Don't think I live this life every day. When college starts, I'll have to stay sane long enough to pass my exams."

"You're not really gonna tell me you're some kind of bookworm?" Lauren doesn't understand, so I ask if she's really so dedicated to her studies.

"If there are any special evenings, I go out. There's a band playing at the Chaplin on Friday. We can go together if you like."

"Yes, of course," but maybe that's another lie.

Lauren gets up to go to the bathroom, so I call Losco. There's no connection. I ask the waiter if he can give me their wi-fi password, but even when I try again, the call gets lost.

Hey man, what happened to you? I'm out.
Let me know if everything's okay.
Please let me know how you are.

We walk along the waterfront, towards Poole, on the other side of Bournemouth Pier. I let Lauren tell me about her brothers, about David's jealousy every time there was a boyfriend to check up on.

We laugh.

I look at her and the sea - they both seem to be made of the same matter. Scientifically, I could say they are, different is just the way the elements that formed their matter are combined.

I've never been a very good listener. Lisa used to say that was my worst flaw.

Lisa was taciturn, but she loved stories, she loved to help others, to be supportive. I was the blabbermouth. Lisa and I had rituals. One of them was to imitate an exam. She'd play the part of the professors and ask me questions. Of course, I'd suggest the questions. All she had to do was change her voice a bit and pretend to be a teacher. Sometimes we could be serious, but most of the time we'd end up laughing. Her voice was really funny. I told her she wouldn't stand a chance as a mimic or a radio operator.

With great sadness, I now understand that she was perhaps looking for a way to reveal her inner talent through singing. Lisa used to praise me because I came out with top grades, got a scholarship and a job so easily.

I often thought that if I deserved the rest, Lisa was the exception.

"Are you okay?"

"Yes, sorry."

"Am I talking too fast?"

"A little bit, but it's okay."

We go up a street that takes us to a park and benches. We sit on one of those benches on top of the cliff, arm-in-arm, facing the sea. Now it's less dense, less full-bodied and rough. To my eyes it seems that the shards of light walk on its blue mantle like little golden beings. The relief I feel is deep and makes me forget Lisa.

When I meet Lauren's eyes, while she is still talking and moving her rose mouth, I see the sea in hers, those little luminescent men walking or running over it. I am so enchanted that I lean towards her, cautious. Slowly, slowly Lauren closes her eyes, and when they are closed and perfectly aligned with the stars, my lips close on hers too. It's just a quick kiss.

I've been wanting to touch her lips since the night before.

Then I draw back.

"I couldn't resist, sorry."

"Interesting. You're warm."

"I'm thirsty. I think I'll buy a bottle of water."

So we get up and she takes me downtown. First, though, we cross the park and stop for a minute to hear a guy playing a guitar. I drag her away and she stops again, this time in front of a juggler. I pull her by the arm, but very gently as to me she is like a delicate leaf – so fragile and light that I'm afraid she might break or get blown away.

I love this lightness she has.

5

I keep forgetting the names of her friends. No, wait, I know the names. I can't relate them to faces. Matthau is easy to memorize as he's the only guy in the group. He's black, from France. I have to correct myself again, he was born in France to a French mother and an English father. He's shouting in my ear that they moved from Metz to Southampton ten years ago.

"My father got tired of speaking French. But honestly," he says, and I find his fusion of French-English cadence amusing, "he never learned very well."

"How come?"

We talk loud because the music is deafening us. The girls are at the counter getting cocktails. Matthau and I, instead, are in the corner pretending to dance.

"The English aristocracy, long ago, used to speak French, so some English terms are the same or similar. However, there are some differences. Bras are the top girls wear to cover their boobs, but in French, it's the arm. Well, my father often made similar mistakes, mixed the two languages and you couldn't tell what he was talking about."

I'm not used to this clangour hammering my head, but it must have reactivated the effect of the mushrooms because I feel taller, more energetic, more muscular. I don't know how to describe the feeling other than I feel *more alive*. All negative thoughts and inhibitions have dissolved.

I move my legs in a kind of passive dance, it's impossible not to move in some way.

We took MDMA, and when I say we took MDMA, I mean, Lauren, me and Matthau. Lauren, however, is convinced that our mutual friend will take something else later on. She asked me not to overindulge because she wants to get me out of this mess.

For me, this mess is really exciting.

Now I understand my sister, and Fabrizio even better. At the same time, I'm aware that it's something that won't last forever, I have it now, but I'll let it go soon.

I just want to feel better, not think about the future.

"What does your father do?"

"He's a merchant," Matthau answers and makes a gesture with his hands. "He's a white man who likes blacks and money."

"You don't seem to have, how...?"

"Consideration for my father? Are you asking me if I have high regard for my old man?"

"Yes. That's right."

"I respect him because he's never let us go without

anything. I have three other brothers."

"Like Lauren," I say quietly.

"But he's always complaining about everything. Before he met my mom, he was an alcoholic, but he'd built a good career anyway. After that, my mother forced him to drink less and do more business. So he became even richer. I know what your next question is."

"What?"

"Do you want to know if they love each other?"

"I would never ask you that."

"My dad likes big asses, and my mom has big tits and a big ass. She's not fat, but 20 years ago, when she gave birth to me, she was shapely and attractive. My dad couldn't resist. They love each other, yes; otherwise, I think my mother would have kicked him out of the house."

"What are you doing in Bournemouth?"

"I'm at the university."

"Yeah, I know, but what are you studying?"

"Girls at the moment," he laughs. So as not to disappoint him, I laugh too. "Accounting, finance and economics."

"Interesting."

"Not at all."

"I don't understand?"

"I'm a YouTuber?"

I'm surprised, I tell him. I'm not a big fan of this new fashion of young people behind a camera, but I have my favourites. Lisa and I used to follow some of them - she was the one who found them. They entertained her. I found some of them ridiculous, but for a while we didn't miss a single episode of Yotobi and Michael Righini.

The girls try to get through the crowd dancing in every square metre of the room. It's a dark place. If it wasn't for the coloured lights in the headlights, I'd feel like I was in an abandoned house. It smells like marijuana, discarded cigarettes and something bitter like malt.

Lauren gives me a pint of cold beer. They've already had two rounds of shots and water on ice so as not to dehydrate. I need it too, but first I'm going to finish this delicious frothy beer.

I'm only halfway through when Lauren starts pulling my shirt like a cat wanting attention. I put my beer in a corner by the girls' water glasses, then I follow Lauren into the crowd. She walks backwards and keeps pulling the collar of my shirt. I don't say anything. I don't feel like talking, looking at her is all I ask. She moves well. Her skinny, sinuous body slinks around in her dark dress, like a caterpillar moving through the branch it has chosen as its home. She throws her head here and there, spreading spells that smell of alcohol and cosmetics.

I try to dance in front of her, bending my knees a bit, moving the feet like a tango dancer. I'm ashamed of it but Lauren doesn't seem to care, she just wants me to dance nearby, to feel desired. She often looks for contact with me and finally I give in, I get even closer, so much so that she gives me her back and rubs herself up and down against my body. I let it go. I close my hands on her hips, taste her softness and squeeze until I touch the bones of her pelvis. She likes it, I can feel it. I know it from the way her body vibrates. And I know it from her kiss on the side of my chin, a kiss still cold because of the drinks, a kiss that is a statement of something deeper.

I look up and see Matthau dancing around Lauren's friends. There are six of us in all: Vivian, Hannah and Katie. The last one's a mix like Matthau; part of her family's from Russia according to Lauren, who had tried to fill me in before we met them, so that I would feel less of an outsider to the group.

I didn't really care.

I listened to her to give her a chance to express herself, to continue to enjoy my company.

I don't know what time it is, and I don't know what happened to Losco. No messages on my phone. They've all gone for a smoke in the back of the club and I'm in the lobby. I asked the bouncers if I can pop out for five minutes for some air.

I've never got into smoking, maybe because I spent a lot of my time studying, making my parents and Lisa proud. I figured if my siblings couldn't get a degree, I had to be the one to do it. But then the truth is always something else: I didn't like the idea of work, and studying allowed me to stay away from the world of work.

I was lucky, one day my biology professor invited me

to talk to Riccardo, the head of a chemical laboratory in Milan. We liked each other right away. He was looking for an apprentice and I was looking for something I could learn without feeling like a perfect idiot. It was a short apprenticeship, I was fresh out of studies and easy to train. I bought myself a car a couple of years later, met all the instalments and repaid my debt a year early.

I'm not a good driver. Whenever Lisa and I could, we used public transport. Then came scooter summer. Lisa wanted one. I tried to talk her out of it as I was afraid she'd get hurt, but, in the end, with her parents' help, we bought one.

It was hers, but that summer she made me drive it all the time.

We weren't even sharing a house yet, and I don't think we had even really talked about it. Lisa, a mobile phone salesperson, finished around 5:00 and picked me up at the lab at 5:30. We used to tour around town elegantly like flamingos. I'd park near San Siro and we'd walk for an hour along the paths in Trenno Park. Sometimes we dined there with a pizza or bread and mozzarella bought in a local dairy.

The scooter didn't last long. It was second-hand and, at the beginning of October, hard to start. We realized it needed some parts changing but, with autumn and winter looming, we decided to sell it.

It was a good summer.

If I decided to stay in Bournemouth, dreaming a new

life, I think I would buy a scooter like Lisa's. Lauren would like it. Maybe I'm stupid to think about these things. It's still too early to decide on the future.

I have my ups and downs - moments when I'm a bit confused, but my head works better. On the other hand, maybe I'm lost forever.

When the condemned man accepts his sentence, there is no longer any fear in his heart.

Am I like that death row guy?

Other small groups come out to the front to meet up or to have a smoke. Girls look at me; surreptitiously, they glance in my direction whilst chatting to their partners. Maybe it's just an obsession of mine, but I too am attracted by these thousand daring, sexual eyes, eyes that are asking for something: we feed in the exchange of irises. In the distance that separates them, we inject a sort of libidinous substance, which is food for our pupils.

I'm just euphoric, that's the point. I see subtle things. The world travels at two speeds: its normal speed and then a slower speed as it traverses my mind, a slow race full of sensitivity, of connections that I would not commonly perceive.

I go back in. I need to see Lauren, touch and hold her to my body until I absorb her all the way. I walk among people and I find Matthau wandering about.

"Where are you going?" I ask him.

"I'm going out for half an hour. I'm meeting a friend." There's some irony in his sly smile. "Would you like to come with me?"

I'm trapped.

"They're smoking in the back. If you wanna listen to them talk, go ahead, I'll go out, get some good stuff."

I decide to go with him.

We step out onto the street and into the nightlife of Bournemouth.

"That's my father's second car," he informs me. "He only lends it to me for the summer and occasionally during the college year."

"Rules?"

"Yes," he says and, with a flick of his hand on the steering wheel, he shows me a gesture of anger. Matthau would like to have one of his own.

"I mean, you were telling me you're a YouTuber. What kind?"

"I started a couple of years ago with a friend. We used to comment on games. Like Playstation, I mean, you know this stuff, man?"

"Yes, of course."

I knew games as presents that, before eighteen, all went to my brother. He was obsessed with Xbox, I think he got every new model. I played Pes or Fifa with him, sometimes. Soccer and war games were the only ones that attracted me. His favourite was GTA. If Dad hadn't yelled at him not to spend the rest of his life staring at a screen, he would probably have missed soccer practice and not done his homework for the next day. So, in order not to lose our father's approval, he would acquiesce;

otherwise, Dad wouldn't have bought him the next model.

"We were doing one or two million views at the time."

"Not bad."

"I saved a lot of money. The sponsors came later, but I wanted to do something else. My friend is a famous guy. He says he doesn't make as much money as before but could give up work for ten years if he wanted to."

"What are you doing now?"

"I advise on investments. I make challenges. Do you know what challenges are?"

"Yeah. What kind?"

"Dump stuff, but the guys like them. You show 'em how to get some awesome abs. You show them you can live for ten euros per week. The college kids in the area know me mainly for showing them how they can save and ask their parents for more money. There are a lot of people here who don't need to work. If they work, it's just so as not to get bored, because they have daddy to finance them."

"I can imagine."

Matthau seems nervous. "And you know what they do?"

"No."

"Yeah, they think they're superheroes. They look at you from head to toe, I think they say that, like they know everything from life. They're snobs, selfish, and if you make one mistake, they'll cut you off."

"Sounds like they did something to you."

"You're right. Fortunately, not everyone is like that."

"Four hundred and twenty," Matthau says over the phone.

I don't know what his caller answered. I just observe. Matthau gets out of the car, suggests I wait for him to get back in ten minutes. Then he changes his mind.

"Come."

He rings a buzzer to a dark building; the trees in the garden on the side block the city lights. A robotic voice answers, inviting us to go up.

The inside has a strong smell of cigarette butts and coffee.

Share House, Matthau stated.

The walls are rough - there's mould and abandoned garbage bags on the stairs. We get to the first floor. A long corridor connects the rooms.

"The bathroom is there."

"Maybe before we go."

We knock on a door and wait. A Spanish guy lets us in. He's tall, thin and is wearing a Red Bull hat on his head. When he finds out that I'm Italian, he starts speaking Spanish to me, saying that we can understand each other, that he knows my language a bit.

The television is on. There's a girl with her back to me sitting on the edge of the bed, looking stoned. While she's watching TV, Ben (the Spanish guy) talks to Matthau about a job. He has to get up early in the morning and can't go out tonight.

I don't know why, but I'm relieved.

"Did you just get to Bournemouth?" Ben asks me in English.

"Yes. I'm a friend of Losco."

"I don't know who he is."

Matthau comes to my rescue, makes him understand that Losco is that DJ who sometimes plays in local clubs. He mentions some names but only two words remain imprinted on me: Halo and Camel.

"Yes, I know your friend well. He's Italian like you. He's cool. Do you play too?" he asks, nodding his head.

"No. I came to see him."

They talk to each other again.

My attention shifts to the girl who's staring at me. Every time I meet her dull green eyes, she smiles sadly. I want to talk to her. She reminds me of someone. She was a girl in one of the strip clubs where Umberto took me. But who?

If my mind was clearer, I'd remember, but there are too many distractions. The television's on a movie I know: Snowden. That film was one of the reasons I decided to distance myself from social media. At the time, I had Signal installed but none of my friends used it, except Umberto.

This night keeps bringing me to him.

We used Signal for our evenings. I hid it in an anonymous folder, along with other apps. I knew Lisa would peek at my texts, and I didn't want her to find my secret chat. We had an ordinary life, for Lisa there was no reason to think I was cheating, but she wanted to know about herself, wanted to see if I was talking about her with my friends and what I thought of.

Lisa, however, did not give up Facebook, I remember that the last public message was related to the upcoming musical performance. There was a picture of her on the piano, sat in our living room. A picture of her back. I took that. I told her to turn around but she wanted me to take her profile, so I couldn't capture her immense smile. She was happy that day, happy until I came home at two o'clock in the morning and found her drunk and delirious on the couch in the lounge.

"Let's go."

Matthau says hello to Ben. He says *buona serata* in Italian back.

"Would you like some?"

"No, thank you. I'm not used to..."

"You'll feel great. Guaranteed."

Matthau has a seductive smile and wide eyes. The glimmer of the street lamps reflects on his smooth skin. His charisma attracts me. It's a different attraction. I don't want to have sex with him or kiss him, I just want him to be my friend. I'd like to hug and confess my love for him.

I turn down his offer. "Not now, thank you."

"Alright. But it's free for you tonight. Only tonight, understand?"

I understand.

We get moving. We're back on the street again, in the

jaws of Bournemouth, where a few guys are drunkenly staggering towards their friends.

"What do you do? I didn't ask."

"I work in a chemical analysis lab. We do other things, though."

"Like what?"

"We test the products that will go on the market. We have several sections, but I'm in chemistry."

"So am I, my friend. Me too."

We laugh at his comment.

"Do they pay you well?"

"Not bad." Before the crisis, my annual income was just over 35,000 euros.

"Do you have a girlfriend in Italy? I know you're seeing Lauren, but I guess no one will know..."

"I broke up with my ex. So, I'm on my own."

"You've come to the right place. Now you want to forget your previous story, you're looking for fun, so you came to see your DJ friend to relax a bit. Is that so?"

"Yes."

"You've done the right thing. Since I like you, I want to give you some advice. Do you want some advice from a friend?"

"Of course."

"Don't fall in love with Lauren. She's a good girl, don't get me wrong, but she's young and smart. She attracts men like magnets attracts iron."

"What are you trying to tell me?"

"Don't do anything crazy for her. Do you know what *carpe diem* means?"

"Enjoy the moment."

We're parking. Matthau's speech has kind of shaken me up. Strange ideas about the future have been lurking in my mind, and when I say *future*, I mean a future that includes Lauren and me.

We get out of the car. Matthau calls me, says my name in a kind, almost worried voice.

"I'm sorry about what I said."

"Don't worry. You're right."

"I just want you to have fun. Obviously, I wish you two could be together. I'm just saying don't go too fast. Alright?"

"Understood."

Inside the club, I have a strange feeling of uneasiness, a new synchronicity, as if Matthau, unconsciously, had predicted something. When we return to our group, Lauren is not there. The girls say she went to the toilets but I don't believe it. Usually, the girls stick together, but they left her alone.

Then I think about Lauren's words, about feeling different and not very accepted because of her moral choices. Maybe it's just paranoia. We're both lying, somehow driven by selfishness and obsession.

We chat together and sway with the rest of the people. The music lifts us up, challenges us, seduces us. Katie seems the most interested in me. Her wild animal eyes are lightning in mine. I dance close to her, trying not to overdo it - I wouldn't want Lauren to get any ideas when she comes back.

Katie is the youngest of the group, has the taste of new things, the same things that at first convey wonder and surprise. She's sipping her fruit drink while holding the glass with both hands.

I bump into someone and apologize. I was this close to touching Katie.

There's something else in the air, a presentiment or a presence that I know. It's like finding myself at a party of cousins: everywhere I look at, I recognize someone, but in reality, those faces belong to strangers. Everyone is laughing, drinking, talking and breathing. And then it happens. I see her now. The music is opacified, slow; even the crowd around me has that opaque, slow movement. There's only one shape, just one, who is outside of that modified space and time, and I know perfectly well who it belongs to.

The music comes back high, the movements fast, but I still see that girl's shoulders and hair. She's trying to get through the crowd, she wants to reach the stairs. I have to follow her.

"I'll be right back," I say to Katie.

I catch Matthau's inquisitive, worried look. I'm sure he's still following my gaze to see what the hell I'm up to.

I chase this revealed figure. My heart is beating so fast, it takes my breath away.

Lisa.

No, it can't be her.

She's coming down the stairs. The mysterious girl has the same profile as Lisa, the same dress Giulia gave her at a birthday party. I remember that dress because yellow was her favourite colour and my sister knew it. She used it in the summer. She also used it the summer we spent in Milan on scooters. She wore it to provoke me. It was a fine, unique dress, with bare shoulders. It glided down to her knees, flexing like a skirt.

I'm struggling to catch her, by the time I get to the stairs she's already reached the lower floor. Opposite are the toilets, and on the side is another room full of young people.

I run downstairs, breathless. I must stop her. I have to see her face to be sure that it's all a joke, but when I get to the lower floor, she has disappeared, dissolved in that world of dancing bodies. I wander into the crowd. Everything is dark, sweaty and has a thousand eyes and teeth.

And finally, I see Lauren. She's talking to a guy much taller than her. I recognise him: he's my neighbour. They're pretty close and are talking fast, maybe having a heated argument. They seem intimate but, at the same time, they're torn apart by something they have to work out.

I don't want them to see me, nor that they think I'm a jealous person.

The girl in yellow is gone. There's nothing down here I want to see anymore.

I go back up.

But of course, I know I'm jealous.

"Are you okay?" Matthau yells in my ear.

"I'm great." I smile, showing all my false sincerity.

"How about a round of white?"

"Okay, but I don't know what that means."

"Trust me."

I follow Matthau to the bar. Out of the corner of my eye, I see Lauren coming back into our group. I'm relieved.

"You need to loosen up," Matthau tells me.

"I'm in your hands."

"Then let's toast. You know how to do it, don't you?"

Yeah, Lauren taught me that. Let's put the salt on the side of the hand and take the shot down. Matthau orders another one. I'd like to pay for it, but he refuses.

"Next," he says. "This one's for our friendship."

We knock the shots back straightaway. My head is spinning, everything is dense and malleable at the same time.

"Alright, I want another one." I'll ask the girl at the bar to serve us some more. She fills two shots and we knock them back in one go.

Why did I do that?

To ward off jealousy. I would have gone to Lauren in an unpleasant mood, messing her evening up. So, when we get back to our group, I drag her into a corner, dancing for a few minutes, and then I kiss her as I had imagined throughout the evening.

6

We walked hand-in-hand before I threw. We walked along Bournemouth beach, on the Poole side, before I ran into a corner to do it.

The last time I did that was a long time ago. School was finally over, exams were behind me. I was so angry that all I wanted to do was to tell my ex-girlfriend to fuck off.

I hate to remember that now.

Lauren strokes my head and keeps reassuring me that *everything's fine*. I believe her.

I overdid the shots, after the three with Matthau, I got two more with the rest of the group. The girls needed them to keep their spirits up. They were trolling for boys. Before I left with Lauren, I saw Matthau go out back with Vivian, leaving Katie and Hannah alone. Someone got lucky. So did I.

"No, lie down."

"Why? You should sit down for a minute."

"If I lie down, I'll fall asleep. I'm dizzy... *gira tutto.*"

Lauren pulls a weird face because I must have spoken a little English and a little Italian. I laugh and I'm glad to hear her laugh too. I'm bent on one knee, with one hand leaning against the wall trying to support my torso, my head tilted towards my chest, open-mouthed and ready for the next retch.

Lauren is at my side, one hand on my hair and the other on my left shoulder. It's a fragile, complicit and important contact. I've ruined our walk on the beach, but she seems to have the situation under control.

As we were chatting slowly, we noticed the starry sky, a crescent moon and the song of the sea. Lauren confessed that she never stayed until the end of night out; she preferred to leave around three o'clock, take a walk on the beach and then go home. Sometimes she would make an exception, sometimes the drugs would push her to dance for hours.

"I'm sorry."

"It's okay," she keeps saying.

I vomit for the last time: it's horrible, it's nerve-wracking, I'm out of breath. I spit out excess fluid.

"Please, let's go."

"Stand up."

I'm holding on to her to stand. It all turns. The sea and the sky seem to have switched places and keep mixing. I screw up my eyes, heavy as if they were full of compressed air.

"Do you have any sweets?"

Lauren hands me a mint. "I must have horrible

breath."

I hear her laugh, but I don't focus on her smile. Her hair brushes my face but I can't smell it. I need a bath. I need to wash away this sensory deafness. I want to feel the world again, especially Lauren.

"Wait."

I bend forward and throw up against a wall. Maybe it's a restaurant or perhaps it's the entrance to the animal museum near the Bournemouth Pier, because as I turn my head, I think I can see the drawing of a fish and the Ferris wheel. There's something else. The view is blurry, but I can see the girl in Lisa's yellow dress again. That's why I saw the Ferris wheel. If only I could raise my head - if only I had the strength - my eyes would still find her there, not more than twenty or thirty metres away from us.

"I'm sorry."

Lauren strokes my back, just like Lisa did that night.

I screw my eyes up tight, trying hard not to remember, but it's impossible not to. It's them, those damn mushrooms, they keep showing me what I've been hiding from myself for the last few months.

Can you shout without being heard?

Lauren might get scared.

I feel better now, stronger. The square at Bournemouth Pier is empty, but we can hear the cars and the noise of young people coming from the street above the park. There's still something left of the girl in yellow.

It's nothing more than an ember in the air, not physical, not visible in any way; it's more like a melody. Someone is playing the song that Lisa sang on the piano for the spring recital. The school concert was still a few months away. She never got there. It was a two-year-old song she rediscovered during Covid-19. She told me that I had nothing to complain about anymore, that in addition to Michael Jackson, she would now play Lewis Capaldi's album.

I didn't like those scratched and melodramatic songs, but I had learned to appreciate Forever. It was at that time that she decided to buy a *pianola* to cope with the lockdown imposed by the Government. She bought it on Amazon and started taking a course on YouTube. Like all the things she was passionate about, her dedication to piano soon faded. Within a fortnight, we were back on the couch watching old episodes of Game of Thrones or The 100.

"Can you hear that song?"

"Are you feeling better?" Lauren asks me, caressing my face.

I, on the other hand, want to know from her if I'm the only one who can hear that voice.

"I'm fine, don't worry. I just want to know if you can hear the song too."

"Yeah. What's so special about it?"

"Who's singing it?"

"Lewis Capaldi."

"I mean, now."

"Some dudes on the bridge."

I look up and see them. At the head of the group, there is a girl dressed in white who's jumping and singing.

"Let's go," Lauren encourages me.

I let it go and focus back on the task of walking with Lauren's support. Halfway through the park, I tell her I can walk without any help.

"You'll stumble."

"I just need a moment."

I'm making progress but I have the balance of a rookie tightrope walker.

"Look, I can do it!"

The girl's voice has now faded behind us. I want to listen to her a little more but the sound has been swallowed up by the night.

I grip Lauren's side and we walk towards the town centre.

We don't talk. She giggles, I have a clumsy gait that amuses her.

I met Umberto in high school. An only child, of robust size and banana face.

We didn't bond immediately. Our real friendship started in the third year when we used to talk about our future. We were strong in chemistry and physics, and often there was a kind of competition between us.

One day, he told me he was going to study to be a pharmacist. That's when I considered biology. We had a few things in common; we both read the Lancet in English and subscribed to an Italian natural science journal. Umberto already spoke English well and helped me to improve. In the last two years of school, I went from satisfactory to eight in my report.

Our friendship had many ups and downs. When I got engaged, it was natural to spend less time together. Often, on Saturdays, I would stay for dinner at his house. His parents would order pizza and then go with us to the Navigli. But that wasn't the only time we spent together. Even though we lived in two different towns, I frequently went to his house to prepare myself for the next day's exam. We were a team that worked.

Sara cooled our idyllic friendship, which was like a blood pact. I didn't stop studying, but I consumed almost all my leisure chasing her, discovering the pleasures produced by the physical body.

When she broke up with me, I said nothing, I was ashamed to have abandoned Umberto and to have ruined our friendship. He, however, found out we'd split up and asked me to help him with his final year dissertation, that we could work together, just like the old days.

So, in the final half of our fifth year, we became friends again. I was at his service, and I indulged him in everything he decided to do. I felt guilty but I didn't understand why. I just knew that his closeness was enough to ease my pain.

After the exams, I would go to his house almost every day, bring a change of clothes to play football in the outside area of his condominium and get some money from Dad for ice cream or other treats we fancied.

We knew at that point we only had one summer. Umberto was aware that we would separate again. It was his idea to go to a birthday party of an acquaintance of his. He was the one who dragged me to Lisa's friend's birthday party.

"We're here," she says.

We're going in. We use the stairs. I have no idea how many. I have no idea where exactly we are. I just know it's Lauren's shared house.

"You need a shower."

Her room is large, clean and white. There is a queen-sized bed in a corner, a low table on the side, a shower cubicle on the wall opposite the two windows and a couple of wardrobes for her things: books, clothes, cups, makeup and more. It smells of sandalwood or something.

"Take off your shoes."

I put them next to the shoe rack, which is already full of hers. Lauren takes my hand and walks me to the shower. She takes my clothes off, staring me in the eye. I am confused, clumsy. I have nothing to say to her.

She unbuttons her shirt and immediately presses her cold hands on my chest. I wrap my hands around her waist and pull her dress off in one fell swoop. While she undoes my pants, I undo her bra. We laugh because our arms cross each other, making it difficult to move.

Her bra and my pants slide down at the same time. I'd like to touch her breasts, but Lauren says she's got something for me. I watch her walk away, enjoying her slim, slender silhouette.

Lauren puts on music, says she likes Ed Sheeran and his acoustic live shows. I don't comment, I'm fine with anything.

"Let's dance a little."

We dance as I look at her breasts, full of desire. We turn around on ourselves but, after a while, I lift Lauren from the gluteus, kissing her hard. She lets go, grabs my arms to support herself and sinks her tongue into my mouth.

"Go to the shower," she says.

I do it while I keep kissing her.

With her free hand, Lauren opens the glass door and pushes the water knob up. We go in together, taking off our final items of clothing and yelling like kids because of the freezing water.

"Have you woken up?"

"It's too much," I protest, but I don't care.

She tries to adjust the temperature as I kiss her shoulder. I bend over like a branch laden with fruit. I kiss her washed body, which is white, which is fire inside and air outside. I descend to her felled forest, the centre of her apex.

I am confused and excited. The primordial cry I had in my chest a few hours earlier is now a wolf hungry for flesh. I devour Lauren, I devour her skin, her moans, her lips constantly searching for mine, her tongue digging into my mouth and our rapid panting in and out through our noses.

Our screams go beyond these walls now; they are no

longer held back by any inhibition. We shout because at our age we don't care about rules, we want to live with noise and derision.

I take Lauren's body and soul as my trophy. I possess her by giving her all my fire. Now she's the guardian of my passion.

I close my eyes, the last thing I see is *Lisa's face* telling me I can sleep *peacefully.*

***

It's a dream within a dream. So, my question is, who's dreaming this new dream? Is it always me, or is it myself I dream about?

Umberto never touched a beer. It was just water, Coca-Cola for him, or a glass of wine when he went to visit his grandparents. That evening I had bought a beer. He thought it was such a stupid thing to bring, but I told him I needed it to cheer up.

The party was in the tavern. I knew some of the guys there, a couple of them were from my class, but I was more interested in girls than talking to another bloke. I tried to pick up one of them, asking if she wanted to dance, but she turned me down. I took that rejection badly; it was like being dumped a second time by the same person.

Outside of Umberto's supervision, I started to go around the table, nibbling and drinking. I drank wine. I noticed the girl sitting alone at that table. She was pretty but I avoided her so as not to be rejected another time.

I had no more interest in that evening. She told me it wasn't a good idea to drink all that wine. And I told her that no one was drinking it, that I was doing everyone a favour.

I felt funny, she sketched a smile and told me her name to distract me.

"Nice to meet you, I'm..."

"Are you a friend of Luigi's?"

"Not really, but I know him. We were in the same school but in different classes. And how do you know him?"

"I'm a friend of his fiancée. She's throwing this party."

"What school do you go to?"

"Marie Curie. I've just finished my fourth year."

"I'm just done."

"How much did you get?"

"I came out with top marks. Not bad, right?"

Lisa seemed astonished, she made to speak but then hesitated; she hadn't expected such talent from someone like me; I was still intent on draining the last drop of wine from the *tetra pak*. It was the Baileys though that dealt me the final blow.

Someone brought it over and gave everyone a drink. I drank mine and Umberto's.

I threw up by the fireplace, relieving myself of the evening's pasta as well as some of the wines.

Umberto came to my rescue. I remember his slap and

the worry in his face. I told him I was sorry; he called me *an idiot*.

I couldn't stand up and someone complained about the mess I'd made and that I had to leave.

"I'll clean it up, I'm sorry."

Others laughed, had fun.

Umberto plucked up strength to help me clean my vomit up but it was not enough, I puked again. I wanted to cry and leave but I was at the height of drunkenness.

Lisa stretched out her arms and helped me sit down. I let her guide me with kindness while Umberto cleaned up my mess. She did as Lauren did on the beach, caressed my head and spoke in my ear to distract me and not think about the mess I had made.

It made me feel better.

I owed her a lot.

After the first few dates, I asked her why she'd agreed to go out with a drunk guy.

"I don't know. I thought you were interesting."

"And what did you find interesting about me that night?"

"I thought, you just wanted to have some fun. You just went too far, but I never thought you were bad."

"Thank you."

"For what?"

"For thinking I wasn't bad."

"But I'm warning you, if you change my mind, we're not dating anymore. If you lie, sooner or later I'll find out."

"Is it a deal?"

"Call it what you want."

I wonder where we are. I see this memory, I see the light of this memory, there is a park, a stone table and a wash basin to wash your hands. We're sitting under a tree, a big poplar tree. That's where I first kissed her.

The next day she would leave with her family. I didn't want her to go and I think she would have wanted to stay. I promised I'd wait for her, and Lisa said *only lovers wait for lovers.*

That's when I kissed her.

The sex would come much later.

She went away for 20 days. I swear, during that time I never wanted to see anyone the way I wanted to see Lisa again.

7

Lauren's still asleep. I pull the hair away from her face to see her better, to make sure she's real. The lipstick has faded from her lips, and has managed to make its way in smears to the corners of her mouth. The black eyeliner around her eyes now continues down in a single perpendicular line like a clown's tear. I try to wipe it away with my thumb, but Lauren mumbles a weak dissent by moving her hair back to cover the face.

On the bedside table, there is a clock radio. It reads one o'clock in the afternoon. I thought it was later than that.

I get out of bed, still staggering, I haven't learned to walk on the rope yet. Maybe I need a coffee; I'm thirsty for sure.

I see my face in a little oval mirror. I've got a reddish scratch just under my unsightly left dark circle, a tiny souvenir from Lauren. I had guts to do what I did. When I think about it though, it wasn't just me: it happened because of Lauren and the MDMA.

Now, I'm looking for my cell phone, and while I'm waiting for it to turn on, I come out of the room and head toward the bathroom.

Losco still hasn't responded.

8

The beach is shining.

I asked Lauren how long the MDMA effect might last and found out that I ran out my fuel, which is why I can't explain what the sand gives off.

I didn't tell her the truth.

"I was just curious," I whisper, looking at the sea.

We made love before we ate a sandwich and went out. This time it happened in bed, pulling our pillows, biting each other and sweating away the remnants of energy we had left.

From the beach I can see the imposing white building beyond the cliff. Behind it, along Manor Road, is the flat that Losco rented for us.

Lauren asks me if I have seen someone, and I tell her that I am worried about my friend, whom I haven't seen since the beach party.

She shrugs. "I thought you knew him well."

We lay a large blue tarp over the sand and sit on it. Lauren opens a beer. I bought a large bottle of water to quench my thirst.

"We have things to do together, I just wish I knew why he's not answering my texts."

Lauren put on a pair of sunglasses. Her skin is sensitive to the sun, so she asks me to rub cream on her shoulders.

She lets herself be massaged in silence but the sound of her thoughts is so loud. I can hear them.

I can't go on like this, I want to get back to normal.

The sunscreen on Lauren's skin looks like it's full of coloured beads. Intense colours, little more than disco strobe-lights.

Finally, she breaks the silence.

"People say things about him."

"Like what?"

"He is bisexual."

"You mean he likes both men and women."

"Yes, that's right. Some people think he hasn't decided which side to take."

"I didn't know. Do you think it's true?"

"I'm bisexual too. Did I tell you that?"

"No. We've only known each other for two days..."

"I'm not ashamed to admit it, I have other friends like me. You want to know what we do?"

"I..."

"I was kidding, I'd never tell you," she says, laughing, moving her feet up and down like she's crushing something with her heels.

"I'd love to get into that."

"Silly."

"Have you ever seen him with a man? I mean, Losco."

"No. But he has a good following of girls. Honestly, I don't know him very well. He's a nice guy and he seems to see a lot of people all the time, but apart from letting me into his evenings, I've never had a chance to talk to him like I do with you now. Once we were at the same table in a pub downtown, but there were so many of us that we couldn't chat for long. It was really confusing."

"Glad he could find some friends."

"Why?"

"In high school, he was a guy... what's the word? Introvert?"

"You mean he wasn't friendly?"

"He was but only to a degree."

"If you live in a place like this and want to be a DJ, you have to get busy - you can't be introverted."

"You're right."

Then Lauren turns and kisses me, pinching my side.

"You're mine, remember that," she declares.

"I can't forget it now that you've hurt me."

She's still poking me, so I push her down and force her to kiss me even if she turns her head to avoid my lips.

"Your breath stinks."

"It's not true," I protest. "I ate the sweet you gave me."

"Then your armpits stink."

"That's true, it's too hot."

We laugh.

Then I take off my shirt and lie down, covering my eyes with one arm. The light is everywhere today.

"Ask Matthau."

"What?"

"They'll be here soon. He knows a lot of people. Maybe he can help you find your friend."

That's a good idea. When Matthau arrives, dressed in a dark vest and fluorescent swimming shorts, we embrace and he shows me how to do the boys' greeting: punch, slap and punch again.

I let Matthau and the girls settle in, lie down, have their drinks and start a conversation. I need to close my eyes because of the glitter, pretend I still want to sleep, that my hangover isn't over. After a short while, someone takes a dip in the sea, Matthau shakes me, insisting that I join the swim.

"Alright, I need it."

Then Lauren follows us after a while. Eventually, we're all in the sea slapping water in our faces. I have to regularly cover my eyes, pretending that salt or something else is disturbing my eyesight to avoid confessing the truth. The glow is much stronger on the shore; the sun's rays make it unbearable.

I hide my face against Lauren's skinny back, making her laugh. I pretend to be a shark, then someone who wants to drown her or just to hide from her water toys.

"We're going off for a walk."

I let them go, even Lauren follows her friends. They

tell me they're going to walk to the pier to buy some cigarettes. I stay with Matthau, standing on the shore listening to him tell me about his evening with Vivian. He describes her body and confesses to me that they did it at the club and then at her house.

"How did it go with Lauren?"

"Good. We went to hers but I was so drunk, I don't remember anything."

Matthau laughs and punches me weakly. "I hope you haven't disappointed her."

"If I'm still here, that means it went well."

"I underestimated you."

"Oh, yeah?"

"But I should have expected it from an Italian." He laughs at his own joke and to please him I sketch a smile showing my embarrassment.

"Can I ask you something?"

"Of course."

I ask him how well he knows my friend Losco. First, he swings his head and then he says: "Not much, but he's quite famous around here. When I arrived in Bournemouth, he was one of the first DJs I saw live, he played at a student night. Do you know Halo?"

"No."

"Monday. Yes, I remember it well. My friends brought me, said the DJ was Italian and had style."

"He's been missing for two days. He hasn't answered my messages and he wasn't home last night."

"Perhaps he's there now. Maybe he's with someone."

"Maybe."

"Are you worried?"

"I just wish he'd text me back."

"As soon as the girls get back, we'll drop by your place and you'll see he's there with someone."

Maybe Matthau's right.

The elevator goes up, he and I stay quiet. When we get to my floor, I notice the neighbour's door is open. There are bags outside – it looks as if someone is moving.

I look for the keys and open the apartment.

I let Matthau through, and out of the corner of my eye I see him, the guy who was with Lauren on the lower floor of the club. That's him. Now I have confirmation. He nods at me and I wave back. Then I go in.

It's quiet in the flat. Well-ordered. There's light everywhere, but it's less bright than it was at the beach. That's a relief.

"Losco, are you home?"

Matthau looks around, says he likes the house and that I live in luxury. I don't answer. I let him wander around.

I take a bottle of water from the cupboard. I notice that if I drink more, the glow gets less intense. Then the effect of mushrooms hasn't fully worn off yet. I'm in a trance and I don't know how to get out of it. I'll drink a lot; perhaps that's the only way to get back to normal.

Losco's room is how I remember it, but I'm sure there's something different about the bed. Someone must have slept there last night. It smells different, too.

Matthau calls me. His voice is coming from the living room. Before leaving the room, I notice the incense burner. It's new. It wasn't there before.

Losco has been here.

"I've found this."

Matthau shows me a piece of paper written in Italian so he can't read it.

I'm busy. Enjoy the ride, my friend.
Know that I'm always with you.
You can see me everywhere.

Cryptic. He says one thing and then contradicts it. A very busy person can't be there at the same time.

I look around while my Anglo-French friend asks me what's on the note.

"He says he's busy, not to worry."

"I have something to tell you. I'm sorry, but it's just occurred to me."

"I'm listening."

I walk towards the pic of the Buddha. It is a remarkable, attractive painting that has the power of resoluteness and peace: it reminds me of the last evening with Losco.

"Your friend is playing Friday. I have the notification on Facebook. Friday, I'm sure. DJ NB."

"That's him."

"Two days away."

"I hope I see him before then, 'cos I have a flight to book."

Matthau smiles, then spreads his arms, putting his back to the big window and, while he advises me to stay here forever, I see the glow on the sea.

***

"Certainty, he's a real weirdo. First, he invites you to stay with him and then he doesn't show up," Lauren declares, when we're alone.

The others are on the shore, chatting. Matthau is planning to spend another night at Vivian's and I don't know what to do. I'll go home tonight even though Lauren's constant thinking and her delightful slow way of speaking try to persuade me otherwise.

"I'll tell you what, I'll come with you to that night. If he doesn't show up, I'll take you to this Friday night. We'll have fun. Is that alright with you?"

"I agree."

She hugs me. We play a little, pinching and kissing and caressing. She tells me about her life with three brothers and how she wanted a sister.

Lisa dreamt of a sister too.

"What did you do with the boys? With your boyfriends? I guess you couldn't bring them home."

She's amused by the question. "No, I couldn't. David was jealous. If he saw me holding hands with someone, he would make a scene."

"My God."

"Yes. Some people mistook us for lovers. One of my last boyfriends in college thought I was cheating on him with David."

"And you didn't tell him he was just your brother?"

"Yes, but not right away. I wanted him to be jealous."

"You're terrible."

"It's good for you boys to be a little jealous, so you don't betray us."

"Or perhaps we betray you out of jealousy."

"What theory is that? Never heard of it."

"Then listen to me carefully. Some men will betray you because they think they will be betrayed."

"That's not true."

"It is true."

"Have you ever done that?"

Nothing comes out of my mouth, I had a denial on the tip of my tongue but a memory suppressed it. I saw again, in my thoughts, the girl who was with Ben. There was something about her that reminded me of a place that the head injury made me forget.

I'd like to tell Lauren that I'm a survivor. The scar on the back of my head, covered by the regrowth of my hair, is a sign of my truth. A truth, however, that I still don't remember.

"You are a coward, a liar and a traitor."

"I swear I have never done that."

She comes back to play with me. She wants me to get away from her, but at the same time, she picks up my hands to be touched.

"I don't believe you, you're... I don't know, but I don't believe you're like that."

"I swear I've never done that. I swear I haven't."

"Would you ever do that to me?"

"I don't know."

Lauren moves away from me firmly. She's confused by my answer and doesn't know whether to laugh or take it.

"I'm not one to do these things, but I've learned that anything can happen in life."

"I know I'm not technically your girlfriend, but I like you, so play nice or I'll change my mind."

I take the hand that she left between us and I drag her to me, moving the towel as well. I think that's what she wants: to play. And I like playing with her.

9

The loneliness now has its own gravity. It is solemn, deep as the silence that I have been hearing in this apartment for two days. It's a house made of silence. It gives birth to silence and spreads it. This non-existent noise is swollen, full, and I cover my ears as I feel its heaviness. I need noises, draughts, slamming doors or squeaking hinges.

I should have asked Lauren to stay with me, but I preferred to keep this rebellious loneliness immaculate.

"Call me if you get lonely," she said.

Maybe I will.

And then with her, I broke one of Losco's rules.

I need a moment to myself.

The glow was exhausting my eyes, but after I drank more than two litres of water, it disappeared. Now that I can see the sea through the large window, everything is calmer. I wonder when the Mother Wave will come, as Losco called it. I wonder what it means. Is it a real wave or a metaphorical image?

There are cheese, sauces and vegetables in the fridge.

I don't feel like cooking, so I make a plate of spaghetti. I find a tin of tomato sauce in one cupboard and pasta in another. That'll be fine.

I turn on the kitchen radio, someone is talking about 2020, the year of Covid-19. I have a few memories of those days, when there was so much confusion and contradictory information. It was never clear how and why this virus was able to spread so much: millions infected, hundreds of thousands dead. Lisa was terrified. She said if she contracted the virus, she would surely die. I told her she was too young to die. Well, I was wrong. You die from so many things in life, there's often no cure or vaccine.

The water boils, and so I pour the pasta in and wait.

The DJ on the radio puts on a piece of Lady Gaga. Sounds like she's back to her old style or maybe it's just an old song. Anyway, I'm fine with it; I need to move this body that's asking to be recharged. The music charges me.

I'll follow Losco's advice until he can tell me what's happening to me.

And then I have a feeling: I won't see my friend for a while.

If I'm right, I'll book my return flight for next week, or maybe extend my stay to be with Lauren. Something occurs to me, something I haven't foreseen, but I need to understand if the well-being I feel here is due to drugs or to a new awareness. The answer will have an immediate effect on my future and, at the moment, I am still waiting for it.

I can't sleep. I sit in the living room and pretend Losco's in front of me, like the other night, last time we were together. He made me close my eyes and ask me to focus on my breathing. I do it again: imagine breathing the room around me. It's tough without his guiding voice, and the silence doesn't help.

I breathe in.

It's not working.

I breathe out.

All I can think about is Lauren and her soft, smooth, fragile body. Between my fingers I have her bones, her saliva on my lips, but I wish I was still at sea to hide my face in her back. Playing. *You're at my fingertips.* I'd love to tell you, send you a message but you'd think I'm crazy.

I inhale.

I can't breathe in this room because I breathe in you.

I breathe out.

Then I open my eyes again. I don't know how it happened, but... *it's daytime.* Maybe I'm going crazy or perhaps something keeps drugging me without me realizing it. What I see out of the window is a new sunny morning. The sky is clear and the birds are chirping from tree to tree.

I get up in disbelief.

The outside has only one problem, and that's the sea. The rest is quiet, bright, but the water seems to have receded from the beach at least twenty metres.

I shudder.

It only happens when a tsunami is coming but there is too little distance between the English and French coasts for such an event. I focus on a very marked blue line. It occupies the whole horizon and marks the border between the sky and the sea.

A tsunami.

"It's just a dream, it can't be."

I grab the bottle of water I left in the living room and drink half of it.

When I turn around, as I thought, it's all over.

10

It's the policeman, again. Open the door for him.

"Good morning," I say.

"Good morning, kid. You alright?"

"Very good, sir. May I help you?"

He writes something on his bloc-notes using a black pencil, one of those with an eraser in it. Today he has a pair of sunglasses on his head and the transceiver attached to the strap of his uniform. Someone is giving him information but his voice is distorted by frequencies. I don't understand a word of it.

What a bother these guys.

"I'm here on a reconnaissance mission. I received a warning. I was taking this opportunity to let you know we found out what happened two days ago at the beach party."

"About Saber?"

I'm asking the questions...

"About the seagull you call Saber. The video we recovered shows a group of four boys hurting him. They were very astute."

"Will there be a penalty? Or a consequence?"

First time you fuck up, boy, you could pay dearly. Watch your attitude. We don't like foreigners.

"Obviously, we'll issue a penalty as soon as we get the punks' facial recognition."

I can't wait for him to go. I hope he doesn't notice the little drops of sweat on my forehead or think I'm hiding something.

"Are you still alone in the house? Can I talk to the other guy, too?"

"I'm all alone. Losco... I mean, my friend went out to work."

I bet you a hundred quid, he's in his room with a whore.

I can hardly contain my laughter. I cough.

"Sorry, I swallowed wrong."

"Alright. Your neighbour came back yesterday. Do you know him?"

"No. Never seen him."

"But you must have noticed there's someone there?"

"Yes, but I didn't see anyone."

He's taking notes. Then from one of the pockets of his uniform, he pulls out a card. He hands it to me.

"I know you're a good kid. We like nice kids."

I nod, but I already know what he wants.

"Don't hesitate to call us if he comes back."

I read on the card: Mr Mike Kelly.

"I will."

He doesn't say goodbye; he just leaves.

I go back in. I lean my back against the door and I stare at that name. Kelly was Umberto's favourite strip club, and Mike was the owner. He was an American who had made his fortune in America and wanted to expand his business in Italy.

Mike Kelly was his name.

Life is ironic.

Losco was right about one more thing: Stage three has begun and I don't know what to do.

I must have got a text message as I can hear my cell phone vibrating all the way up here. I'm walking to the living room, breathing slowly. I dry my forehead and then I open WhatsApp's chat room.

Hey, man, it's Mat.
Vivian and I are going to Hengistbury Head.
What are you and the princess doing?

Lauren asked me to meet her later as she wanted to go downtown. She needed some food supplies. She'd been to three different night clubs in the last five days and kept forgetting to stop by Holland and Barret's for supplies. I asked her if it wasn't cheaper to go to Lidl or Tesco, but she wanted her stuff.

"Besides, I'm not much of an eater. At least what little I eat I want to be healthy."

Lisa didn't eat much. She was actually thin, the same size as Lauren. She had breakfast with whole grains, often low-fat yogurt and fruit. She wanted to keep her figure and didn't like to feel fat.

Personally, I rarely ate breakfast. If she was already awake, Lisa would make me coffee and then I'd have another one at work. We had a snack machine at the lab, and in the middle of the morning I'd eat a sandwich or a chocolate bar. My biology professor said that a square of bitter chocolate a day was good for the heart, but the chocolate bars I took to stop hunger were very sweet, not exactly the height of well-being.

I sit on the couch and aim the card. If I suddenly remember so many details, the madness that Losco introduced me to is working. There are things I struggle to bring to the surface. The last few months, for example, are the hardest to unravel. Something inside me keeps refusing to bring them into focus; the outside, this reality to which I am imprisoned because of those mushrooms, however, tries to wake me up, just as this name cannot just be an accident.

Mike Kelly.

I text Lauren.

After a while she answers.

We're going to go to Hengistbury Head.

Matthau's happy. He says not to eat *too much*. He's got something for us. I'm not sure I dare today, there are too many things buzzing around in my head.

I need a drink now.

11

A little quartz in the palm of my hand.

"This stuff is for shamans."

"What does that mean?"

Matthau gives Lauren a speck of it, too.

"My mum likes esoteric stuff. I mean, to cut a long story short, the masters use this stuff for their meditations or to prepare for a speech. I'm not familiar with it, but I think you got it."

I shake my head, making Lauren and Vivian laugh. They don't care. They are on their final days before returning to university, so they just want to enjoy this almost windless day, full of the scent of flowers. Here it's not much different from Bournemouth, but there's a better view of the coast, maybe because we're a little bit higher than the neighbouring countryside.

I swallow down the little quartz with some water. Today I'm prepared. I put two bottles in my backpack and I'm going to drink them both.

"Let's get on top of that rock. The view from up there is even more awesome," says Matthau.

We walk on the cliff surrounded by air that smells like fish and burnt grass. Lauren looks for my hand, says that if we stay close, maybe we can reach the peak together.

"That's a nice idea," I tell her.

"I've been thinking about you all night," she says when we're alone.

Matthau and Vivian are up ahead, chatting and playing with each other.

"What were you thinking?"

"I wish you'd slept at my place."

"Yes. I would have liked that. Sorry. I had things to do with Losco but he didn't come home last night."

"You look really concerned. What did you have to do?"

"Spend time together. We haven't seen each other in years. And then he wanted to take me around. I mean, we had ideas." I don't know what to tell her.

"You have to admit he gave you more than you hoped for. Am I wrong?"

"What do you mean?"

"Three days after your arrival, you're already hand-in-hand with a girl. Either you're some kind of talent or his influence has helped you."

"I hadn't thought about it. You're right."

I give her a kiss. When I move, she holds me back because she wants another one.

"Now don't think about it. We'll get him on Friday

for sure."

Let's go higher. I admire the rock, the cliff and the blocks of flowers on the lawn. I'm strong and calm.

"Sit there."

"Sure."

Vivian and Matthau have already reached the top. Perhaps they won't stop.

From the top, looking towards Bournemouth, the view is immense, divided between sea and land. Everything is flat, small and green. The coast is shaped like a centipede. The hinterland is the Garden of Eden, I'm sure.

We climb over the wooden fence and sit on the ground, with our feet dangling in the void. I feel no dizziness, no fear. I look at that short precipice as part of the whole. Lauren holds my hand, her skin is embers, and it's like she's throwing fire into my veins. The sun in front of us is a golden hot-air balloon, and neither its rays nor its heat burn our limbs.

I wish I felt like this all the time.

"What would our life be like if we felt like this every day?" she asks me.

It happened again, but this time I'm not afraid.

One day Umberto told me that if he could choose a superpower he would opt to read people's thoughts. He said that reading people's thoughts gave you an advantage, that could improve our lives and the lives of others. "For example, I'd know for sure if my girlfriend was cheating on me."

Now, I know what it means.

"There wouldn't be wars, I guess," I tell her.

"Really? Yes, you're right. No one would ruin such a beautiful, magical world. Can you feel the magic?"

I nod, I can't answer her. My fingers are resting on the earth and they are the earth; they are the earth, the worms, the water and every mineral of which the world is composed. I feel like an extension of something bigger.

I wish it would never end.

I hear her thoughts, I admit it. All I do is smile and giggle when she keeps saying that everything is *magnificent*.

Are we innocent and stupid? Or just fragile?

One thing, though, is certain: she can't see the sea as I see it.

***

Lauren and I are sitting in the back of the car, her head resting on my legs, still in her bliss. We're going to have a bite, then spend a few hours in a pub to keep our spirits up. How long it will last I don't know, but hopefully as long as possible. I'm in their hands.

I look out the window while Matthau talks about something that makes the girls laugh, and I have the impression that parts of me are slipping away with this constant motion. I am nothing anymore, the placid delirium in which I am wrapped is a comfortable shell. The head does not think: it is immersed in a state of deep freedom from the fog that usually obstructs it. I keep thinking about Lauren's words, the ones she didn't say, but I caught them: *I would like to feel like this all the time.* I would too, my love, but in this life the excesses are paid for, sooner or later chemistry will issue the bill. It is inherent in the nature in which we live, that the more it gives, the more it takes away somewhere else. It's called balance or homeostasis.

I caress her face as I continue to watch the houses crumble because of the speed of Matthau's car; I hear the thoughts of all of them, they buzz in my head and are blind flies, hidden chills, ephemeral desires. It's obvious that Vivian would like to grope Matthau's testicles while he is driving, as she keeps touching his leg, bringing her hand closer to the middle of his jeans. Even though I can't see them, they're throwing glances of consent. They're waiting out of respect for Lauren and me.

Lauren, on the other hand, isn't just thinking about me, there's someone else in her thoughts. That makes two of us. It should upset me, but suddenly I don't care; what matters is that I'm well now, I'm out of the tunnel, maybe for a while, possibly just for one last night.

Lauren begged Matthau to park in Boscombe to get a burger at Plant Hustler. He wanted to go to a typical club, maybe Mary Shelley's downtown, mix in the crowd, gorge on beer. I said I'd like to try something different and, in the end, I let Lauren win.

Matthau looks around like he's in prison, says he likes the pictures on the walls of the club and the quiet atmosphere. When our orders come in, we eat in silence.

Then we're out again, in the fresh, dirty air of Boscombe. The smell of garbage and putrid water are part of this wide street in the centre.

With them at my side, I feel like a movie star, a rocker ready to perform live.

I hold Lauren close to me, kiss her forehead, and then we're off.

12

There was a time when I talked to someone about starting a family, having kids, buying a house to live in. I know who I was talking to about it, but those moments remain a remnant, a sound similar to what scientists intercept from the universe.

The never-ending spread of the beginning.

Lauren dances in front of me, moving her body like an eighties girl under the notes of Irena Cara's *What a Feeling*, imitating Jennifer Beals in the film Flash dance. One brunette and the other blonde. They seem to be two separate things; but my mother was a fan of eighties films and sometimes watched them with my father. He would gladly accept that suffering because he didn't want to be disturbed when his favourite football teams played on the weekend. They had a sort of pact. Maybe that's what family means: to bear together, united at any cost. That film used to be shown, and I'd listen to the music and the voices dubbed in Italian. I knew many of the lines by heart.

I remember my mother and me being in the kitchen, my dad not yet home and the song *Maniac* playing in the background. Giulia was looking after Matteo in the bathroom and Fabrizio had run away for his aperitif with friends. I helped Mum to set the table by taking the cutlery. She told me that we'd also need knives because there were potatoes in the oven. I tell her that Lisa and I had found a house to rent and we wanted to move in together. Mum was happy, exclaiming a "finally" that Giulia also heard from the bathroom. Giulia already knew everything; she'd known about Lisa and me for a while.

"And when?"

"Next month."

"Do you need money for advances?"

"No, Mum, we don't need it, I just wanted to tell you."

"When are you having a baby?"

"We're moving for the moment. There's plenty of time for a child."

I liked the idea of living together. I needed more space and some peace. Since Giulia had gone to live with Sebastiano, a couple months ago, I had taken her room, so Lisa often stayed with me. That meant we could make love without fearing that Fabrizio would return at any moment. It had happened. He had caught us in the act. Luckily, though, we were under the covers.

I think it was on one of our evenings, in Giulia's former room, that the idea of living together gathered momentum, going from chatter (since we had talked

216

about it before) to action.

That evening Mamma cried, she said that time passed quickly, that it seemed like only yesterday when her children were little and messed the house up with their toys.

In Lauren's mind, there is not the faintest desire to have a family. She wants to travel, meet a lot of people, have fun before a degree in chiropractic takes her away from all this abundance of smells, colours and movement. I can't feel sad about it. I just wish I didn't know, that I could let it be, live in the moment.
Carpe diem.

I'm lucid now. I bought one shot for Matthau and me and promptly downed a litre of water straight after. I wanted to get to this moment of lucidity with all of my faculties intact.

I'm stroking Lauren from the thighs up. She's lying on the bed, trembling from my hands touching her soft skin. She wants to tell me what background music I should put on, but I tell her she has to accept *whatever I put on.*
"What is it?"
"Italo disco."
"You know, maybe your friend played it too?"
"Interesting."
That's all we talked about. I kiss her pubis and then

her clitoris. She moans and grabs my hair. She says something I can't hear but, from the movement of her legs, I understand that I have to help her take off her panties completely. They're pale yellow and have a sort of bow in the middle. I'm going up, crawling up her belly with my nose all the way to her breast. I kiss her chest, behind the neck and I get to her mouth. I've breathed every inch of her and now we're ready to explode.

I just wish her hair and the things in the room around us weren't so *goddamn* yellow.

Faults

1

Lauren collapsed from exhaustion. I watched her for half an hour before I decided to try Losco's meditation again. Inhaling, exhaling and inhaling again.

It happened just like the other night.

The daylight is an opaque colour against the curtains of the two windows. Just one strip of it filters through, bisecting the space in the room and falls on Lauren's feet, at the end of the bed.

There are a couple of messages on my phone but nothing from Losco.

I take the bottle of water that I left in a corner near the bed and drink all the contents.

I'm irritated. I can't call him, and he doesn't answer my texts. He's a spiteful ghost. I still have his note in my jeans pocket.

I get dressed and leave the room. The guys in this section of the house share a kitchen and two bathrooms. I need to urinate and I'm really hungry.

In the kitchen, I find tea bags and a water heater. I fill two cups and go back to Lauren's room.

She moves across the bed, going from side to side, mumbling. She fell asleep naked, just as my love rush left her.

I put the two cups on the bedside table and crawl across the bed looking for her breasts.

Lauren giggles, tells me to stop, that she still needs more sleep - much more.

"Tell me exactly how much more sleep you need," and I pull her to the edge of the bed.

"Stop it. I want to sleep all day."

"Did you know that in a spoonful of sugar there are as many grains as the stars you can see with your naked eyes?"

She pulls her hair out of the face and looks at me as if I'm crazy.

"So, is your need for sleep this big or much bigger?"

"Much bigger than a stupid spoonful of sugar."

"So let's say, if we widen this spoon at least 12 kilometres in diameter and fill it with sugar, we could put in all the stars in the firmament. Is it big enough for you now?"

Lauren slips out of my arms and goes back to her side of the bed. I reach out and bite her side, sinking my teeth and tongue on her soft flesh.

Let's play for a while. We play so much that we forget the tea.

We ordered two croissants, cappuccino, and Lauren

also wanted a glass of carrot and apple juice. I taste her juice and I think it's delicious.

"Have one for yourself, too."

"I prefer coffee."

"But then you're really Italian. You can't be wrong."

We laugh. It's nice to do it together even for stupid things like this.

Lauren's face is flushed, the heat's brought out the freckles on her nose. I love watching her. She's the most real and unreal thing that's ever happened to me in my life. As she talks about her studies, while I chew my croissant, I see her reflected in the oblong glass, the juice glass. She's enthusiastic, alive, full of energy. Last night Lauren moved above me as if she were riding a prehistoric creature. She overwhelmed me, forced me to change position, to possess her in every breathable square metre of the room.

"What is university like in Italy?"

"What, sorry?"

"Weren't you listening to me?"

"Yes. It's just that you changed the subject quickly and..."

"I know, I do it all the time."

Lauren kisses me on the cheek like she wants to make it up to me. I can still smell the wild fragrance of her body, it hits my face along with the cold of her kiss.

"I don't know what it's like. I mean, I studied a lot and I was already engaged."

"Have you ever lived with her?"

"No."

"Didn't you love her?"

I'm sipping cappuccino to stall.

"It didn't work out."

"What about the scar on the back of your head?"

I almost forgot I had some kind of war wound. When did you notice it?

"An accident. Head trauma."

"That can't have been a good experience. What happened? I'm curious."

I'd like to tell her I don't know, and that would be the truth, but Lauren spies on me with her eyes. I'm afraid she can even hear my thoughts.

"I went off the road. I remember it was raining and I lost control of the car."

Yes, it was raining. For a moment I saw the rain of that cold afternoon. I also saw the inside of my old car.

Petricore.

"Were you alone?"

"Yes, fortunately." The heat must have reddened my cheeks.

"I get it," Lauren gives up, "it's not something you want to talk about."

"Sorry. It was a long time ago. Bad time."

"I'm sorry. I'm thankful you survived."

I don't answer and instead turn my attention to the last piece of croissant, which I pick up off the plate.

"What do you want to do today?" I ask her.

"Shopping. I have things to buy. Do you want to come with me?"

"I need to go home and change. Maybe I can see you

later."

Lauren seems disappointed. "Alright."

"I'm not leaving right now. I meant in a while."

"Alright. Let's take a ride to the beach, go to your place."

We walk hand-in-hand on the sand - a warm, deep, breathless sand. The pier is behind us and so is the sun. We catch people's glances, the air, the words of others and the squawking of the seagulls. I watch a crow fight with a pigeon and see dogs sniffing the wind. Lauren greets a group of boys who are bathing.

"Friends from college," she says to me.

When we get to the zig-zag, we put our shoes back on and, still a little sleepy, sit on a bench. I gaze at the sea with discomfort, but it is apparently quiet. I start to get thirsty and I don't want to endure another hallucination. Today things are silent, relaxed and remain in their place, fixed in their unknowable origins.

"Will you call me later?"

I nod and hug Lauren with her head against my chest.

"No party tonight. If Matthau calls, don't answer. You promise?"

"What about your friends?"

"They're not doing anything today. We've been going from one night to the next for a week. And then tomorrow we'll see your friend. I'd rather rest today."

"I agree."

"So, you'll call me later?" she insists.

"I will."

"Maybe your friend is back."

"I don't have any messages from him on my phone. I think he's still somewhere."

"I wouldn't worry about it if I were you. He can take care of himself. What did Matthau tell you?"

"He says Losco's like a star. He only hangs out with people of a certain calibre."

"It's true. He knows most of the local club owners and I think all the major DJs from London to here. We'd often see him at other musicians' nights; he'd be with them. And then he was friends with someone very important."

"Yes. He'd met someone important in London, opened the way for him."

"I hope you'll stay."

"Where?"

"Here in Bournemouth with us."

There is no answer in my thoughts, nor on my lips.

"You don't have to answer me, don't worry. I was just saying that."

Lauren gets up and looks at me. She presses her hands against my face, covering my jaws. She has bright, very clear eyes. They are the eyes of the sea. Mine are dark, a brown colour, not particularly attractive.

Giulia said girls liked me because of my ruffled hair. She told me that when we were both underage. She wanted me to find a girl and, in the end, I did.

"I've never met anyone like you," Lauren confesses to me.

I'm surprised, if before I struggle to find the words,

now I'm *struggling* to breathe. There's so much I've wanted to say to her during our time together. I've wanted to thank her for the comfort she's given me. If she only knew the hell I've been through, maybe I would be able to tell her, tell Lauren that she is saving me.

There's something else.

Lauren shifts my focus, kisses and hugs me.

"So, I'll see you later."

Powerless. I can't read thoughts anymore and I'm relieved.

She waves to me as she walks away with her sad smile and her sea eyes.

I've never met anyone like you.

I told Lisa that during our first summer. She'd come home from vacation with her parents and I was eager to see her. She came back changed, looking more serious and distant. She kept going out with me and we just kissed for a while. One night, however, she told me that we shouldn't see each other anymore; so, I went to her house and pleaded with her that she couldn't leave me right now because *I had never met anyone like you.* I saw her crying, a soft cry, as sad as Lauren's smile a few moments ago.

I took Lisa out to dinner. We drank some white wine and on the way back, in the car, we sang out loud some Lucio Battisti's songs.

Our first time was in my car, in the back. Not very romantic, but nobody cared. I had some beach towels in the boot and we used them to cover the side windows.

Someone could have seen us.

They're confusing, faded memories.

I get up and join Lauren. I force her to turn around, and I kiss her. I don't tell her that she's saving me, or that she almost convinced me to stay. But I'm grateful.

"Why?"

"Because I missed you."

"But I waved at you five seconds ago."

"I'm sure it was five days ago."

She calls me a *romantic fool*. I tell her she had to expect it from an Italian. Then, I watch Lauren leave while the wind gently lifts the edges of her yellow dress that I wish was of another colour.

2

The neighbour's door is wide open.

I stay very quiet, straining to hear noises but there aren't any. Maybe I should call that Mike Kelly or, perhaps, I should mind my own business. I crane my neck to look inside; the walls are light pink and the floor is tiled.

It's weird. There's something familiar in there.

The flats in this building have hardwood floors, but only the bathrooms are tiled.

I approach the doorway holding my breath. Now I hear the background music: light, distant, almost external. It's the notes of a piano, I know them.

C. A minor. F. G. Four quarters.

"Hello?"

I knock. I call out again, but there's no response.

The interior has something special that catches my attention: maybe it's the paintings on the walls or the smell of frying. It's the same feeling as when you seem to recognize someone but you don't really remember who they are.

I go in. My hands are sweating, and I can hear my heart beating. I don't have the guts for these things but the melody that's getting louder has certainly made this man brave.

"Hello?"

Nothing.

C. A minor. F. G.

I try to recall the sequence of the notes. Lisa had taught them to me but, even if as a boy I tried to get a band going, I never showed much interest in what she did with music.

On the left, in the kitchen, there's nobody. Not even in the first bathroom on the right. Halfway down the corridor, I stop. The living room door is ajar, but from the knurled glass of the entrance window, I notice a fluid movement, like someone swinging the head. Someone sitting down. That someone is playing in sequence the notes that Lisa taught me and is humming Lewis Capaldi's song to herself. Slower than the record, it sounds as though she's rehearsing or trying to learn it by ear.

"Excuse me."

Whoever's behind the knurled glass has stopped what she is doing. Her blurred image, as rosy as the walls dividing the corridor, rises from where she was sitting. That movement freezes me.

I can't go any further. What could I possibly say to her now? She is coming towards me, and it is clear that she wants to meet the intruder. But just at the point at which I expect her to appear in the corridor, the reflection disappears as if sucked by the edges of the knurled glass. And finally, I feel a shudder, a sort of light air that smells of washed sheets rising up from below and lightly touching my spine.

Silence returns.

I don't stay a second longer. I turn around and walk away.

The scare has made me hungry again, and thirsty.

Losco has some precooked brown rice, and I decide to use his vegetables as a side dish. I find some white beans in a cupboard. I also decided to spend the afternoon doing shopping, maybe buy some fish to eat with Losco. He'll be back. He couldn't have really left me to myself.

Besides, Lauren would be happy knowing that my 2:00 lunch is entirely vegan. Maybe I'll add some cheese, but I won't tell her about that later.

While the vegetables are cooking in the water, I do a recce of the living room, looking for something, maybe a hidden message from Losco. Nothing. The Buddha is still in place, the plants are in their pots and the silence has the same fullness as the silent explosion of an atomic bomb.

After checking both Losco's room and mine to make sure I am alone, I turn on the kitchen radio. It's the same reporter as yesterday, arguing with someone about Covid-19. There are several unresolved issues and unclear information. Some people believe that not all the deaths were caused by the virus and so it's an inflated death toll.

I try to tune into another station, but it looks like the radio can only pick up one, so I turn it off. I unlock my phone and play a list of selected songs on YouTube. Meanwhile, I think of all the things I'd like to do with Lauren. I'll probably spend the night at her place. It's an exciting idea that puts me in a good mood.

***

I try to call Lauren, but the line's busy. I'll wait. Then I try to call Giulia but there's no signal. I'll call home, I'm sure my mom will answer.

No signal.

I move to another room, try in mine, then Losco's, even the bathrooms. No one answers. I try Lauren again, but the line's busy, so I decide to leave a message.

Hi, how are you?

I send the message. I go back to the living room and lie down on the couch. I have no other way to contact them. I'll wait. I'm sure Lauren will get back to me soon. The meal and my growing tiredness weigh down my eyes. I'm going to close them for a few minutes and then perhaps go out for some air afterwards. I suddenly feel like taking a dip in the sea.

I wake up and, to my surprise, it's late afternoon.

There's only one message on my phone. It's Matthau asking me if I want to go for a beer.

I try to call Lauren, but the line's still busy. If she hasn't seen my message after three hours, she's probably fallen asleep like me.

Matthau's message was an hour ago.

Alright. Come pick me up?"

I text him.

I go to the bathroom, need to wash my face and brush my teeth. Meanwhile, I undress, throwing my clothes in the sink. A warm shower will do me good.

The cell phone vibrates on the protruding base under the mirror. I grab it eagerly hoping it's Lauren, but it's only Matthau replying. He says he'll be at my place at 9:00.

I'll be waiting.

3

Matthau, pleased, shows me an Italian ice-cream shop inside of the Arcade in town centre. We managed to get ice creams even though it was closing. We made the girl assistants laugh trying to teach Italian to Matthau, using this banter to persuade them to give us some refreshment. I didn't really feel like ice cream but I hadn't put anything since lunch.

Leaving the shop, we pass by Mary Shelley's. Matthau says it's a cheap place and it will be good for us to be in the middle of the mess.

"Go sit down, I'll get us two beers."

"But the next round's on me."

Matthau ignores my comment and after memorizing our table number, he lines up.

I sit down and watch, locked in silence. There is a mixed clientele. Families are sitting at the tables in the centre, while couples are reclining on the sofas or in the far corners of the club. The groups of youths are the loudest. They toast by banging their glasses against each other, singing or commenting on the rugby game that is on television.

Some security guards are watching over the entrances. Earlier, Matthau had told me that there were often fights in the place, but that we could be quiet anyway. I'm not afraid of anything now. I keep my attention between the outside and my cell phone; Lauren hasn't answered me yet even though it's past seven.

Matthau comes back with two pitchers of cold, frothy beer with two fingers of foam on top.

"Don't pay attention to these weirdos," he says as he points to a group of guys my age running around in women's clothes.

The colours are the ones I'd like to avoid seeing: yellow and pink. The visions seem to have disappeared but with my heart and mind in turmoil today, I would prefer some normality. I've recovered more memories in the last few days than I had in the previous six months, and that was what I wanted. It has worked, but now I don't know what to do.

"Don't worry, it's not so weird. I mean, men dressing up as women. We can see it in old Japan where people dress up as women to entertain their audience."

"You're like a professor. You know a lot."

"No, it just occurred to me that it's not that weird. Have you ever noticed that in the seventies and eighties many metal bands used to dress really ridiculously? Women's pants leopard print. Makeup?"

"Oh yeah. I saw that movie on Netflix, *the dirt*. Crazy people."

"Would you have thought the same if you were a fan at that time?"

"Probably not. Now our idols are musicians with expensive cars and half-naked women. Muscles and money."

"It's the new concept of power. Some time ago, I read a book on psychology. This professor explained that it has been scientifically proven that money doesn't make you happier, that what gives us total satisfaction is our inner effort, the will we put into making our dreams come true, the things we can share with others, like the experience of a trip or even food. This makes us happier."

"Money would be a palliative."

"We have to buy to keep this system going. Anyway, I wanted to ask you why you called me. Is everything okay with Vivian?"

Matthau swings his head, stares at the inside of the beer as if he could observe the flow of his thoughts.

"Yes. That's not bad."

"Complicated?"

"Complicated," he replies, smiling. "How's it going with Lauren?"

I take a deep breath, I'm not sure if what I'm going to say is true, but I don't feel like talking about myself. Talking, saying something about my life, that's really complicated.

"It's not bad," I say, imitating his mood.

"I overheard you're going to the event tomorrow?"

"Yeah. My friend hasn't shown up yet. Are you

coming?"

"Obviously," he says emphatically, patting me on the arm. "I'm not missing the opportunity to meet a famous DJ. If there's one thing your friend and Lauren teach us, it's be smart and make lots of friends."

"It works, I admit."

"Have you decided whether to stay in Bournemouth a little longer or...?"

I shake my head, I haven't decided anything right now other than to find Losco.

The feeling is that everything is so fragile and illusory. This cheerfulness that floats around me, this sour and spicy flavour that I can taste: they are lovely at the time, but they don't last long.

Yet I give in, I can't resist, everything is seductive, soothing, capable of transporting you far away. The comfort of beer in my body is relaxing, so I don't want to think about anything else.

On Matthau's skin and in his eyes, I see something that I missed, that I didn't catch but that has always been in front of my eyes: rebellion. Deep down we know that our daytime lives suppress something more important within us. They block us, humiliate us, imprison us. Deep down we know that our nightlife is just a way to give a damn, close our eyes for a moment and not think about the next flash. We live in the present. And that's what Matthau is trying to do.

"Do you know anyone who might know where my friend lives?"

"I thought you lived over there on Manor Road."

"No. We're renting."

"You don't know anything about him, do you?"

"I thought I knew but, as you can see, I was wrong. You know more about him than I've ever known."

"It's hard to communicate with someone far away."

"We haven't heard much from each other in the last few years. I'm sorry because in college we were very close. I'm sorry I missed so much of his life."

"I had a friend, too. He lives in France, in Metz. We were much younger, but we grew up like brothers. His family wasn't wealthy and he often came to our house. We played football. We watched films together. And now I don't even know what he's doing."

As he confesses it to me, he gazes at something behind my back, meditating, maybe even dreaming about those two boys playing football along the Moselle or in the shadow of ancient Teutonic passages. I wish I could touch those memories, those shadows that no longer belong to the world, that are dreams, images but no longer alive.

I'm sorry.

"Let's toast to friendship," he says, inviting me to raise my glass and strike his.

"To friendship," I repeat.

We drink the last half. I'm not used to alcohol, it makes my head spin quickly. I promise myself to stay sharp, not to go beyond two beers and just one shot.

"I've only just met you, but I like you already. I really hope you'll stay."

"You'd be disappointed if I stayed."

"Why?"

I'm confused, and I give him a shrug.

"Come on, tell me what you think."

"I'm just saying, I've led a different life. I'm not used to this," and I point to my beer.

"Don't worry, you don't have to do that. I mean, have a juice if you want one or a coke, no one will judge you wrong. You want to know what the secret is?"

"I want to know."

"The company. I prefer vodka, I only drink beer with you."

We laugh.

"Then I'll offer you something different."

"Alright."

He tells me what he wants and I go to the counter. I check my cell phone again, but still there's nothing from Lauren. I guess she's asleep in her white bed that smells like lavender. She sleeps naked on her stomach, her head covered with blonde locks and her pillow on the floor - a beautiful fairy resting. The world is her dream. I wonder if it is love that is saving me or this feeling of hallucination that is sometimes light and sometimes ruthless.

I go to order our drinks. I want some water, but in my perpetual deliberation about what I should order, I forget it.

Matthau drags me to a strip club. I tried to dissuade him, arguing that if someone sees us there, there could be trouble with Vivian and Lauren.

"Vivian's taken a night off and your better half sure is buzzing in her bed. They've done nothing but go from party to party for the last month. Trust me, don't think about it."

I want to but I can't.

The truth?

We pay ten pounds to get in. A tall, sturdy black man greeted us at the door, asked us for our documents and wanted to know if we were drunk. Matthau donned his best smile and said we'd only had a couple of beers.

A couple of beers are acceptable, the guard answered.

We walk through a dark passageway. The lights are red and green with white flashing intermittently as a sort of emergency signal. It's twenty past nine and the club has just a handful of customers.

"We won't be late," Matthau promised me.

I don't want to be here. The air is full of perfume and I breathe something like marijuana. I stay behind Matthau until he finds a place for us.

The music is only moderately loud, so I don't need to shout to communicate.

"The show starts in half an hour."

"What kind?"

"Haven't you ever been to a club like this?"

"No."

"The girls walk down the catwalk, dance and undress. What are we drinking?"

"I don't know. You decide."

"Stay here. If one of them comes near, tell them to

wait." He's pointing me to groups of girls all over the room.

I try to relax on my leather armchair and I avoid staring at the showgirls; I don't want them to approach just as Matthau is at the bar ordering our drinks.

I've been here before, not in Bournemouth but in a place like this.

Mike Kelly.

I still have his card in my jeans pocket and I can't really explain why I'm carrying it around.

I turn my phone on, pretend to be interested in something that isn't there. I've been shutting down social networks for a while, too many memories left behind. I asked Fabrizio to erase everything. No notifications. No messages. No photos. I have Signal left though. I find it in the folder where I hid it. Umberto's last message was more than six months earlier: our last night. Our last night before I forgot everything.

I don't have time to open the app before Matthau returns with our cocktails. He has some sambuca and prosecco with berries.

"How many times have you been here?"

"Not many. It's just to pass the time. I have trouble falling asleep, I'm often still awake at 2:00. So I think, maybe if I take a ride, have a drink with a friend, then I'll come home tired and sleep well."

"Does it work?"

"Depends. Sometimes it works, sometimes it doesn't."

Alcohol doesn't help, but I don't think this is the time for a lecture on wellness.

"I have to get drunk to sleep. The problem is the next day. Vomit. Nausea. And weakness. So, at night I'm back to the same problem: I need to go out and dull my senses."

"Not a healthy thing to do."

"I know."

"What are you doing at university?"

"This may sound strange, but I don't have this kind of life during the school year. I couldn't afford it. Dad gives me all the freedom in the world as long as I finish my degree on time."

"A deal."

"Yeah. I only try to go out once or twice a week. Drink without getting drunk. Little tipsy. It cheers me up."

He laughs and knocks back his shot of white sambuca. I copy him.

"Here they come."

"What should we do?"

"Relax. Let's just chat."

"They'll want something in return. Right?"

"Buy them a drink. Now relax or you'll scare them away. It's only a game."

Alright. It's just a game.

One is a brunette, has wide hips, generous breasts, Eastern European features, and is very nice-looking. I imagine she doesn't really want to stay here, but the wage allows her to study and live decently.

The other is blonde, thin and has fishnet stockings that reach halfway down her thigh. She moves like a ballet dancer, perhaps because she really did dance before this job.

"Hey, guys, what's up?"

I let Matthau do the introductions.

"Italian? Really?"

"Yes."

They show me their funny knowledge of my language, mimicking the classic duck-billed hand gesture.

"Can we keep you company?"

The brunette sits next to me. Matthau takes the blonde.

"What's your name?" I ask the girl.

"Anna."

Her eyes are deep, intensely green, the same green as the woods in summer, early in the morning, a bright, firm and carefree colour. The skin on her face is white, without cracks or marks. The makeup under the eyes is more accentuated, but only a little, just to highlight her natural features. I can see that although she appears on the outside to be pale and fragile, inside she is as strong as a lion. I wonder how a woman can stand all this.

I tell her my name and while I'm doing that, I forget about Matthau with another girl. I hear them tittering, but I don't understand the reason for their laughter.

"I've seen you before," she confesses.

"Where?"

Anna looks at me as if she were looking for signs of honesty on my face, but I really don't remember who she is.

"Sorry, I see a lot of people and I thought I knew you."

I buy her a drink, and then another one. We talk, she stretches her legs to touch mine and does the same with her hands. She keeps looking at my body.

Meanwhile, the shows have started.

What time is it?

I feel dizzy.

We move, go to the sofas in the corner of the room, giving way to those who want to enjoy the show.

"We'll be right there," says Matthau, and I watch him leave with the blonde girl who keeps pulling him by the arm.

"Are you nervous?"

"No," but I swallow.

Her hand is on my leg. Sometimes it crawls up and down like a snake, often resting. After a short while, I cross my fingers with hers and we talk close together. I can smell her breath which smells like prosecco and a sweet whose flavour I don't recognize.

I wonder if my breath is as good as hers, but she doesn't seem to care. Whilst the blonde pulls Matthau's arm, the brunette lures me with those fairy eyes of hers. I'd like to touch her breasts, which are copious and are bulging out of the neckline of her dark dress. She must have seen that I keep looking there, because she smiles and swings her torso, making fun of my weakness.

"Sorry," I say. "It's just that you're very charming."

She turns red, thanks me and touches her hair to quell

the emotion.

"It's hot now."

It was hot even before; we'd just drunk a lot.

She gets so close, I have to put my arm around her neck. I'm sweating and holding back my embarrassment by telling her what I've been studying and about my work. She pretends to be interested.

"Do you have a girlfriend?"

"I'm dating someone, but she's not my girlfriend."

"Do you like me?"

"Yes, of course. Why do you ask?"

She pulls my hand onto her chest and makes me feel her heart.

Her angel skin forcing me to perpetual damnation.

She had the same eyes: emerald green. I told her they were *emerald*, one of my favourite colours. She asked me which one was the first and I told her *blue*. I told her it was the colour of my girlfriend's eyes.

"Do you want to smell my perfume?"

I said yes, but I had no idea what she would do. She offered her generous cleavage and asked me to smell it. I thought it was a *game*, and so I played along. I plunged my nose into her cleavage and inhaled that immortal smell with lust and curiosity. Then I felt her hands on my head pushing my face even deeper. I squeezed her hips with both hands. She wanted me to kiss her, so I kissed her. She wanted me to bite her nipples and I did that too.

I awaken from the dream and look at my five fingers

in the middle of Anna's breast.

I'm terrified.

I need air. I need to get away from her. Away forever.

"I'm sorry," I say to Anna, standing up. "I've drunk too much, I don't know what I'm doing. I... I can't."

"It's alright," replies Anna in a sympathetic voice, the same as my mother's for the last six months.

It's okay.

No, it's not okay.

I walk away.

I don't see Matthau, I look for him in private spaces and even in bathrooms. I decide to go outside as I really need some air. I get to the entrance, where the guard stamps my wrist and tells me something I don't understand.

What I do is throw up a couple of metres further down the street. I vomit against the wall of a side street, next to some rubbish bins.

I threw up, yeah. The feeling that comes up from my stomach, though, has nothing to do with my excess alcohol; it's more to do with shame. I'd like to go back in time but I can't.

I don't know how he did it but Umberto caught up with me, maybe he saw me running out of the club.

Kelly's Strip Club.

It was rated four and a half stars. Umberto and I were among the reviewers. That was our third time. Umberto begged me to come back. He'd fallen in love with a Polish dancer. I told him he'd fallen in love with her long white thighs. Umberto even gave her a puppet and a CD with his favourite songs. She promised him that if we came back, she'd treat us like kings.

Kings puke?

Maybe they do.

We were treated like kings.

What was her name?

Anne. Emerald green-eyed *Anne.* I chose her on the very first night. In life, some souls are polarities that need to unite. The further away they are, the closer they are to each other.

"Last time, promise me?"

Umberto promised.

I had fallen in love too, I made fun of my friend but the truth was that since I met *Anna* I dreamt of her all the time. I even said her name while I was making love to Lisa.

That's all I remember.

But I remember that after the kisses on her chest, we went up to the private rooms. I thought she still wanted to play. I thought it would be over soon.

"Ten minutes," she promised me.

She sat me down, said she liked it when I stared at her. She got excited, and the more excited she got, the more she undressed. I wish she hadn't taken off her bra, but then *Anna* sat between my legs naked, unveiled, making me breathe her frankness.

"Hey mate, you okay?"

Matthau.

"Yeah, I just drank too much. I'm sorry."

"Don't worry. We can leave if you want."

We don't talk in the car. Matthau's chortling to himself, maybe thinking about his blonde friend from the strip club. I look out the window wondering what punishment I have condemned my soul to, what guilt I must seek redemption for. What indeed?

The emerald-eyed Anna. I remember now. She was right.

We'd seen each other before: here, in Bournemouth.

***

Swollen eyes and a dull smile printed on the bathroom mirror. That's me. There's still Lauren's scratch and the toned, smooth skin of my 20s. That tells me it's not over yet.

I rinse my face several times, angry at myself. If only I'd drunk some water, I wouldn't have hallucinated and vomited outside the strip club. I'm on the ropes, I'm a professional boxer in the final seconds of round 15.

From the kitchen, I take two litres of water with me into the living room, where I lie down. I focus on closing myself down from this alcoholic melancholy that presses my eyes and recalls sleep.

Then... there's nothing.

4

Lauren didn't text back.

Losco neither.

I take a shower, smiling at my reflection, and have a breakfast of milk and cereal a bit later.

A grey sky awaits beyond this window overlooking the sea. It must have rained during the night: the streets are wet and the branches of the trees are dripping. The weather forecast says it will rain down during the day with several sunny intervals in the afternoon.

I open the book that I brought from Milan. I read the first lines but I keep getting distracted. I don't want Lauren to disappear from my life too. I check the time on my phone, it's almost 11:00.

I try to call her but the line's still busy.

I get dressed. I've got a hoodie in my suitcase; I think it'll protect me from the rain.

The floor is immersed in its own silence. Fortunately my neighbour's door is closed and I hope it will remain so for today. To be safe, I decide to bring a bottle of water with me. There are still hundreds in the utility room, enough for another week, thankfully – I've learned from my mistakes.

Petricore.

I heard it on the air a few days ago, but I can't quite remember when. It's a word few people know.

I walk down Old Christchurch Road with hands in pockets, hunching up my shoulders against the cold. It's raining but it's a fine rain, a kind I've never really tolerated before, the type of rain that's constant and annoying.

I go into the cafeteria, order two vegan pastries, two cappuccinos and the same juice as last time.

"Takeaway, please."

The guy at the counter understands that I'm Italian, and so while preparing my breakfast he tells me that he's from Sardinia. I tell him it's a wonderful place and that I spent a summer there with my sister, Sebastiano and Lisa.

It was only for a couple of days because our real holiday was actually in Punta Ala. It had been Sebastiano's idea, which we enthusiastically went along with. We had never seen Sardinia, except in photos or documentaries. We reached Piombino by car and from there we continued by ferry for several hours. I got seasick when we entered open waters, but Lisa took care of me. A friend of Sebastiano put us up in his house, and we sailed his yacht to Maddalena, where we saw dolphins and pink jellyfish. It had all been spur of the moment.

We got back to Punta Ala tired; Giulia had burnt her back and I was still nauseous from the ferry. I always had a weak stomach.

"Thanks Matteo, see you soon."

I leave the cafeteria along with my memories, which are nothing but faded images of something I vaguely recollect, images not nearly as sharp as those you find in a new movie. Our film caught fire, and what's left of it, is ghostly and shadowy.

My hands are sweating and so I rub them on my jeans.

I ring the intercom for number 8. Lauren answers right away, her voice soft and distracted.

"I've come to see you."

"I was on my way out. Do you want to come upstairs?"

"Yes."

I go up. As I walk in through the half-open door, I find her looking in the mirror, combing her washed hair. She looks at me from there, from our reflection. It's embarrassing, but the desire to see Lauren, to feel her and even to breathe near her, has been unquenchable.

She seems to understand that.

"I got these for you."

I show her my take-away. She smiles and comes towards me, takes the shopping bag, peeks inside, breathing in the good smell of freshly baked croissants and then places it on the shelf of her wardrobe.

She hugs me and presses her head on my chest,

wrapping the hands tightly behind my back. I kiss her blonde head, resting my nose on it. I would like to breathe her in until we become one.

Before I got to her flat, I'd asked myself how it is possible to love someone whose existence you were unaware of, and to have the feeling that you have always known her. Maybe it is my lack of her. Perhaps, the desire to understand each other. Or maybe it's something spiritual that escapes the laws of science.

I don't know.

"I'm sorry."

"I thought you must have fallen asleep."

"I did. But it's not just that," she replies, sinking her head even deeper into my damp hoodie.

"You're cold. Do you want to take a shower?"

"I want to have breakfast with you. I like having breakfast with you."

She giggles at me, moving like a cell phone when it vibrates in your hand.

"You're silly."

"I've just missed you."

She stares at me with her watchful eyes. I feel she wants to tell me something, but she's having second thoughts.

"Shall we eat?"

"Only if you're hungry."

"I am. I was going out for coffee."

We sit on the floor, our backs against the side of her bed. Lauren tells me not to dirty the floor because the upholstery is hard to clean.

"You know me now," she admits, putting the carrot and apple juice between her legs.

So as not to get dirty we help ourselves with napkins. For a while, we don't talk, just chew and glance, laugh softly and breathe hurriedly.

That's all I need.

"I wanted to write to you."

"Why didn't you do it?"

"You won't understand."

"What am I supposed to understand? If you explain it to me, you'll increase my chances of understanding."

"Don't play the scientist with me."

She elbowed me.

We're on the bed, hugging and, above all, dressed. I caress Lauren as she talks to me and kiss her protruding shoulder bone. I like this bone. I told her that I would like to take it home, that every day I would take a piece of her home, so that the next day I would give it back to her in exchange for another one; but today I would like that one, her protruding bone as fresh as the air of this dreary summer day.

Lauren rejoices, showing her well-aligned white teeth. I see all her youth in the rosy flesh of her gums, the absence of wrinkles when she squints, and the agitated sound of her words. There is no calmness in a young body, one must live in haste, speak in haste, even make love in haste; for even if no one tells us this, even if we do not understand it, we know that this time will pass. So, we want to devour it all. All and now, before *an after* takes it away.

She doesn't say these things but expresses through them what she does. Lauren is my teacher and I love her because she keeps teaching me things that I possibly never knew, or perhaps I'd just forgotten.

I want to live as she does, in a hurry, a hurry that doesn't think about time but takes it into account. It's the rush of when you have to get ready and you want to make yourself beautiful, but you're late and yet it doesn't matter. It's the rush of when you want to go home after a day at university, it's not in time, it's in the thousand things you still want to do. Your day should last 48 hours, so you have to put all your haste into the minutes so that they are worth more.

It's the same rush that makes you forget what day it is, that doesn't allow you to hear the alarm clock: you arrive late to work or to a lecture, and you apologize but you don't care because your rush has already brought you to the next chapter, to who you have to meet, to the words you want to say, to the messages you still have to read and to the *Likes* on Instagram that require your attention.

But hurry consumes us, it often remains unresolved, it's a hole in the centre of your time and you don't know how to fill it. You want to live a day of 48 hours but you're not capable of it. So along comes alcohol, drugs and chemical love, love that you don't have to explain, it's a passing thing, it will last just long enough to occupy your hurry, keep you at the right pace.

I wonder if I'm part of her rush, but I already have the answer.

"I'm really sorry I didn't answer. I was just thinking."

"I understand."

"I don't want to go out anymore. I don't like it when it's so grey outside."

"You don't have to," I say.

I look for her lips and her little tongue holed up in the mouth. She lets me climb on top of her and keep kissing her. Then I undress her. I do it slowly, loving that body as it lifts itself up to slide her clothes behind us; loving her hands looking for my legs, loving her hair interfering in our kisses; loving the spasms, the drops of sweat that will soon come; loving the smell of the room, Lauren's breath that smells like coffee; loving her closed eyes that see the pleasure shake every inch of our limbs; enjoying the rush of our wanting to love each other and give everything immediately but resisting to prolong our time together. But we are unable to command time now, and it is precisely in our haste that we take refuge.

I throw the last layer of her behind me by holding up her leg. She is my Everest, the tip of her feet are the valleys, the eyes the summit from which to look at the world. I bite her calf, making Lauren laugh, then I sink, I fall towards her belly hiding my head between the legs.

***

I don't remember what it was like to have sex before

Lauren.

I drink my water.

"I can't make it tonight."

Her statement freezes me, but I try not to show my embarrassment. I'm sitting on the side of the bed. She's behind me, lying down.

"What happened?"

"London. I have a train in the afternoon."

"What time?"

"5:30. I'm sorry."

"It's okay, I'll go by myself."

"What about Matthau?"

"Yeah, I almost forgot, he's gonna be there too. I'll call him later."

I can feel Lauren moving, then her hands come in and the next second she's resting her head on my shoulder.

"Are you angry?"

"No."

"Disappointed?"

I shake my head. The truth is I don't know how I feel.

"I wish you were going to be there."

"I know. I promised you, but I just can't. I should have told you yesterday. Dad's arrived in London. A surprise. He asked us to spend some time together for a few days. I was supposed to leave yesterday but I put it off."

"Alright, don't worry. What does a few days mean?"

"Maybe I'll be away all weekend. Promise you won't leave right away?"

"Okay, I promise. But you have to promise you won't stay away too long."

She detaches herself from me. I don't know how, but even though I didn't see her face, I felt her mood change.

"If you order me a pizza, I'll tell you the truth."

I drag her back against my body, sitting in the middle of the bed.

"Alright."

"I thought I was done with you. And I thought a few days away from Bournemouth would help clear my mind."

"I get it. But I'm here now, so why waste time?"

"I know what a long-distance relationship means."

"You know? I don't."

"I was with a guy before you. But then with college and his work commitments, we decided to stop seeing each other. It was a story that had been going on for five years. We loved each other."

I think about my neighbour, the way Lauren looked at my building, Matthau's *carpe diem* and more. I'm jealous. I wish I didn't have those jealous thoughts. I wish I didn't know anything about her past life. I wish we could start afresh from here but, afterwards, could I call myself a man? Doesn't the beauty of people lie in their lives and in what has shaped them into what they are? And, is it not exactly what they are that drives us to love them?

"But I'm here," I tell her.

It's not enough for Lauren. She moves her head to the side like people do when they feel misunderstood.

"I'm sorry. Go ahead."

"There's not much to say, but I can assure you it's heartbreaking."

"Where is he now?"

Uncertainty appears in her eyes and Lauren starts to tremble at the response that barely comes out of her lips.

"I don't know," she replies slowly, avoiding looking me in the face.

"Then let's put it this way," I begin, moving her face with one hand to focus on me. "What would be better? Would it be better to end it here and maybe not live out the time we have left? Or would it be better to embrace what we have left and build good memories for us both?"

"I don't know, otherwise I would have called you, don't you think?"

Her words hurt me. That's not the answer I wanted to hear.

"Alright. Then you go and I'll wait for you. Let's say I'll wait for you for a while. When you come back, I want you to promise to see me and to tell me what you've decided."

Lauren nods. "I will."

"Shall we watch a movie?"

"What time is it?" she doesn't ask me, I let her look over my shoulder at the digital alarm clock. "We have time."

"Have you packed your things yet?"

"Not all of them."

"I'll help you."

She hugs me and I understand she doesn't feel like

talking anymore.

I'm not allowed to wait with her on the station platform. We say goodbye with a promise. Then I watch Lauren leave, hoping to see her again soon, feeling a strong sense of emptiness that I would like to turn into tears. I resist because tears have never been able to bring back time or fulfil our dreams.

There wasn't enough time between us to say it was enough. We didn't wear ourselves out enough to say it was enough. We haven't yet had the courage to tell each other things that lovers promise each other all their lives. And the sex wasn't monotonous enough to separate our bodies enough. I know I'll look for her in my thoughts and those memories will allow me to feel Lauren on my fingers.

5

Still petrichor.

I'm under my building, indoors. Above me are tons of concrete, ten floors, people busy or lying down watching television. Our apartment has no weight as it's still made only of silence. I could say it was silence that built it.

I'm waiting for Matthau. He'll be late, twenty minutes, but I couldn't stand Losco's empty room any more with Vishnu staring at me in my darkness. The illuminated Buddha in the living room is the origin of that silence, a source that gave light to another beginning: the forms.

The *petricore* is there because of the water from the sky and the humus of the soil.

I drank a litre of water before coming out and I have another one here with me, waiting to be consumed. No more visions, I'll find Losco at any cost and put an end to this tragedy.

I need to make peace with myself, forget the pain and get my memories back. An exchange. I'll give away my pain in return for forgiveness.

I need to remember what I did to Lisa, I'm sure when I see her face again, everything will be truly enlightened.

I asked Matthau to send me the poster of the evening via chat to be sure that the event is real. Losco will go on after midnight.

I can sense the presence of the sea in the sound of the rain, as if the ocean is pouring on the earth in drops. I wonder what it would be like to dive into the clouds.

Lauren's absolutely right, I am a *romantic fool*.

I can't remember if I was like this before, but it's like I've finally rediscovered myself.

Five days without a headache, physically active, strong and healthy. I found a picture of myself on my phone from when I was 19. It was in a hidden folder because Umberto had sent it to me through Signal. Our last message. I have no memory of the reason and I didn't want to read what we wrote to each other. In that photo, Umberto and I are young graduates taking their first selfie as free men, because it was just how we felt.

Free men.

What does that even mean? I don't know now, and so we certainly didn't know eleven years ago.

We took that picture on our way out of school, his idea. His iconic words in my mind, I never lost them.

"*Now our life begins.*"

I'd like to call Umberto, tell him he's always been right, but sometimes being proper means doing things you regret later.

Losco made up for the lack of Umberto in my life for just one turn of seasons. I was so happy during that first year at university to have found someone to share thoughts, silences and stupid parties with, so much so that I didn't care about the past anymore, about Sara for example. I think Losco looked at that world in an attempt to find himself somewhere, putting himself in someone else's shoes; or perhaps just trying to imagine himself differently, a more social person for example. He would hatch his thoughts and create himself in his own mind, and all the while I was oblivious to his metamorphosis.

Even though we talked a little bit about everything, he kept the most important thoughts to himself.

And then, one day, Losco simply told me that he wanted to change his life, that he wanted to leave. There was no *before*, no *precedent* or *warning*, nothing. There was just a sudden detonation and, even at that moment, I didn't understand the extent of his feelings.

Every now and then I met Umberto, sometimes on the subway, sometimes in a bookshop or in the gardens of the university area. Often we exchanged fleeting greetings, distant glances; other times we would sit on the benches outside the University and talk about how things were going. He would always ask me about Lisa and was always surprised when I told him we were still together.

"You're lucky," he confessed to me one day.

We both had an important exam. Third year. It was one of the last exams before graduation. My father had asked me if I was going to continue studying. I told him that if I got a master's degree, it would increase my chances of finding a well-paid job.

He believed in me and urged me to give everything I had, and so I did.

Both Umberto and I didn't want to end up working in a fast-food restaurant or in the call centres of big companies. We had ambitions and we worked hard to achieve them. Umberto ended his five years with me, but I would have found out later. Much later. After the third year I lost sight of him, but I often thought about him and his healthy obsession with life.

There's Matthau.

Adding to the assault by the rain, the wind has whipped up.

I run to the car in an attempt to protect myself from the bad weather. I'm still wearing the jeans I wore when I arrived, and I have a white shirt under my dark hoodie, which shields me from the rain. Lauren wanted me to lend her my hoodie for her stay in London but, in the end, she left with only the last image of a boy with a promise in his heart.

I throw myself in the car.

"How's it going?" Matthau asks me.

"I'm ready."

I greet Vivian and Katie, who are in the back. I become aware of a change in smell from the petrichor of outside to the chemical scent of clothes.

Matthau asks me if I want some MDMA, but I turn it down with the words: "Not right now. All I want is a beer."

That's not really true, but it seems like a good excuse to avoid pills again.

"Let me know if you want to take a ride," he says with a wink.

We put loud music on, singing the songs of Ed Sheeran and Taylor Swift. As I don't know the words, I just shout out loud, trying to imitate their well-tuned voices. The girls laugh and someone touches my shoulders, maybe it's Katie sitting right behind me. Her touch is delicate and every time she moves her head to laugh or sing the highest notes, I can breathe her essence in the perfume she has carefully chosen before leaving the house.

I imagine Katie making herself beautiful in the bathroom, constantly looking at the mirror, trying on different clothes, putting on her favourite colours.

She's looking for someone, but then we're all looking for someone, aren't we?

Eleven o'clock and we're at the entrance to the club. We queue up under a big black umbrella found in the boot of Matthau's car.

Katie grabs onto me and I'm forced to hug her.

Vivian complains that if we don't go in now the rain will ruin her hair and makeup. I notice Matthau's discomfort in the secret language of his mimicry that he hides from his girlfriend. He's annoyed by her constant complaining.

Katie chatters quietly; she's kind, caring and keeps asking me if I'm comfortable, if I'm protected enough under the umbrella. I tell her everything's fine, but the truth is: half my body is exposed to the rain.

After a while we're inside. We pay the entrance fee and a bit extra so that we can leave our sweatshirts in the cloakroom.

The music is loud, deafening and there's a lot of people coming and going. The girls are dressed in short skirts or shorts. I watch Katie fix her hair. She has on a white tube top that is tight around her breasts. Shorts reveal her legs up to half the thighs. She looks around with nonchalant eyes, like when you fake little interest just to attract even more attention.

I see her deciphering a code I've never noticed before, but which Umberto tried to teach me a long time ago. He used to say that girls sometimes pretend to ignore you, but if they're interested, they'll keep looking out for you using the most trivial excuses. And then, there are the caring ones who want to have control over you. They touch you, dragging you slowly into their web.

Katie is a mixture of the two. In the car and during the queue she was very lovely, helpful, but now, finally showing the hours spent in the bathroom to make herself beautiful, she wants to be admired. That's her reward.

"I'll be right back," says Matthau. "I'll leave the umbrella in the car, or I'll lose it here for sure."

I stay alone with the girls. We move around in the crowd, in the screams stifled by the music at full volume, in their haste, the one I was thinking about with Lauren. I'm overwhelmed by the heat, the rush and the joy of the dance. I've forgotten my bottle of water, so I ask the girls if they want something to drink.

I leave them by some seats, asking them not to move.

I order some water with ice, three beers and a whisky for Matthau.

Before I get back to the girls, I drink my water, taking my time and watching the chaos, the highs and the excitement.

Vivian and Katie are dancing on their heels, with their eyes closed, enjoying the euphoria caused by the bass frequencies, the lights and the carefree feeling of still being immortal.

I pass the whisky to Matthau, and he's happy. "Just what it takes to get off to a great start."

"Vivian was telling me that this was a church. Is it true?"

"Yes. Didn't you see the entrance?"

"I thought it was a purpose-built place."

"Come on, let's take a ride."

"And we just leave them here?"

"Don't worry, we'll get them back. They can take care of themselves."

We pass through the middle of the crowd, having to shout to each other over the other shouts. I feel silly but I'm fine. This music falls on our heads like a tension, an electricity that I can't explain, as if someone is continuously defibrillating my body. It's impossible not to jump, not to sing or not to say something unwise.

"Have you seen Lauren?" he asks me, screaming in my ear.

"She left for London to meet her family."

"Alright, then?"

"Alright. What about you and Vivian?"

"We've made up and now we're here. You know how women are, don't you?"

"No, I don't know," I provoke him.

"They have to complain about everything. I don't understand this. They complain and they want control over your life."

"She basically doesn't want you to hang out with other friends alone. Right?"

"She's very jealous. Listen, do you mind that we brought Katie along?"

"No. Why should I?"

"I don't know. I shouldn't tell you this, but she asked for you."

"What do you mean?"

"I don't know the details, but Vivian told me she was glad you were coming."

I'd like to say something but I get stuck. Matthau

laughs at my uncertainty, so I knock back all my beer to stifle the embarrassment.

"Maybe she's a little too young for me," I defend myself, because I feel as though I have to.

"Maybe or maybe not. She's 20 this year. Remember: the woman decides, not you. If you're okay with her, there are no moral problems."

"I know but..."

"Don't worry, you don't have to do anything. If you don't feel comfortable, don't do anything. Someone's probably already asked her to dance while we're here."

"And you're not worried about Vivian?"

"You don't know her. She has a temper. As long as I'm here, she won't do anything because she knows I'm the type who could easily go with someone else."

"You like to play games, don't you?"

"Let's say we keep our relationship alive. She's a nervous girl, she needs to fight. Sometimes I feel like fighting, but sometimes she's just unbearable."

"I haven't asked you how long you've been seeing each other."

"A couple of weeks."

"Listen, I need the bathroom. Where is it?"

Matthau shows me the way. "I'll get some more drinks. I'll wait for you over there, where the girls are. Okay?"

I struggle to get through the crowd, but eventually I get to the door of the men's room. I go in. There's an occasional coming and going with blokes washing their hands or drying them under the hand-dryer.

I lock myself in a cubicle to relieve myself of some of the water I've drank.

I'm a little confused, or perhaps I'm just indecisive. There's Lauren on the one hand, who said goodbye to me at the station leaving with promises between us that we might not be able to keep. And on the other is Katie, who Matthau was telling me about, with her fake lack of interest. I have no real reason to make that mistake, and I have no reason to betray Lauren even though we officially never said we might be in a relationship.

I leave the cubicle to wash my hands and face. I look for something in my rejuvenated look, and it's Lauren's scratch that convinces me not to pursue Katie.

"I'll wait for you," I whisper to myself in the mirror.

I down half the beer in one shot. I'm thirsty. I need bubbles to lift my spirits.

Soon Losco will appear, up there, where a DJ is already unleashing our frenzy. I'm excited to see him again after five days. What am I gonna tell him? What will he think of my rejuvenation? But most of all, will he be surprised to see me?

I turn my attention to my friends and realize I'm alone with Katie. She's dancing around me. It's like she's circling me. I'm the earth and she's the moon.

"What's up?" I ask her to neutralise the awkwardness.

"Everything's fine. How are you? Are you having a good time?"

Katie studies Fashion Design in London but her

family lives in Poole. She prefers the big city to the more local universities. She's undoubtedly talented but doesn't seem to be interested in showing it. I'm asking if she designed the dress she's wearing.

"Do you like it?"

"A lot."

We start a conversation that I do not understand. She talks about fashion brands and fashion shows, but the most interesting part is when she says she has her own collection of drawings.

"Someday I'll produce them."

I don't think she's taken drugs, but I can see the effect of the alcohol in her every word and gesture. Katie speaks softly, as if she has to measure what she explains, then concludes the sentences by lowering the tone of the voice even more.

Someone pushes us even closer, a group of guys literally surrounding us, looking for the table they reserved. They're so close to Katie that after each beat of drum, our arms touch.

I look for Matthau, once again he's dumped me for a girl. I swallow. My throat dries up. I finish my beer but I need something stronger.

It's almost time for the truth.

I take Katie by the hand without saying anything. She allows me to whisk her away, she's light as a feather. We walk through the fray, making room for both of us. Her cold hand and my warm hand are the Yin and Yang of meteorology. I think stupid things, maybe that's what happens when embarrassment takes over.

"I'm sorry, I needed another drink. What do you want?"

"Would you like a shot?"

I'll order one, white. Salt goes on your hand. The lemon ready in the other one.

"What shall we drink to?"

"I don't know," I say, "you choose."

I keep smiling at her, but my intention is just to stall her and not to feel like a complete idiot.

"To us."

As I knock it back, I cough. Katie laughs, puts her hand on my shoulder and asks me if everything's okay.

"Fine. I'm not used to this."

"You could have told me."

"Don't worry. You want another one?"

She shakes the head, looking disappointed in something.

"Let's dance."

I wrap my hands around her hips, dragging Katie back into the crowd. She has soft hips and a tight waist. I am behind her but at a certain point she turns her head, showing me the oval of her eyes, which are like Egyptian effigies, as ancient as the seas. I smile at her. I force myself to do nothing else.

At the centre of our chaos, as my head starts to turn from too much alcohol, we dance, Katie against me, almost as if detaching herself could become fatal. We're both innocent and victims.

Katie flicks the hair against my face. She has a seductive, pale, mortal nature. If I give in now, everything could disintegrate, but the reason for this awareness is unknown to me.

Then I notice something, I recognize someone. I step on Katie's feet. I apologise, but she doesn't seem to care. There are two things now that have shifted my focus. The first is Ben and the girl with him. The second, and most important, is Losco.

I recognize his slightly curved shoulders and the shape of the head and his helmet of ruffled hair.

It's just as I thought: that girl Matthau and I saw in Ben's room a few nights ago, is the same girl I met at the Strip Club - Anna with the emerald green eyes. I'd like to join her and apologise, but Losco takes priority.

He's up there, talking to the DJ. He's going to perform soon. Other people have joined them and are near the deck, and so I can't get a clear view of Losco's face.

"I'm sorry, Katie, my friend is here. I need to go to him. Do you want to come over?"

She seems disappointed and irritated by me.

"So I'll be back in a few minutes, okay?"

She nods.

We separate. I run to the stairs and she keeps dancing, caught in the crowd closing in on her.

I'm sorry.

I'm glad but also confused.

Since I've been here, I feel something else, something deeper, mystical and open. In my previous life, I would have laughed at someone like Lauren who lives a healthy vegan life but at the same time uses drugs. In my previous life, the one in Milan, I was a nervous, distracted and lazy guy. Apart from trying to start a rock band, I never had many passions. I read my twenty books a year, not as many as Lisa, though, who was a real fan of novels. I tried to study, avoided novels, preferred essays or science papers. I liked to see the same people all the time and never strayed too far outside my boundaries. Sebastiano brought something new into our lives but it didn't last long.

I'm confused because I no longer understand who I am. Am I the one *before* or the one *now*?

I'm at the top of the stairs. I push through the couples and a guy stops me before I get to the deck.

"I'm a friend of the DJ. NB DJ."

"You can't go any further."

I beg him to let me through, telling him Losco's real name. I want him to check, to verify that he knows me.

"Your friend has just left."

I look beyond his bulk in the hope that Losco will recognize me and move this brute out of my way. But he's gone.

"Where did he go? I need to know."

"I don't know."

"Could you ask your friends?"

The guard puffs, then goes to the guys by the desk. They exchange jokes, giggles, gestures, and finally he comes back to me.

"He's not coming."

"But his name is on the poster."

"We know, but he had a problem and had to leave."

"What kind of problem?"

"I don't know, I'm sorry."

"Can't you even tell me where he went?"

He shakes his head, bothered by my daring. I, however, am more annoyed than he is. I'd like to smash his head.

"Please, I need to talk to him."

"Sorry, the guys behind me don't know where he went. He had an emergency. He had to leave."

"Thank you."

I look around and suddenly this place doesn't make any sense to me anymore.

My night is over.

I rush back to the dance floor, bump into someone and apologise. I go out into the open in the rain and, like a sniper, I look for the best vantage point I can find. On the right is the cinema with its shops, on the left is the centre of Bournemouth. People move from one side of the street to the other. Taxis are picking up a few people and policemen are watching over the rest.

I have to choose a street, a direction, and so I head to the left of the centre. Then I change my mind, deciding to go behind the cinema towards the car parks. I don't remember if Losco has his own car, so I run and finally I find myself in the park, wet, disconsolate, with a strong desire to scream.

I call Losco from my mobile, but there's no line. It's a joke, now I think it is all a joke. Lauren is a joke, even flirting with Katie. We're all actors. No, I'm wrong, they're faking it, they're the actors. Losco set up this tragedy to test me, to put me on the ropes, to punish me for hurting someone who didn't deserve it in the past.

I tried to commit suicide because of the shame I felt and I came very close to paying for my sins, but life thought it would take me back to give me a second chance, and for days, I've hated this *second chance*.

Losco, though, has given me a third option. Now I can't go on anywhere, I want the truth, I want out of this absurd movie.

What are you playing at?

What are you getting at?

What do you expect from me?

With my hands on my head, partly to protect myself from the pelting rain and partly out of desperation, I run towards the centre, hoping to find him chatting to someone. Losco is well-known but suddenly nobody knows what he does, where he lives and who he's seeing.

I walked an hour up and down Old Christchurch road, a long road, crossed by drunk, loud, begging people. I'm tired, I've forgotten Katie, left her alone.

I'm running in the rain, getting cold and hungry.

"What are you doing out here in the rain?"

Matthau, Vivian and Katie are outside, under a canopy, sharing a cigarette. They look at me with apprehension, but I'm glad they found Katie.

"I'm sorry. I don't know how to explain this..."

"Have you seen your friend? He was at the desk, but then he left."

"Yes. I asked a security guard to explain, but he couldn't tell me where he went. So I looked everywhere outside for him."

"You're out of breath. Have you been running?" Vivian asks me.

I can see her rush to smoke that cigarette. She reminds me of someone. Now that I'm thinking of it, they all remind me of someone from my past life.

"Yes, I've been running."

I have to get back, find emerald-eyed Anna. I don't know who the others around me are, but I know who she is. And Anna is the closest thing to the end; and the end means Lisa. Lisa is the end, the last door, the key to dissolving this little theatre.

Losco wrote to me that he is close to me, around me, promising me that he would always be by my side. Yet he runs away. What if I'm the one who's running away? What should I run from?

Memories.

"I saw Ben earlier."

"I haven't seen him," replied Matthau, but I can tell from his eyes that he's lying.

Vivian must have noticed it too, crushing the last cigarette butt under her heels as if she wanted to shred her boyfriend's head.

"I'm going back in. I'm cold," I say.

Katie follows me. I tell her I'm terribly sorry, that I really need to talk to my friend.

"I knew you were here for him, but I had no idea you were so desperate."

"I'm sorry, but you're right, I'm desperate and I need to find him."

"How can I help you?"

I'm freezing. I need the electric hand-dryer inside the men's toilet. Raindrops drip from my hair onto my lips and neck before descending into my shirt. Some I'm forced to swallow.

"I don't know."

Katie puts her hand on my forehead, lifting the hair that had stuck there. From her pocket she pulls out a handkerchief and tells me to dry myself a little bit.

"I'm really embarrassed," I admit, and she starts laughing. "I need the bathroom."

Katie nods. I, meanwhile, go into the men's toilet. I dry my hands under the hot air from the electric dryer, then my hair. I sneeze and apologise to the people inside this bathroom. A guy asks me what happened and I explain it to him while I'm swabbing my forehead with Katie's handkerchief.

"Good luck," he says.

When I re-emerge from the bathroom, Katie's gone. I walk zombie-like between people, avoiding the tight fray, and finally I find them. Vivian and Katie are sitting at a private table - they must have asked permission to rest their feet. Vivian took off her shoes because she twisted one of them.

"Are you alright?"

She's fed-up. Vivian answers without looking me in the eye. "I just stumbled. You'd better get to your friend, or he'll leave."

"Matthau?"

Katie is silent, gripped in her uncertainty.

"Yes. That asshole!" she yells.

"What happened?"

"Make him tell you."

Katie pushes me aside and tells me to go, to come back later.

"Alright. Thank you."

I leave feeling her eyes on my back. I turn to meet her gaze, I have an intense sensation, almost a presentiment. Katie has puzzled eyes: they express something that resembles my mood but I can't stay, I can't stop now. And because I know I'll never see her again, I mouth "goodbye" followed by "Thank you for everything."

Katie nods imperceptibly as my mind fills with that final image of her, that look of total abandonment: her arms hanging limply next to the hips, a corner of her mouth turned downwards, and those ancient light brown eyes of hers now downcast. I see the tubular top showing off her navel, the shorts showing off her skinny, smooth legs, and finally the sparkling glitter around the nose almost like the reflections of light on the water. Abandoning her seems to me like I'm abandoning something of myself, and God I really want to know what, but there are no answers.

Out in the open, I meet Matthau.

"I've been looking for you. You met Vivian, didn't you?"

"Yes. She was pretty angry. What happened?"

"Ben's friend works at the strip club, remember?"

"Yes." Emerald green-eyed Anna.

"Well, Vivian heard from her that I went to the strip club yesterday with a friend."

"I'm sorry."

"It doesn't matter. Let's go, shall we? We'll come back for them later."

We are on the street now.

"Sorry you couldn't talk to your friend."

"Do you still have some MDMA?"

"Do you want some?"

I have an idea. Actually, it's not the first time this idea has crossed my mind. There is no more time, and even though I have recovered many memories, a new me emerges that I have never known. If I take that pill, my body will ask for more liquid, and that's when I'll face my demons.

"Alright. But I'll pay you."

"Don't be silly. Just buy me a drink."

"Listen, I'd like to ask you something else."

"I'm listening."

We pass near the pier in Bournemouth and, while I talk to Matthau, I think that when Lauren comes back, I will take her for a ride on the Ferris wheel.

"Do you mind if we stop by my apartment?"

"Are you hoping he's there?"

I nod, knowing I'm lying to both of us. I realise this is something I have to figure out on my own, and I know a way to do it. I don't remember Losco's rules very well, but he recorded them on an old little portable tape recorder, the ones with audio cassettes the size of a stamp.

I just want to hear the rules.

"What do you want to do next?" I ask him.

"There's a private party. I know someone who can get us in."

"In a club?"

"No, it's a party. It's like a birthday."

"Alright."

We pass Landsdown towards Boscombe. The road is clear apart from the fine rain, the type I can't stand, the type that gets you wet before you realise.

Matthau's in a good mood again, driving slowly, just afraid the police might stop us. Apart from the MDMA, and the whiskey I offered him, that's all he took. As for me, I'm drunk. Mentally, I still have reasonably decent control, but physically I'm not so good.

We leave the main road and shortly afterwards we're at a roundabout on Manor Road.

There's something on the horizon. Matthau must have noticed it too. I find it hard to focus on the couple who are crossing the road less than twenty, or maybe thirty, metres from us. The car slows down, so I ask

Matthau why.

"Didn't you see them?"

He parks with the engine running. I crane my neck to get a better look through the windscreen but it's difficult to see clearly, partly because of the rain and partly because of alcohol-induced confusion.

"It looks like..." but I can't say it.

The couple stop to talk on the other side of the street, in the open space in front of my building. Her back is towards me, but his face is pointing in our direction.

It's my new neighbour.

"Maybe we should come back later, don't you think?"

"But... that's not possible. Lauren…"

I wanted to use the word *gone*, but I can't get it out of my throat. It's blocking every other word. The second thing I'd like to say is that maybe we're wrong, but the more I look at them, the more convinced I am that we're not wrong.

"She didn't tell you?"

"What?"

"Didn't she tell you the story about her ex-boyfriend?"

"Yes. A complicated relationship."

Matthau is silent and I finally understand. Her ex, my neighbour - the new one, the one with the pink-walled apartment that reminds me of a place I must have lived in.

"I'm sorry, man."

We watch them move toward the building.

Now alcohol is going to create a protective mantle

against negative emotions.

"Maybe it's not what it looks like."

"Isn't it?"

"I don't know her well, but..."

"That's alright, Matthau, thank you. She's not my girlfriend, we were just having fun together."

Matthau takes something out of his pocket and shows me the pill I asked for. "Shall we go have fun?"

***

We arrive at the party half an hour later.

We are welcomed by a couple of homosexuals. It is their home, a residence overlooking the sea.

The first thing I do is to go out in the open air, walk on the terrace and look at the stars that are so numerous tonight. I am surrounded by a multitude of people; my head turns and I lose my balance, but I have the lucidity to observe this moment and feel good.

I don't know if that girl was Lauren but now it doesn't matter. We only promised to see each other again; it wasn't a promise of love.

I thought it was, though, I really did.

A *romantic fool*.

Even though it's pathetic, I like to see myself this way: a romantic fool.

There's another reason why I have come outside to see the stars: I realize that my real compass, all this time, is the water. Other people don't see what I see, or maybe they see different things. I'm sure that at least this detail is mine, mine alone.

The Big Wave is coming.

The beach is deeper, the sea has receded at least fifty metres, and I laugh.

I go back in. I don't feel like talking to anyone.

Matthau is with the two owners, chatting emphatically, along with a friend of his who suggested we gate-crash here. There is a DJ in charge of the music sitting in a corner, surrounded by a group of single women, most of them much older than me.

I go to get a drink. All I'm gonna do tonight is drink whatever I can lay my hands on. There's even food, fresh food and forgotten food, like the already started slice of cake that I've just stolen from behind a pillar - good, sweet and creamy.

I continue my cocktail tour, oblivious to what I'm drinking or eating, having lost the last shred of lucidity.

Destroyed, I sit down and stare at this crowd smiling with their beautiful clothes and drinks raised without a care in the world. All the alcohol and food has anaesthetised me. I need to go to the bathroom to empty some of the excesses but, if I get up now, I'm sure I'll fall down.

There's someone else sitting at the other end of the table that I'm leaning on to look less pathetic; it's a girl. I'd like to talk to her but I can't see that face clearly. I rub my eyes to bring her into focus but it's like someone's erased her face.

Her lips are red, deep red. Straight hair, straight up behind the shoulders. She smiles at me. I don't know the colour of her eyes or her features.

I smile at her.

I get up and I don't notice tripping over and knocking over a couple of glasses on the table. I just want to talk to her.

Then I see Matthau's face. His voice is in my head, telling me it's time to go, that we have to pick up Vivian and Katie, but *I don't want to leave*; I try to beg him to give me ten more minutes.

"Let's come back later, alright?"

He convinces me. I greet the girl at the table with one hand. She seems sealed in her position, a forgotten bronze statue. Between us, in the space that separates us, the silhouettes of other people come, while Matthau drags me away and I forget everything again.

"You went too far, man."

"I'm sorry."

I ask Matthau why he's laughing.

"I'm as drunk as you are. If the police stop us, it's over."

"I'm sorry."

"You've been saying you're sorry all night. You don't have to be."

I lean against him as we stagger to the car, laughing uncontrollably. We're far from Bournemouth, far from Manor Road and the sea. Yeah, I'd love to see the sea, maybe with Lauren or the girl from the party.

They're the same.

"*Proprio non mi reggo in piedi,*" I say in Italian.

"What?"

"*Dicevo che non mi reggo in piedi.*"

"I don't understand you. Speak English."

I sit in the car and hear the door slam on my side first and then the driver's side. I feel as if I'm going to throw up. Meanwhile, Matthau keeps laughing.

"Why?"

He starts the car.

"Why what?"

"Why are you laughing? Am I funny? Are you making fun of me?"

"No, man, you've already asked me that."

"I can't remember."

"Yes, you've already asked me that."

Outside the window, the world turns, spinning around with my head that is drumming in rhythm to the beats of my heart.

"No, I said I don't remember a thing..."

We're on the street - I can tell by the lines between the two carriageways. And it's raining. It's slow but it's definitely raining. It's no longer that fine rain that I hate; instead it's a calm, almost musical downpour.

Matthau asks me to tell him what I don't remember. He wants to know so that I can help him stay lucid, that maybe he needs to stop, that he doesn't feel like driving to Bournemouth, that it would be better to call a taxi.

Yes, I answer him, *let's call a taxi.*

In the meantime, my mind switches off and my eyes

blink like babies' do when they fall asleep.

"Tell me this story. Tell me what you don't remember."

I tell him slowly, as slow as this damn rain. It's the same rain as that night, the night of the accident. I was waiting for Fabrizio that day and suddenly I remembered what I'd done to Lisa. I'd like to confess. May I confess? I stammer trying to confess at least to Matthau but if I talk I'll throw up. I don't want to throw up. I want to be fine, that's all I want right now.

I want to be fine.

And your forgiveness.

I've studied a lot in my life. So, I knew how to die, intoxicated by the smoke from my car. I evaluated the moment and I knew Fabrizio wouldn't make it in time. We just had to get my stuff out of the apartment, the one with the pink walls. Lisa's parents had already come, they had taken everything, even Lisa's keyboard; and the flowers, yes, all the plants and flowers she'd taken care of.

It was my turn. I had decided to face that apartment alone, Giulia had advised against it but I had gone there and asked Fabrizio not to say anything to anyone. But he offered to help me, he didn't want me to be alone. I told him that I was going first, that I really needed to do some thinking.

The music made me remember everything.

I know that now. Lisa had the same recorder as

Losco. She used to record on these little cassettes her singing practice, so that she could listen to her voice again, to improve her singing of that song she was obsessed with - the Lewis Capaldi song.

We had a garage where I had some equipment and also chemical stuff. I used to dabble in doing little experiments or playing with guncotton. I wanted to die. I locked myself in my car and waited for the fumes to kill me. I would have suffered of course, but it was also the right price to pay for what I had done.

"The police!" exclaims Matthau, bringing me back to reality.

But still, even in the face of this, he kept laughing. I'd like to tell him there's nothing to laugh about, that we're in big trouble, but I can't.

Matthau pulls the car over.

Mike Kelly comes towards us. He comes forward with his little white light, gun in his trousers and serious face.

"I know him," I admit.

"Is he a friend of yours?"

"No. We gotta get out of here or we're going to jail," I declare, remembering I read his thoughts.

"We haven't killed anyone, he can't throw us in jail," he replies, finding my remark amusing.

Then he does something I really didn't expect.

"To hell with it." He switches gear and gets back on the road.

The last thing I see of Mike Kelly is his incredulous

and annoyed expression as he tries to get back to his car to chase us.

"Now we've done it big time. We're in trouble," admits Matthau.

"I didn't think you'd do it."

"Neither did I."

We hear the siren. The car's behind us. Out of fear, Matthau accelerates without looking ahead.

I close my eyes hoping that this is really just a dream. When I wake up, I'll be somewhere else and will be able to tell someone about this strange story.

Matthau shouts, says something in French that I don't understand. The car is spinning too fast, it's like it's slipping and then nothing, it's the same feeling as when the walls of houses shake during a strong earthquake. You no longer know in what space-time you exist.

Finally comes the bang. It's so raw and sudden that you pass out.

Atonement

1

And you, can you hear the music?

I hear it. It's weak, like it's playing far away, covered by the sound of rain. Besides, it's all fucking wet.

What happened?

I'm not drunk now, but my head and arm hurt. My left arm. There's a flashing light, red and white, or maybe it's green not white. Or perhaps it's white and green. I mean, there's this light, and the flashing light is accompanied by a siren whistling and flooding the music I was hearing.

The voices.

Matthau's gone off the road. I hope that boy's alright. Mike Kelly will take care of him.

Now, let's see what happened to me.

I close my eyes, I take a deep breath in and then I exhale again and again, until the sound of the sirens disappears and I no longer hear Mike Kelly's voice.

I open my eyes again.

I'm where I'm supposed to be: sitting in my car. The windshield is broken and the door on the other side is open. Through this opening, I see the country road and rain.

There's something else, someone lying on the ground in an uncomfortable position.

I breathe in.

It hurts to move but I have no choice. The view gets blurred and I almost lose consciousness.

I exhale. And when I exhale, I wake up. How long has it been?

I don't know.

The blood runs down my forehead and behind my neck, it's cold and fluid. I breathe out quickly, terrified. I force myself to move, to get out of this smoking junk.

There's a sleeping girl on the country road.

I must tell her to wake up or she'll catch a bad cold in all that rain.

What am I saying?

I know what happened.

It's terrible.

I open my eyes again wide. I'm in Bournemouth and Matthau's car is behind me. I crawl on the wet tarmac towards the figure walking in my direction. It's a girl. I thought it was Mike Kelly but this vision has a pretty, thin silhouette and she is wearing a yellow dress that comes just above her knees.

Lauren.

No.

Lisa?

"Lisa?"

With my blurred vision I can't see well, but I recognise her movements. She is close by. In a few steps I will have her feet in front of my nose but she stops and kneels down, reaching out one hand to me.

"Closer," I tell her. "I want to see your face."

With difficulty I stand up and so does she.

We're on Manor Road and that's my building. There are no more cars behind me, no more sirens, no more Mike Kelly.

Maybe I'm dead and this is the time for redemption.

I'll take it.

The girl invites me to follow her and, hobbling, I go after her. I don't have the agility to keep up with her: my head aches, my limbs hurt.

When I get to the elevators, she's already taken the one on the right. I get in the other one and press the button for my floor. I look at myself in the mirror. My clothes are wet, soiled and my face is as it was when I was in my thirties. That sort of magic that the mushrooms gave me has dissolved.

The elevator opens directly into my neighbour's apartment: the flat with the pink walls. But this is exactly the house I shared with Lisa. I could already hear the music as I reached my floor - its slow, sweet, deep notes. She had taught me how to play it but I kept refusing to learn, and out of spite I changed the chords, showing her a round I had invented.

C. A minor. F. G. I told her these notes sounded better than Lewis' but it wasn't true, I knew it. She got mad because I didn't take her seriously. That was true too.

I saw in Lisa what I hadn't been able to realise myself. Maybe the failures of my youth didn't allow me to be happy for her, for what she could do with music. Giulia had once overheard Lisa singing in the shower from outside our room. We had been staying in a small village in the mountains, where Sebastiano had taken us skiing. My sister had asked me, with a fair degree of annoyance, why I had never told her that my girlfriend could sing so well.

Lisa was in tune, and when she sang, she would keep the tempo by clapping one hand on her leg. She even learned to do certain Michael Jackson moves, or at least the simplest ones. In the car, when we were travelling alone, she would sing Michael's songs, imitating his tone.

I can't remember what I was thinking at the time.

Here are our pink walls. Kitchen on the left, bathroom on the right. I walk down the corridor enraptured by the beauty of those carefully played notes, almost like whispers, and through the knurled glass of the living room I see the same silhouette as last time. She hums, she tries to learn the words in English, often by making mistakes.

I arrive at the door with my heart beating in my temples. Finally, I see the apparition of the girl. She has her back to me, the hair gathered in a ponytail, hands pressed on the keys of an old second-hand keyboard. The paper on the lectern shows the real notes of the song. I see a Db written in block letters.

There's someone else in the room. It's a guy sitting on the couch with a Bluetooth headset on his head, watching a TV show; he's got a serious expression, his mouth shut in the shape of a zero and he doesn't seem interested in the melody his girlfriend is playing.

They don't notice me and yet I'm just over the threshold of the living room.

The guy puts his headphones down and says he's hungry, needs a snack. I know that's not true. He's got a message and he can't read it there. I used to do it every time Umberto wrote to me on Signal. I used to run scared that Lisa would find out about us.

She found out about us in the end.

I observe myself passing by. I don't look to see where he's headed because I know those habits by heart. Instead, I walk up to the girl to study her. I look over her shoulder, which has escaped the confines of the fine-wool sweater she is wearing. It's winter but the apartment is well heated. She's wearing a skirt and skin-coloured stockings, showing off her thighs with refined sensuality, thin and apparently made of an invisible velvet.

Her legs used to drive me crazy. Lisa and I made love everywhere. For us there was no ugly or beautiful place; it was we who made those places special. It used to happen in the car. Sometimes I'd rent a motel room. We did it on the stairs of my building, at night when everyone was asleep. I had a garage big enough to accommodate the two of us as well as my dad's car and his old bike. We even stayed there for a while.

I couldn't say how long it lasted, but I guess not long. After Losco's departure, my life literally fell apart. University kept my spirits up; the idea of pleasing my family and standing up to Umberto stimulated me to commit myself to my studies.

We've had ups and downs, Lisa, and yet you've always been there for me.

I reach out to touch her shoulder.

She sings. She sings of a love that was never a promise, only a chance. After all, she sang our song, what we became.

"I never said that we would die together..."

No, none of us ever said that.

I'm going to move my hand away, because if I disturb you now, I won't hear you sing your song. I'm listening, my love. I'm listening to you like never before. And I'm sorry, because you were so happy to finally have the chance to take part in your school's musical recital, but I wasn't able to protect you until then, and now there's nothing that I can do to put things right.

We're done. The fallen angels have been damned and God has punished them all, not one saved. And even though this angel had not been among the fallen, I managed to bring her down with me. For that God has punished me through this eternal suffering that grips my heart, and now I feel and understand it all while she sings about us.

*"I wish you all the love you're looking for...
darling..."*

I let that last word vibrate in the vacuum while she takes her hands off the piano.

Please, my love, grant me one last turn, don't stop singing, before God condemns me forever. Let me hear you for the last time.

But Lisa gets up and looks out of the window. Everything's different now. We're in Bournemouth in my apartment, and outside there's the sea. When I say the sea, I mean a sea that is advancing with all its might.

The Mother Wave.

The tsunami has powered over the cliff, twice as high as the buildings opposite and is coming straight at us – no, not us - the Mother Wave is only coming for me.

Lisa's gone.

The old tape recorder is on the hall table. It's identical to the one Lisa had. I take it. I press play. The cassette wheels are spinning, but there's no sound.

I can't scream even though my fear is total. The wave is banging against the window and it's overwhelming everything.

I breathe in. Then I close my eyes, waiting for the icy touch of death.

2

Umberto is talking to the friend who invited us to Luigi's party. I count at least twenty steps between them and me.

The tavern is spacious. There is a fireplace in the corner, the kitchen to the side, some folded spare chairs and at least twenty people. I think there's music in the background but I don't hear it. I don't even hear the boys' banter, nor Umberto and his friend.

Everything seems to be moving without sound.

I'm thirsty, I want to drink to death. But I'll control myself, I've already drunk enough, being sick again is no longer an acceptable option.

Someone knocks my arm, but I don't feel the contact, only the displacement, like an involuntary reflex of the muscle.

I say something to the guy who bumped into me but apart from moving my lips, not a word comes out. I'm deaf and dumb, fortunately I can see. And I see her, the girl sitting at the table, alone, clutched in her gentle female form, staring at her glass half full (or half empty) with sparkling water. I'd like some too, but I'm tempted to drink the wine that someone hasn't finished.

I walk towards her and she notices me. She smiles at me with her red mouth. I don't know whether she'd overdone her lipstick or whether I had a distorted recollection of her lips.

"Hi." I finally hear the sound of my own voice.

"Hello," she answers me by squeezing the glass with both hands.

"I'm sorry, I just wanted to... let's say disturb you a little bit. Aren't you having fun?"

She swings her head in response.

I tell her my name and I sit on the other side of the table.

"Lisa," she muttered, keeping her eyes down.

She reminds me of someone else, a girl I met a few days ago. I can hardly remember her name. I can see Lisa's face now, but I can't remember the name of...

"What are you drinking, Scotch?"

I make her laugh but, deep down, it's always been sufficing with her. I already know many things about her, things that I would have discovered with time. For example, that she was still reading Mickey Mouse, and that those stories put her in a good mood. Then she abandoned him, started following the Youtubers, and persuaded me to do the same, which I did to a certain extent. I also remember her laughing at ridiculous things, humorous cartoons that I found meaningless. Lisa laughed at the way I used to run. She said I looked as though I was limping. She laughed when I was ironing a shirt or trying to figure out how to turn on our first washing machine.

She thought I was funny.

Not a romantic fool, but a *funny one.*

"It's just water. And you, don't you drink anything?"

"No. If I drink this all goes away."

"What?"

"I know, it's weird. I mean, if I start drinking, then I'll end up throwing up tonight and I don't think that's a good idea."

"Are you flirting with me or something?" she asks me, pretending to be offended.

I smile at her. I've seen that clever expression on her face at least a million times. I used to tell Lisa that when she did that, I wanted to bite her. I'd nibble her shoulder and she'd pinch my hips to make me stop. We'd start out like that and then we'd end up making love.

Maybe we gave so much of ourselves for the first three or four years that people thought we were one, a symbiosis, that we weren't realizing we were consuming each other, and losing a little bit of ourselves. Mum was happy, hoping that after graduation I'd decide to marry Lisa. But after graduation, there was work, and for a little while longer we just thought about having fun.

I made a decision. The truth is, I made another choice. She deserved it. I loved her and I really wanted her, but I only knew one aspect of the meaning of love - and if I've been able to know it, it was because of you.

I didn't love Sara, it was just a matter of sex and pride. I hated the fact that she dumped me for someone else. Maybe that was something I never got over.

"No. I mean, I'd love to, but... Can I ask you a question?"

"Yes, come on. Shoot."

"If you could choose... if you loved someone but knew you couldn't make him happy, what would you do?"

"Does this someone else love me?"

"Yes. He loves you too. Very much, I'd say."

"If we love each other, how can we not be happy together?"

"I don't know, let's say you saw the future, and you saw that you weren't happy, then you go back to the past and make a choice, what would you do?"

She lifts her eyes to the ceiling, meditating - another of her usual gestures. She often did it when we discussed work or studies, during our sleepless nights when we talked about the future and on countless other occasions. Lisa used to raise those virgin eyes of hers to the ceiling in search of an answer, a reflection or a mystery that I never knew.

"It, actually, is a difficult question. Let's say I would go back and try to change things, because I could never give up on someone I love and who loves me."

"Whatever it takes?"

"Whatever it takes."

I nod, lowering my head; I can no longer face her blue eyes, her familiar gestures and, above all, that innocence. I'm sorry, I ruined everything. I was a bad partner, I'm so sorry for so many things that I can't talk to her about anymore.

"What about you? What would you do?"

I bite my lower lip, squeeze my eyes so hard that when I open them again for a few seconds my vision is blurred.

"Are you alright? You need to..."

"No, no, I'm fine, thank you. I was just thinking."

"Have you by any chance seen the future?"

I shake my head and puff, considering what she can't imagine.

"Why are you here alone? Don't you like the party?"

That night, many years earlier, I never asked her why she stood there alone watching others make friends. Nor did I ever ask her afterwards. The only thing I really cared about was having her as my better half.

"I'm tired. I want to go home."

"How come? What have you been doing?"

The water inside Lisa's glass vibrates without her moving it. With one hand I touch the table to make sure it didn't wobble under the thrust of our legs.

Lisa looks at me confused and I tell her that a couple of beers must have made me a little tipsy.

There's not much time. These things defy the laws of physics.

"I mean, what do you want to do? If you had a choice, what would you do?"

She's doing that eye gesture again, but I'm distracted by the water shaking in the glass.

"You mean now?"

"Yes."

"Go to sleep."

"And do you have a dream?"

"What's with all the questions?"

"I don't have a dream. Umberto, my friend, wants to become a pharmacist. I still don't know what I want to be. I'm curious."

"Maybe a singer," she admits, without hesitation.

She'd never told me that in all the years we were together.

"I have to go now. It was nice to see you again."

"See me again?"

I smile at her as I look right into her blue eyes, aware that as soon as I turn my back on Lisa, she will disappear along with all this silence made of shapes. She opens her eyes wide as if caught off guard, but it is too late, I have decided that she deserves another chance.

I wish that eleven years ago I'd made just this choice, to leave and forget her, suffocating my desire to find someone to replace Sara at all costs.

I'm doing this for you, Lisa, because I love you, because you deserved to have a different future. Ten years later I'll kill you. You'll lose your life in a senseless accident while we fight because I cheated on you with *Anna-with-emerald-green-eyes* and you found out. My betrayal will kill you. It wasn't my neglect to drive, no, it was because I betrayed you: I betrayed your trust and out of anger for myself I've lost control of the situation.

"One day we'll meet again," I tell her, turning around.

I notice that in my pocket I still have the recorder on, I can see the tape that keeps rolling. I'm no longer in my distant memory but in dense limbo, deep blue. Indigo. And Lisa has vanished, sucked into her time.

Then a voice that I recognize: Losco.

"On the count of three, you will awaken. Are you ready?"

"Yes," I say.

"One."

It's daytime. I'm sitting on a bench by the sea in Bournemouth. I'm still holding the tape recorder and I notice that the tape is spinning slower; time is holding it back.

As soon as I lift my eyes, the wind carries a smell I have inhaled before, which I know very well.

"Excuse me."

A girl walks towards me, coming from Bournemouth Pier. I know who she is, but she doesn't know who I am.

"Hi," I reply, inviting her to talk with me.

"You're not from around here, are you?"

"Is it that obvious?"

"Bournemouth in the summer is full of tourists. You recognize them easily."

"I'm Italian. You caught me."

She dresses like the first night we met. She's beautiful, radiant. I am a fool, I had the truth right before my eyes throughout my five days in Bournemouth, and yet I never noticed their resemblance. But this was more than a likeness.

"Do you mind if I ask you to take a picture of me?"
She gives me her phone.

"Alright."

She wants to take her whole body and see the sea clearly behind her figure. I look at her through the lens of the little camera, a miniature Lauren, and think of all the incredible moments with her. With each flash I see something of us, our intimacy, the chatter, our impractical promise and, above all, hope.

Maybe this person I'm looking at is Lisa's other life, or perhaps there are things so subtle that you can't explain.

I give her back the camera. She looks at the pictures and tells me *they're perfect.*

"Thank you very much. I felt silly taking a selfie."

"I hope they're really what you wanted them to be."

"Yes, perfect. How do you say *perfect* in Italian?"

"*Perfetto.*"

"*Pefetto,*" she says, trying to mimic my pronunciation. "Sounds very similar, doesn't it?"

"Yes. Very much."

"They're having a party here tonight, do you know that?"

"Yes."

"Ah, great. Then I'll see you later. I'll be here too."

"Yeah, I'll see you later."

"What did you say your name was?"

I tell her my name. She repeats it and asks me if she pronounced it correctly.

Yep, she was very good.

"*Pefetto,*" she comments, smiling with her white mouth I'd like to kiss but I have to leave forever.

"I'm Lauren."

"Nice to meet you, Lauren."

We shake hands in the heat of summer, with the wind messing up my hair and moving hers backwards. Seagulls fly far away, making circles in the air, people walk and chat and this is really our last breath together.

Lauren goes off to meet the sun rising above the pier in the distance. She returns to the light; where will I go through?

I sit on the bench and pick up the tape recorder. I wait.

"Two."

That's me before Lisa. Even before Umberto. Sitting on the grass of a football field, I look around with my eyes half-closed.

When I was a teenager, I used to come to the soccer field and do nothing but be silent. The ball is near my right flank. In this memory there is also my first guitar, the one I could never play. My first and last. It's a special day because my friends wanted me to leave the band, at least until I learned to play an instrument well. I never learned to play any instrument. In fact, the guitar lying on the grass is broken. It has a hole in the side made when I threw it to the ground and then kicked it violently.

My father had never wanted to buy it. He said it

would distract me from my studies, but my mother had managed to convince him.

I don't look sad or worried; I'm the sort of person who sees the future as an opportunity to change, to think differently, just like Losco when he was hiding his real thoughts from me.

I turn my back on that young me as I hear Losco's voice on the tape recorder saying: "Three. Welcome back, my friend."

I exhale. I'm in the belly of the ocean again. Light hits the surface of the water, crosses it and descends into this abyssal cavity where I am lost. The sun is a flickering ball above me. My feet are suspended in the void by floating in an unreal dimension; and even though this ocean surrounds me, I do not feel wet.

Not far from me, facing my own horizon, Lisa is sitting on her piano playing a melody. She has the headphones on that she used to listen to the songs and then try to perform them on the keyboard. Lisa swings her head, whispering Forever by Lewis Capaldi. She has the dreamy air of someone who is daydreaming.

I try to go to her but I can't. A sort of current drags me away, but with wide-eyes so as not to lose another instance of her. I waited to see her face again for months and finally I did it. Her figure becomes smaller, fades slowly, slowly into the belly of this ocean that for a moment raised you from death. And I feel that through that song you speak to me, and I'm sure that if I still want to listen to you, in the future, I will play that tune by keeping our secret.

The Secret

1

I open my eyes, panting. I must look horrible. I can tell from Losco's sad face. He's in front of me, still sitting in the living room. Beyond his shoulders is the big window where I see Bournemouth's sky in red and orange.

I don't know what time it is. I don't know if it's another dream or (sub) reality.

"Forever."

An echo. It's so faint that I don't dare speak and I thank Losco mentally not to interrupt what I feel with bitterness.

It was different before; I couldn't remember before. There were photos of us that Giulia had taken away from me. I saw images: her hands on the piano, her back, the way she had of putting up the hair at the back.

I'm convinced it's not a dream.

I get up and with one hand I point to Losco to stay still, I just want to check something.

In the bathroom, I look for Lauren's scratch on my face, but that's gone. There's nothing in this look that I remember from before. I come staggering out of the bathroom and I go through the living room door. My legs give way with exhaustion. I feel destroyed and breathless again. I lean against the doorstop and cry, trying to stifle the sobs. I'm ashamed.

Out of the corner of my eye I see Losco move. I signal to him not to come, to stay away from what is just a moment of awareness; so often awareness hurts at first. Now I know. I would like to ask him again for those mushrooms, to have another go but I hold back that request, quelling it with my tears.

"Go away," I yell.

I'm confused. I feel nauseous and feverish. My heart's beating erratically, but it's okay, I've been taking drugs, so I shouldn't expect to feel better.

One last round of tears, one last breath before I return to Losco. He is still in the Lotus position he was in the last time I saw him. Days ago, maybe weeks. I really don't know anything anymore.

I wish I hated him for what he has done to me. I wish I had never come. I wish I hadn't known this pain, but it is another emotion that I drive away as I try to get up to receive the final answers.

I look at Losco. His sad face will give me those answers. I have the tremendous certainty that he has never moved from there, I can tell by the way he feels uncomfortable and I can't say how I know; maybe it's because he keeps massaging his left foot or because of the way he's moving his neck – like you do to loosen it after a day of staring at the computer.

This is reality. The living room is all intact, the window is in its place, Losco is here with me and there are some empty water bottles in the corner.

Wiping away the tears running down my face, I sit down in front of him.

"What day is it?"

"September 22nd."

"It's not possible," I say, sceptically.

"We've never moved from this room."

I shake my head, I trust him but it's hard, hard to accept. Too much has happened.

"And you've been there all this time? And me too?"

"Yes. We never moved. I mean, we never left the apartment, if that's what you're asking. I saw you dancing. I heard you crying in the bathroom. We put on music and drank most of the water."

"I don't know what to say..." I put my head down.

The memories are still there. She's still there. I feel like I need to cry and I do. It's a terrible pain. I had to forget. I had to try and attempt suicide. Even now that I know everything, it feels impossible to carry on existing.

"I'm sorry for what happened to you."

Losco hugs me. He's never done that before; I don't resist; instead, I let his hands pull me to his chest while I keep crying.

"Shall we play a game?" he asks me.

Bizarre question, but I move my head to gesture that

it's okay with me.

"You tell me your story and I'll tell you mine. Are you up for it?"

No, I don't feel like it.

"Then I'll start. Do you agree?"

"I agree," I say, pulling away from his comforting chest.

We both sit at the table. We look out the large window. The sky is clearing, and the sea is blue with darker patches scattered offshore. A true blissfulness.

Our mobile phones are on the table next to the old tape recorder.

"I think I'm gonna throw up."

"Go to the bathroom and take your time."

I throw up in the bath as I was about to take a shower. The stomach cramps started while I was undressing, so I lean over the first basin I came to. The stench brings on another gag that I can't contain. Just liquids.

I pull myself up, my hands are shaking and now I notice some back pain. We've been standing in an uncomfortable position for almost six hours.

I meet my gaze in the mirror. My hair is ruffled and greasy, as if it is sweating just like skin. There's a white tuft of hair that I hadn't noticed before. I wonder if it had been brought on by the psychophysical shock of what I have just been through. I flick it with my fingers as if smoothing it might turn it back to black. That tuft saddens me as it seems to be a sign of destiny, one of those inexorable signs, something that reminds you that time is not your friend but rather a companion that forces you to surrender.

I rinse my face. I don't know what's causing the dizziness, but the shaking of my hands is disturbing me. I can tell from the dark circles under my eyes that my body must have made an incredible effort to endure that drug.

Now I'm aware of what I feel.

I know, for example, that the irregular beats of my heart are due to a feeling of pressing anxiety. I know that the nausea must be due to tiredness, or that my body is trying to expel what I ingested.

Then I need to urinate, which I do in the sink. It's only water and little else. When I've finished, I kneel down with my hands to my face. Suddenly, everything I've been through overwhelms me. It's not something the human mind can stand for long.

I open my eyes, again.

"Where am I?"

"On the couch. I found you passed out in the bathroom. How are you feeling?"

"I feel weird."

"You've slept for four hours."

"I can't figure out which is the dream and which is the reality."

"The mushroom effect is over," he replies with a

smile.

Losco is comforting even if I have the feeling that the body is in continuous free fall.

"Today you will rest. Then we'll talk."

"I'm hungry."

"I know. I'm making soup."

"But I don't want to eat."

"You have to put something in your stomach or you'll get worse."

I nod. Losco goes away and soon comes back with two bowls of steaming soup.

"I didn't make it too liquid; you've had enough already."

We sit at the table. It's broad daylight. The light bothers me, so after the soup I sit quietly on the couch. I close my eyes because the reality is still excruciating as my mind continues to relay to me the memories I had forgotten.

***

It's late at night and Losco is asleep, snoring.

I try not to make noise, I need to urinate.

When I'm done, I go back to the living room. I sit at the table, watching the night paint the trees, the sea and the buildings along the coast in black, a dark velvet cloak that rests on everything.

I don't understand how I feel. There's a deep sense of unease that has no name, a desperate anxiety that squeezes my chest. This indefinable frenzy begins to stir panic in me. I go back to the sofa; if I fall asleep I won't have to remember. If I sleep for a while, I'll be fine. But I'm not sleepy. I'm wide awake and so my memories remain with me.

2

It's mid-morning.

Losco, who has prepared tea for both of us, asks if I want some biscuits, but even though hunger rages, the idea of swallowing food makes me feel sick.

"Shall we go for a walk? Do you want to?"

I tell him I want to. "Not much, though, I feel bad."

I walk slowly but after about ten minutes, I'm out of breath. We don't talk, we just breathe. That's what Losco told me before we came down: "*Breathe.*"

I knew from the beginning that it wasn't going to be easy, but there was really nothing to make me think it was going to be that difficult.

It's like I've aged a year in one day.

"I need to stop," I say, before we reach Bournemouth Pier.

At that hour only elderly people walk along the seafront.

We sit on a bench and for a few minutes we focus

our attention on the sea and its chaotic, penetrating noise.

"Breathe. Try to stay here, don't go far," he suggests, surprising me.

Without realizing it, I was shaking my leg. It's anxiety or a sense of stress over not knowing what to do or what to say. I have a lot of questions, but I don't dare to bring them up.

"I was 16 when I lost Damian. Did you know that?"

"I knew you were young," I said, without looking at him.

I'm distracted, partly from lack of concentration and partly from physical weakness.

"Thanks, Francis."

"What?" Now he has my full attention.

"I understand more because of you."

"What are you trying to tell me?"

"The curator told me I wouldn't be fully recovered if I didn't give someone else a chance to resolve their inner conflict."

"I'm glad."

"How are you feeling?"

"Injured. Tired. And... lost. In fact, I'd say lost. It's like I'm here, but I'm somewhere else too."

And again I hear him say: "I'm sorry about what happened to you."

I smile. A worn-out smile, of course, but the fact that Losco keeps saying he's *sorry* makes me feel better.

"Apart from what happened to me, I'm the one who's sorry for you, because I never knew, because now I realise I've been a horrible friend."

"No, not at all, Francis. You don't have to say that. I put up those walls. The times you asked me to tell you, I turned you down. Nobody's to blame for that; that's just life."

"What now?"

"What do you want to know?"

"What should we do now?"

"Enjoy our life. Whatever it takes."

I fill my lungs with air and I tell myself that everything will be alright, that guilt won't hurt me anymore. It's a hope, I know, but this blind sea, this deaf air and the mute light of day cheer me up. No matter what happens to me afterwards, everything is perfect now. Losco by my side is a relief.

"Tell me your story."

Losco nods and looks intensely at me. Then he shifts his gaze to the beach and we both watch a dog run across the sand scaring seagulls.

"As I told you, I was 16 when I lost Damian. Not a good age for someone to die. No, not really. At 16, you think nothing can stop you, you're a superhero, a rocket at full power. You do all the shit you do at that age. You smoke. You sneak out at night. Sometimes you smoke a joint or maybe snort cocaine when you can afford it - just a little bit, but enough to make you feel cool."

"Was it the drugs then?"

"No, not directly, I mean. You may be surprised, but it was an accident."

"But you didn't have any license yet. How did you...?"

"We used to hang out with people older than us. Friends or cousins. I have cousins, as you know, and they're four, even ten years older than us."

"Yes, you told me about it."

"It wasn't often that we did these car rides. Mum would get angry if someone who wasn't married drove me home or gave me a ride to school, but it happened and when it did, it always put her in a bad mood. My dad didn't say anything; he was interested in the workshop, in bringing home the money to support us. One day in front of my mother he said that every time I get in the car with those kids, I put my life in their hands. I didn't care because, as I told you, at that age you're interested in living life to the fullest, even if you don't know what it means, even if you think you've never done enough. In short, you don't give a damn about advice. Mum would find cigarette butts and yell at me, saying that I was gonna be a junkie, but I'm not. Even though I've smoked a few times, and I was in down during London for a couple of years, I don't feel like a junkie. I've finished with all of that. Sometimes circumstances don't help, but the important thing is to recognise that it's temporary."

"Were you with him when it happened?"

"Yes. Just like it happened to you. Really strange life, isn't it?"

"It certainly is!"

"It ended badly. I mean, you think you can live forever but our biological structure is not made for extremes. We're fragile. I understood it that day. I learned that at someone else's cost, but for years I didn't accept it."

Losco's tale is painful: painful for the heart and painful for the mind. I feel lacerated, as if wounds were continuously being opened on my skin with invisible blades tearing at this tormented body. Wounds that open, bleed and then close as fast as the blink of an eye.

I wish I didn't know anything.

I want to close his fiery mouth and throw myself into the icy sea. That would be a relief. But at the same time, there is something in Losco's words that caresses the senses. Even if it's only for a moment, his words stop me from feeling lonely as I realise that I have found in Losco someone who can really understand me.

"The summer before, we had spent ten days together in Rimini. Our parents had agreed. We left with my family and... you can't imagine how much laughter. In the evening we went back to our room so as not to arouse suspicion, and then at midnight we went out to clubs. We'd come back at five or just before six, which was a rule because I knew my father had a habit of getting up early. We were discovered on one of the last nights. We came back drunk and my father was sitting in the lobby waiting for us. It was a bad gaffe, but we had a good time. So, when winter came, we started going out with older people. There wasn't much to do and it was freezing cold outside. I remember the snow. I remember the roads were frozen. And on the very day of the accident, I remember staring at an icy puddle and feeling something, as if God was trying to warn me of danger. But we didn't care, we liked danger. We had secrets. We were the keepers of something unique, something that in our eyes made us unique to others."

"I thought so too at that age."

"There was the AC Milan match. We entered the stadium. We were happy. But halfway through the game, one of our grown-up friends told us we had to come back, that it was getting late for us. It was almost ten o'clock. I had left my mobile phone at home and so had Damian. We knew we were in trouble. On the way back, to get back earlier, we took the country roads. Damian and I were in the back, the others in front. We were speeding. Damian was worried but I kept teasing him, pulling his vest to get his attention. He said we were going too fast. He said he didn't like it. I didn't listen to him. Maybe if I'd said *slow down*, our friend would have slowed down, but I kept teasing Damian because... because I was happy."

"I'm sorry."

"I stopped laughing when a sense of confusion hit Damian's eyes and then up to my back. The car swerved and went off the road, hitting a tree."

"That is so sad."

I started crying and so did Losco. Sweet tears, a veiled sadness, a small smile because awareness had replaced guilt.

"I got out of the car and dragged Damian out. I had no choice. The trunk of the tree had bent the door on his side. I was screaming. I was terrified. I didn't care about the others, I just wanted to know he was okay. I laid him in the cornfield, a hard bed made even harder by the frost. I moved him near the car lights because I wanted to see his face, to see that his eyes were open. There was blood. I thought it was mine at first but every time I touched his face, the blood was there."

"What about the others?"

"They survived. Injuries, fractures, but they're still on this earth. Damian, on the other hand, is no more. The force was so hard, it crushed his chest. I was praying. I told him to stay awake. He looked at me, but he wouldn't talk, he couldn't. Someone in the car called an ambulance; so, help arrived. They couldn't move him, because if they did, he'd be dead. But I had dragged him out and begged them to put him on the stretcher, and they told me that one more movement and I would inflict serious pain on him. It was the longest and most terrible 20 minutes of my life. He died like that, lying in a cold, stiff cornfield, slowly, almost without feeling anything, looking at the world with a sense of bewilderment and incomprehension, forever extinguishing his invincible age, leaving me for nothing. I kept telling him it was okay. I told him I was sorry, that I'd pay our meals at McDonald's for the rest of our lives but he couldn't answer me. So, I broke our promise. I forcibly moved the two ambulance guys over, and I kissed him. I did it because they said he was going, that he was finally going to die."

"What promise, Lo?"

"We were lovers, Francis."

"Now I understand, you loved him."

"Sure. At that age love is not yet clear. It's more of an impulse, a chemical feeling. But we loved each other. We discovered love that summer I told you about. We had understood that our friendship bordered on the love between a man and a woman; and partly as a joke and partly to understand, one night we kissed. Then we even went to bed. We were crazy."

"Is that why you left Dounia at university?"

"She was a pretext. The psychologist advised me to get a girlfriend and so I did. I did it for my mother who, when she saw me, cried, said she had a lost son. And I was really lost. As you can see, we have so much in common."

Losco smiled. I feel our bond become deeper than I could ever have imagined. He'd never expressed his feelings for me and our friendship, but now I understand it must have been important.

"What did he say to you? I mean, when you relived that moment..."

"For me it was different, I didn't have to recover my memory. My memory had been tormenting me for years. I had to get over the desire to commit suicide. And now it's gone. But only thanks to you could I let Damian go too. Now I can forgive myself. I can understand that fate has allowed me to move on and I have to do it for myself. I'll do it for myself and for him too. Damian couldn't move on; he'll stay young forever. I'm going to get older and enjoy this stay on earth a little longer."

"Yes, that's right. But I'd like to know if..."

"You're not my type, Francis."

We laugh. We hug. We love each other.

"I want to find a woman."

"But how?"

"In London, I was Dragos' lover."

"Another thing you never told me, but it was obvious. I mean, it is now."

"We had a fight in Bournemouth and I decided to stop following him. I was tired of hiding who I was, but he wanted to keep hiding it. He was seeing a girl, but he didn't love her. Recently he's tried to contact me again, and has told me that he now feels ready but I have no intention of carrying on a complicated relationship. Besides, I like women."

"Okay, do what makes you happy."

"Yes. But enough about me now. You're still in a state of confusion and you need answers."

"It's alright for the time being. I'm lonely, you know, weak, confused."

"At that moment, when I kissed him as he died, I wanted to give him my life breath, to exchange my life for him. Damian was a visionary, but I didn't give a shit. I had no future prospects. He, on the other hand, dreamed of opening a club, like a pub with live music. But it didn't work. His lips were cold and by the time I'd got up, he had already closed his eyes."

"Yeah, I know how that feels. When I saw Lisa unconscious, I wanted to force God to rewind the tape of time back at least an hour earlier. I would have made things right. I would have confessed my mistakes and begged forgiveness. I would have given my hands, my eyes, any part of me to stop her from having to make that journey to death and thereby force Lisa to miss her one chance at life."

Losco grabs my shoulder and asks me if I want a burger. I tell him that just thinking about it makes me want to throw up, but we get moving. We go into a pub near the pier and order something hot.

We talk again. I tell him everything. I tell him about Lauren, the cop and the seagull. Losco listens in silence. He never interrupts me. I owe him my life.

3

Sanremo. Italy.

I turn the recorder off. I put the tape of Lisa's recordings in a box along with other small items that belonged to her, sealed with a metal padlock. One day I'll be ready to listen to her voice carefully again, better than I did in the past. I would never have recovered these few things of hers if it hadn't been for my brother Fabrizio.

And now, I think I've remembered enough.

The effect of the fungus has almost completely dissipated.

Luca, the one with whom it all started, asked me to perform an act of courage, to dare, to test my mind. After months spent in the Marche, in his house in the country, with the company of his wife Teresa and the many animals that populated it, it was time to get out of the garden of Eden and face once and for all the demons that plagued my mind.

This is what Luca used to tell me: *the worst demons live in our minds.*

Often, when he was away on business, I would spend hours outdoors watching the sun rise behind the mountains or set on the horizon. Teresa would prepare lunch and, if I had not yet returned, she would leave it, covered with another plate, on the top shelf of the kitchen. The cats had been known sometimes to sneak into the house and steal it.

They had a nice backyard and a small vegetable garden. I sat on the chopped trunk of a tree and waited for the day to pass. I waited for Luca to come back to discuss my state of mind. We did some breathing exercises early in the morning and just before dinner. He told me that I didn't have to spend all day thinking about what I had done, but that the day would eventually come when he would ask me to do that.

"Be patient. If time consumes your body, don't let it consume your mind," he said.

I thought several times about running away, packing up and going home, but only once did I really do it. Teresa had gone out to meet some friends, and so I took the opportunity to leave. I got my stuff and headed for the train station. There was a delay, which I thought was a sign of destiny. I hitched a ride to the station, had a hot tea in the bar and missed the train. I sat there for a long hour before I decided to go back. Nothing in particular had convinced me to miss that train. I think the prospect of going back to my parents was far worse than facing personal demons.

Last month I spent some free time with the German shepherd dog who guarded the estate. He kept the cats away from the house by frightening them without hurting them.

One day I suddenly realized that he had gained the respect of the animals visiting our garden. He would play with the cats as long as they didn't try to sneak into the house; he'd allow the cow grazing in the field next to ours to lick him and smooth his fur by sticking his head between the cracks in the fence.

Going down the hills of the estate, we could see other wildlife such as thieving magpies, roe deer and foxes.

King (the German shepherd) and I rested under the poplar tree that had its roots in the outermost corner of Luca's garden. King came to visit me when I was hiding down there; maybe he wanted to make sure I was alright.

***

The questions kept me alive.

They say I lost my memory twice because of the shock. I never lost the questions though. She was dead, and all that was left of her was a faint light in the distance, a tunnel-like abyss at the bottom of which someone held a flickering torch. You cry out in the hope that she might hear you, that with that flash of light she might comfort you more closely; but she remains there at the bottom of her isolation, like the things that sink into the sea, a Titanic that has no other destiny.

It was Lisa who said "I love you" for the first time. No one before her had ever said that to me. It was around Christmas, our first Christmas. I never liked Christmas, but she was a joy. We spent every free day of December walking around downtown Milan. We bought presents for everyone and she wanted me to meet her family.

Lisa and Giulia had already met, months before, but my sister was still immature and thought she was someone like Sara.

Lisa's "I love you" happened just before going to her parents. She was tense. She kept talking to herself, even while we were in the car with Michael Jackson's songs in the background. She rubbed her hands nervously, checking that we hadn't forgotten anything. No, we'd packed the presents days before and had counted them one by one. That night we had put them in the backseat. She'd counted them first and then I did. She'd never brought a boy to her house before and her parents were a bit old-fashioned.

They hoped Lisa would get married soon, find a rich man and have at least a couple of babies.

We got out of the car and she was still tense. We were silent the whole way from my house to hers. Lisa told me rather brusquely to *hurry up* and get the bag with the presents in. So, to retaliate for her brusqueness, I closed the car and left the presents inside. She was furious with me for doing that. I hugged her. She apologised for mistreating me, but I didn't care.

I would have changed over time. My real temperament, sometimes not very patient, it would have jumped up like the rabbit in the hat.

I told her *everything's gonna be fine.*

She said *I love you* without thinking about it, without really realising what she'd just confessed. It was typical of Lisa to brood over something for days and then to suddenly throw it out without warning. It was the same with music, too. She must have thought about it for years and plucked up the courage to try.

There were so many things she wanted to do. We did a lot of them together, but as far as music was concerned, she was on her own. The few times I paid attention to Lisa's passion, it was to joke and change the notes of her songs.

I said that questions woke me up in the middle of the night. I told myself that if I could find at least one answer, Lisa's face would appear as if by magic, maybe a little at a time, like when you put the pieces of a puzzle in its place.

For months, I'd just seen parts of her, helplessly. The doctors kept saying that I would recover my memory very soon, but there seemed to be no definite date for that "*soon*".

I never had the courage to face her parents, but I

promised myself that it would be one of the first things to do as soon as I leave this place.

Now I love everything about her. I'm fully present for her. It's never too late to love someone even if they're gone. I tell myself *love has no boundaries* and I dare to believe it. I like to think that love makes things right, puts things in order, heals the past too. Maybe it's an easy thing to say; maybe a part of me will never find peace even after this. Thinking that I will, though, helps.

I had to let you go too many times, Lisa: first when I had to accept your death and then in those parallel worlds where you were the before and the after.

Life is fragile. We are vulnerable, I know that now. Nothing, apparently, prepares you enough for tomorrow but that's the challenge. That's how we can learn the most important lessons. I want to think about this, to believe that love heals and that it has finally put our past right, that she never died, but rather simply turned from a chrysalis to a butterfly. I imagine her like this, free for the borders of other worlds to give all her light to the nature of infinite stars.

Osho said that a butterfly doesn't care about being beautiful or appreciated; she simply shines. She does what she has to do regardless of any judgment.

Lisa caressed this fragile life with her own frailty, wondering if she was up to it.

You were up to it, Lisa, you were up to everything.

Even in the face of death, which dragged you away like an overwhelming undercurrent, you shone with beauty.

To me, you'll be *forever* and ever until the day we meet again.

End?

"Lo?"

"Tell me."

"How does it work?"

"What do you mean?"

"What you did to me, I mean, how...?"

"Luca will explain it to you soon. Only if you want to know."

"Um."

"I just learned something. I can't give you that answer."

"But I can't explain how I was able to see places I'd never seen before. How can that happen? How real was what I saw?"

"It was real. There's a part of us that's in the shadows. It's called the subconscious. And the subconscious is exactly what makes us do what we do. The surface, our consciousness, is what we think we know about ourselves and reality. But there is a deeper connection that acts in the shadows."

"I don't follow you. You mean, somehow they were real?"

"Yes. We live on the surface of the sea. The surface of the sea is only one layer. The subconscious, instead, is what makes the sea the sea. That is what makes you, you. And at that deep level, everything is linked."

"You mean that we consciously exist on the surface and coexist within the sea, which is the submerged part, the subconscious?"

"Something like that, yes."

"Lauren was real?"

"When you met Lauren at the beach, she was real on the surface. Something happened between you. You recognised each other on a deeper level; you were connected - your memories with her memories. This connection is felt on the surface as a chemical or electrical activity, but you were karmically linked."

"They were all there that night. I mean, the people I was gonna meet in my other life, right?"

Losco nods, then adds: "When I altered your mind, I only brought out the full potential of this submerged part. You were no longer in your own mind, and you were no longer swimming on the surface of the sea. You didn't know those places, but Lauren and I did. Somehow life has evolved in ways that cannot be understood by reason alone."

"Anyway, thanks."

"Now rest. You have a long journey ahead of you tomorrow."

21 June 2017 – 19 June 2020

Milton Keynes UK
Ingram Content Group UK Ltd.
UKHW022133230824
447344UK00008B/619